Payton Edgar's Performance

By M. J. T. Seal

Table of Contents

Payton Edgar's Performance; A drama in three acts

Cast of characters;

Payton Edgar; a popular townsman

Irving Spence; his aide

Grace Kemp; a nursemaid

Aunt Elizabeth; an evil spinster

The players;

Katherine… … … … Toffee Morrell

Petruchio… … … .. . Sir Maurice Williams

Bianca… … … … … Sylvia Pickford

Baptista… … … …. Christophe Playfair

Lucentio… … … … Tony Trace

Hortensio… … … John Nash

Understudy… … … Emma Drake

Director… … … …. Gordon Farringdon

His wife… ……. ….. Rosemary Farringdon

Stage management… Alex Drake

Costumes… …. … …. Ethel Damp

Prologue

Payton's plate
The London Evening Clarion
4th January 1964

What on earth is a Macbeth Salad?

This and many other questions will remain largely unanswered in this week's edition of Payton's Plate, for I left the West End's latest eatery - The Box Office - in a state of complete befuddlement.

There is a little trend that has developed in recent years for the themed restaurant, and while one can permit certain motifs - restaurants themed by ethnicity of cuisine, for example - one draws the line at the theatrically themed establishment. One particular restaurant in Kentish Town has been running for a little over a year. I confidently predict that it has almost completed its run.

Conceived and produced by retired actors, uppity brothers Thomas Dodd (henceforth known as Sour) and Henry Dodd (henceforth known as Dour), the restaurant offers what is described proudly on the menu as "hearty, unpretentious British food".

Unpretentious? Reader, I have never eaten anywhere so dizzyingly ostentatious.

We were greeted at the door with loud overtures by Dour, and shown to our table. The restaurant's interior is bewildering, with countless framed head-shots or cast photos from performances long forgotten scattered all over the place. There is barely an inch of wall uncovered, and I was forced to eat my meal with miserable old fop Larry Olivier glaring in judgement over my plate.

Our orders were taken by Sour, and the brothers continued to share duties throughout the evening. When asked about the chef, Sour explained that the kitchens were overseen by a third actor friend of theirs, and that they took the mantle of "artistic directors" to the whole endeavour. Sour was especially atingle with having The Clarion's own restaurant critic at their table, and so I shall try not to disappoint with my overview of their menu.

As usual, my dear companion Mr Spence joined me at my table - a man far more tolerant of unnecessary pomp and circumstance than I. He even enjoyed the tortuous puns Sour and Dour had concocted for the menu.

For a starter Mr Spence ordered The Taming Of The Shrimp Cocktail, and I the Pygmalion Platter - a mundane and largely tasteless plate of ham with pork chunks on skewers. The shrimp cocktail fared no better - the salad was limp and lifeless and the shrimp themselves suspiciously pink.

Our main courses were so very long in coming that I enquired if we were, essentially, Waiting For Godot, to which I merely received a Sour look.

For his main course, Mr Spence considered the Hamlet Omelette, but instead ordered the Midsummer Nights Bream with a West Side-Salad Story. The fish was just good enough, although a little tepid, but the accompanying salad was unimaginative and far too heavily dressed. I braved the Spotlight Steak with an Oedipus sauce ("How does it come?" I enquired politely of the meat. "As you like it" came the Dour reply). Nevertheless, the steak was overdone and the sauce far too peppery.

The brothers insisted that we also sample the aforementioned Macbeth Salad, which was a confused concoction of red cabbage, tomato, red onion and walnuts.

Dessert was no better. A Curtain-call Cake with custard for Mr Spence turned out to be a tough plum duff which put one in mind of stale school dinners. My Trap-door Tapioca was pedestrian and most certainly did not receive the standing ovation that the brothers Sour and Dour had been expecting.

And so to conclude, I rate this brash, hammy performance with a measly one-star review. If "hearty British cuisine" is to fare well on the world stage, we simply must perform better than this.

Payton Edgar

Act I

Part I

In which Payton Edgar laments over an imperfectly boiled egg

I firmly believe that the start that we are given in life goes a long way to shaping who we are to become as adults.

At the tender age of five, I missed my first day at primary school. I was recovering from the dreaded mumps, and the crusty headmaster of St Augustines insisted - unnecessarily, as far as my mother was concerned - upon a further twenty-four hours quarantine. And so my actual first day at school was everyone else's second, a matter that had prayed on my mind from that day to this. It was terribly unfair, and ever since missing that first day over fifty years ago, I felt that I was - in some way or another - still catching up.

Forever catching up.

However, despite such an inauspicious start, young master Edgar enjoyed a keen brain and grew to be a superior sort when it comes to common sense and intellect. Payton Edgar is level-headed and sensible - a fact as true as the grass being green or dogs being, on the whole, rather revolting creatures. It is also a fact that even level-headed, sensible types sometimes make mistakes.

My marriage was one such mistake.

Youthful enthusiasm would be a fair excuse. Rosemary Jessop and I were practically children when our eyes met over our blotting paper, and we had plunged into a brief and entirely uneventful courtship almost by accident. A husband, a house and a garden was young, dewy-eyed Rosemary's dream, and - if I am honest - I simply hadn't the bravery to deny her this wish. We had precious little in common, and soon found out that married life brought only misery and misunderstanding. It was Rosemary who finally suggested we part ways, but it was a divorce that I welcomed wholeheartedly, for married life with Rosemary proved to be deafening and relentless. Following our separation, she had gone on to share her particular brand of deafening relentlessness with two other poor unfortunates.

Christmas cards and the odd letter were exchanged over the years, and the circles in which we moved touched on one or two occasions, but that was all. And then, on an overcast and insignificant January day in 1964, she pried herself into my affairs once again.

Rosemary had always been a persistent beast, and in recent days she rang the phone off the hook and left numerous messages with Grace, my aunt's nursemaid. I, in turn, ignored the messages time and again. I just didn't have the time or energy for her nonsense.

Unfortunately, one morning as I was preparing breakfast, I accidentally picked up the telephone simply because I was half asleep and the ringing caught me in a moment of distraction while waiting for my eggs to boil.

Rosemary's adenoidal screech woke me sharply. As is her way, she launched into an epic monologue. How could I possibly have ignored her calls for so long? She had things to discuss! Did I not think that what she had to say might be important? Heaven knows she had left enough messages! Did I ever think of anyone else but myself?

I waited for her to catch breath and then muttered gruffly that I was taking my breakfast and replaced the receiver firmly in it's rest. The eggs were top priority, and quite right too. I returned to the bubbling pan and did my best to focus on the job at hand. The ringing began again just as I was at the table, slicing the top off of my first boiled egg.

I recruited my first soldier only to find, much to my dismay, that the egg was perhaps thirty or forty seconds overdone. My heart sank.

Oh, the horrors of an overdone egg!

The second egg was no better, and I ate this and the remainders of my troop with a grumbling dissatisfaction. This was entirely Rosemary's fault.

After breakfast, heavy with digestion, I allowed myself a little rest in my lounge chair, a delightful, recently acquired piece with a thick brass frame and a seat of soft brown leather. I did have some work to do, but the comfort of my dear new seat was all too enticing.

The work pending concerned a polishing of my latest restaurant review, plus a bundle of letters to Dr Margaret Blythe. Dr Blythe is the nom-de-plume I had adopted after being forced to take on the role of Agony Aunt in the London Evening Clarion. Dr Blythe appears weekly, and has been a runaway success under my supervision. I had adopted an unnoticed and badly conceived piece of fluff – Peggy's Postbag – and resurrected it as a weekly comment on the morals and dilemmas of society today. I am a natural problem-solver. Over time, Dr Blythe had become a voice in her own right, and my secret identity had, for the most part, remained secret.

That said, the latest batch of letters to Dr Blythe sat in the satchel at my side, ignored, as I settled down for a rest. Lucille, my dear fat puss, jumped up to settle in my lap.

As if on cue, the telephone awoke.

I lifted the handset with grim resignation.

'Hello, Rosemary,' I said coldly.

'What the devil was that all about? I know that you're there - why didn't you answer when I called back? What were you on about, muttering some rubbish about soldiers? What was that all about?'

'You interrupted the boiling of my eggs,' I replied simply. There was a stony silence. I could practically feel her glaring with exasperation down the receiver.

'You don't change, do you, Payton?'

I fancy there was a touch of affection in her tone. She sighed and went on.

'Well anyway, I am calling about something far more important that your precious dippy drippy eggs.'

'Rather hard boiled and entirely un-dippy drippy, thanks to you.'

'Getting knickers in twists over trivialities, Payton! Still have your little peculiarities, don't you, darling?'

‘This from a woman who refuses to add butter to scrambled eggs!’

I rested back in the chair in a glorious silent victory. Her penchant avoiding butter out of some misguiding notion of health - while allowing herself endless peppermint cigarillos and umpteen dirty martini’s - had always been a matter of some vexation on my part. It was satisfying to revisit the point. Remarkable, I thought to myself, how we could so easily slip back into our old habits. Here we were again, bickering like man and wife.

I prayed that our conversation would be brief. My days of pandering to Rosemary were long gone - I owed her nothing, most certainly not my valued time.

Unfortunately, this was just what she was after.

She urged me to meet with her “as a matter of urgency” and, rather infuriating, refused to offer any details.

‘Can’t we discuss this so very urgent matter over the telephone?’ I asked, entirely reasonably.

‘No, it must be face to face.’

‘I am pretty busy these days…’

‘Busy? Busy idling each day away with little to do? Busy flouncing out to restaurants and having a pop a their sub-par shrimps in print? Busy shopping for neckerchiefs and pocket squares? Busy idling away time doing absolutely nothing?’

‘How rude!’

‘You will be glad you came, Payton, I promise. I need your brains.’

‘Excuse me?’

‘I have a proposition for you. I need someone with your intelligence, Payton - some common sense! Whatever your peculiarities, you have common sense in barrels…’

‘True, true… however I-’

‘That’s settled, then. Four-thirty this afternoon, cocktail lounge at the Mayvere.’

It was only the thought of getting her off the line so that I could snooze under the warmth of my beloved Lucille that led me to concede to the appointment.

I replaced the receiver and snoozed.

Part II

In which Payton Edgar refuses a dying man's wish

Dear Margaret,

My fiancé is urging me to have intimacy before marriage. I am only eighteen years old, and I want a long engagement to be sure that he is the right man for me, but he tells me he cannot wait. I have nobody to talk to about this - my mother passed last year and I wouldn't dare talk to Daddy. I love my fiancé, and don't want to lose him. What can I do?

Petunia, Grosvenor Square

Margret replies; A message to all readers; kindly avoid sending in letters of this nature. Matters of sexual intimacy should remain just that; intimate and – above all – private. Why would you wish to share all and sundry with The Clarion readership? I will, however, offer some sage advice on the issue of marriage; marriage is over-rated and especially perilous when one is young. I am quite certain that it will end in misery and disappointment for the both of you. I see from your letterhead and the quality of your stationary that you are not underprivileged, Petunia. I suggest you break off the engagement immediately and perhaps pester Daddy for a pony instead.

I had been caught in something of a cold squall out on the street, and so was already not in the best of moods as I arrived at the lounge of The Mayvere Hotel.

I took off my hat and shook it, pulled off my macintosh and adjusted my cravat. A hamster-cheeked porter stepped up to assist and I shooed him away with my stick. With my mac folded over my arm, I drew in a deep breath and straightened myself up, pulling back the shoulders and lifting the chin. I took in the room.

I have never warmed to the Mayvere, nor understood its appeal to those of status. For many, it was considered to be the place to be, and quite bafflingly so. The ancient lounge had the proportions of a bus depot and the fittings of a flappers boudoir. It was more than a little outdated, and I did not like it one jot.

A pianist was tinkling in the corner as I searched over the small crowd. It wasn't hard to spot Rosemary in her garish scarlet trouser suit. She had a rather sparky presence, resting with bony legs crossed at a small table, sipping a martini and smiling her gummy smile. Pressed between the fingers of her left hand was, as always, one of her rancid peppermint cigarillos.

Some people do indeed never change.

She greeted me as though I were a long lost cousin and not a barely tolerated ex-husband, throwing a kiss past each cheek in a horrifically cosmopolitan manner. She then sniffed the air and spoke in a way that only Rosemary could.

'Still using that same old hair tonic, darling?'

I was allowed no time to reply.

'Still a slave to your diaries?'

Although I considered myself to be a fair-weather diarist, it was true that I was on volume sixty-four, but I wasn't about to say.

'And that stick! A superfluous affectation if ever there was one!'

Again, as I opened my mouth, she ploughed on.

'And still with the pocket square stuffed in the top pocket!'

This was too much.

'Stuffed? I'll have you know that this is Italian silk twill, carefully folded in-'

'-in a reverse puff! Yes, I know, I know. Still, I quite like that smart olive cravat.'

It was chartreuse green, and I would have told her so had a slight young lady not appeared from nowhere with pad and pencil. I requested a tomato juice and took my seat.

'Alright then, Rosemary,' I began with an uncompromising frankness, 'let's get it over with. What is it that's so very important?'

It was then that I noticed a second martini on the table besides hers - she was not alone. She glanced conspiratorially around the room and then leaned in a little too close. It was immediately clear that she was uncomfortable, and I watched the furtive flicker of her eyes as she spoke. Her voice low and urgent, words tumbling out of her mouth with barely a breath. There was lipstick on her teeth.

'I must just say quickly, before he gets here, that this is an extremely delicate situation. Extremely delicate. I need you to be quiet and careful. It is all about money and pride. Gordon can be so terribly proud. And so I want you just to smile and agree and not to ask any questions, alright? Just smile and agree. Can you do that for me, Payton? Yes? Yes? Good!'

She stood up abruptly and smiled that gummy smile as someone approached our table.

'Gordy! Payton, you remember Gordon?'

Gordon Farringdon, Rosemary's husband of several years, shook my hand weakly and plonked himself beside his wife. I had only met Farringdon in passing once, and it hadn't been a particularly memorable occasion. He was a blunt pencil of a man, as thin and reedy as the most weaselly of bank managers, with a pallor akin to stripped wood. Fine strands of limp black hair rested on a dry scalp. He allowed only a paper-thin smile.

'Edgar.'

It was a curt acknowledgement, which I matched with a dryness of my own.

'Farringdon.'

I studied his features. He had lost weight, and his face was gaunt with dark bags under the eyes. There was something distinctly sickly about the man.

'Christ, I need a drink!' he said, retrieving his martini.

There was, I detected, a certain discomfort about the silence which fell as they sipped at their glasses. Rosemary sensed it too, and she did her best to plough through it with yet more forced vivaciousness.

'We're up in Chelsea now, Payton - did you know? You did receive our change-of-address cardlet? Mmm, perhaps I forgot about you. Lovely area... darling house! Four bedrooms, two en-suite and two garages, not that we drive. I use one as my wardrobe. Kitchen recently fitted with all the modern necessities, a magnificent Aga… and guess what? We have an electronic dish washing machine! Insane! You pop your dirty crockery in, press a button, and it comes out gleaming! Oh, and Gordy enjoys a delightful study in distressed teak. Absolutely stunning! You must come and see…'

Bored of the boasting, I cut in with a question.

'And how is your daughter?'

I had met the poor soul several years back, and recalled a plain girl with bunches and a face like a scone. Wrong-footed slightly, Rosemary looked for a moment as if she had entirely forgotten the existence of a child from her second marriage. She blinked rapidly.

'Oh, Mary-lou? She is fine… I believe. She is at a very satisfactory boarding school in Cornwall, right by the sea. Darling school, top marks! A devil to get to, so we don't go there much. But I'm told she's happy enough…'

'How old is she now?' I asked, enjoying Rosemary's befuddlement.

She continued to falter. 'Oh. well, she must be… that is… she will be past her twelfth by now, I should say. Or thereabouts.' She waved a dismissive hand. 'We send hampers…'

'Shall we get this meeting over with?' Farringdon put in, directing this to neither one of us in particular. He set down his glass noisily and looked me in the eye.

It was then that I noticed and remembered all about the eye.

Gordon Farringdon's left eye was a glass substitute, a ball stared up and slightly to the left, gazing out at nothing in particular with a fixed dryness that can only have been synthetic. Was this a heroic wartime mutilation or something entirely more domestic? Whatever the cause, it was terribly distracting, and I couldn't help glaring back at it in wonder. It was the sort of affliction that is bad form to point out in polite company, but still I was itching to mention it. I was, thankfully, distracted when he issued an alarming statement.

'I am dying, Mr Edgar, and I need to ask you a favour.' This was declared coldly and without compromise.

Rather unexpected, I thought to myself.

It is worth saying at this juncture that Payton Edgar is a charitable man.

I have been blessed with enough money to do as I wish, thanks to my mother's estate and a number of savvy investments, and I try to do all I can to extend a helping hand to the poor and the needy. I have donated to our local Scout's rummage numerous times in the past - items of clothing that once cost a pretty penny but were probably taken as rags and sold for a heart-breaking pittance. I took in Lucille when an elderly neighbour passed away, not to mention housing my Aunt Elizabeth following her stroke, and I am always sure to vacate my seat on a bus for the elderly, the malformed or the unfortunate.

However, I respond poorly when charity is demanded of me, whatever the reason. It is worth making this point, for I was about to be just a little… uncharitable.

‘Gordon! You can’t just blurt it out like that!’ Rosemary gasped, grinning nervously.

‘I can and I did,’ Farringdon replied. ‘I am dying. It is a fact, Rosemary. A fact.’

One had to admire the man’s audacity, and I gave a nod with genuine interest, inviting him to continue. This particular meeting could turn out to be far more entertaining than anticipated. My tomato juice arrived.

‘I need money,’ said Farringdon without an ounce of discretion. Rosemary slapped her knee sharply.

‘Right Gordy, that’s it! If you can’t explain to Payton in a proper fashion, then I shall.’ She turned and spoke to me with the condescending air of the woman on television who does strange things with a wooden donkey.

‘Payton, darling, as you know, Gordon is a man of the arts. His direction has been praised by many of theatre-land’s finest actors and most fearsome critics. He is a legend - widely respected, revered, even. And now he has the opportunity of a lifetime… his life's dream, you might say.’ At this, she briefly placed a hand on her husband’s knee. ‘Gordon is the director of a fine new production at the West End! We started rehearsals at the tail end of last year, with some very big names. It’s all going really rather well, isn’t it, my dear?’

Somehow I doubted this. If it was indeed all going rather well, why should they need me? Rosemary went on.

‘Now, you have heard of Richard Chandler?’

The name did ring a vague bell, but I wasn’t given a moment to reply.

‘Of course you haven’t! I quite forgot who I was talking to! Known as Dickie Chandelier to the press and anyone who doesn’t really know him. Ring any bells? No? Well, Dickie is a notable producer and Patron of the Arts – you would know of him if you were in any way important and had your fingers in any creative pies. Something of a playboy back in the day, made his name producing the very best shows… and he is a dear, dear friend of ours. Dickie owns the Old Compton Theatre, Soho. Well, even you will have heard of that! We went in to a kind of partnership with darling Dickie, an agreement if you like. He has given us the venue – a magnificent, astounding and historic venue - and we provide the capital for the rest, the actors, advertising and so on. Well, Gordy and I can only put up so much towards this, as you can imagine, and recently, we’ve had… well, a bit of a bad run with, well… a bad lot of, well…’

As she hesitated, her husband but in, bluntly.

‘Some poor investments.’

The good eye was cast downwards as the glass eye looked wildly off to the corner of the room.

‘Indeed, some poor investments,’ continued his wife, keen to brush over the details. ‘You see, we had a second stakeholder, Gordon’s cousin, Ham.’

‘Ham?’

‘That’s his name,’ replied Rosemary, raising pencilled eyebrows.

‘The man’s a dog!’ Farringdon spat over his drink.

I leaned in. ‘A pig, surely?’

'To cut a long story short, we need the capital to pay the players, and cousin Ham let us down,' Rosemary said, waving a dismissive hand. 'He's gone. Simply vanished into thin air! We don't know where, and the money - if it ever existed - has all gone up in smoke, and poor Gordon and I are stuck. Dear Gordy is ill, and this was to be something of a last hurrah.'

'A last hurrah?' I whispered. Rosemary sucked on her teeth. That was something I hadn't missed - the sucking of the teeth. I sighed pointedly.

'And that's where I come in?'

'That's where you come in, indeed! We need funds,' said Farringdon. If the man was supposed to be buttering me up, he was failing miserably. Rosemary attempted another gummy smile. She was surely using up her annual allowance of gummy smiles in one afternoon.

'You're after my money. You said on the telephone that you were after my brains.'

'Pah! That was just to get you here,' replied Rosemary with infuriating honesty. 'But you are smart when it comes to finances, and this opportunity... it will be a smart investment, believe me. The show is sure to be a smash hit! It's The Taming of the Shrew with a superb, top-drawer cast, and a very, very famous leading man - a household name, no less. He is coming to meet us shortly-'

'Shakespeare?' I groaned, unable to stop myself. 'I detest Shakespeare.'

Rosemary had been expecting this.

'Oh, but you don't have to watch it, Payton. In fact, you don't have to do anything whatsoever! All we ask is that you invest and then count the profit at the end of the run. You can be as involved or uninvolved as you wish.'

Farringdon turned on her. 'Steady on, dear.'

Rosemary ignored the man at her side and kept her eyes sparkling in my direction. Then, when I failed to reply, she sat back, sighed and rolled them to the ceiling. Like a struck match, another memory came to mind - Rosemary's impetuousness. I recognised that look, and could sense her sudden impatience. I remained mute, and watched as the simmer came to a boil. Her left knee jiggered up and down, and eventually she could hold herself no longer.

'Oh, come on, Payton, just say yes! Heaven knows, you could do with something to fill your time instead of gallivanting out to restaurant after restaurant and calling it a career! It's about time you did something useful.'

She had overstepped the mark this time.

'On the contrary,' I said mysteriously, 'I have been very useful of late, solving murders and righting wrongdoings...'

'Oh, fiddlesticks!'

I maintained my dignity in the face of such scorn, shrugged impassively and allowed her to continue.

'It really is a very attractive proposition, and I know how you adore to be in control. You can consider yourself a partner in the production - and it is a fantastic production. If you stay for a moment you will meet our leading man. A highly respected name - a true headliner. Well, even if you wanted a part on stage-'

'Careful, Rosie!' warned Farringdon again, obviously unhappy at the idea of too much intervention on my part. This in itself was almost enough for me to agree to the proposal - irritating Farringdon could be a rather pleasurable pastime. But Rosemary knew they were safe - she only suggested this as she knew being a part of a theatre crew was the very last thing I would ever wish to do. She was also right about my finances, I did indeed have the savings stashed away doing nothing. I was also a little bored, if I were to be completely honest.

But even so, it was not quite enough.

'I'm sorry,' I stated, pushing aside my drink. 'I'm afraid the answer is a firm no.'

Farringdon jerked his head at his wife and spat through dry lips.

'I told you! Waste of bloody time!'

Rosemary wasn't giving up so easily.

'Well, at least go away and think about it, Payton, darling!' There was a revealing desperation behind her eyes. She whipped out a pad and pencil. 'I will give you our number in Chelsea for when you change your mind.'

'I have had ample time to think about it, Rosemary, and my answer is no. A very definite no! And I will not need to call you, for I will never change my mind.'

There was no point of sticking around, and so I gathered my coat and hat, bid them a curt farewell and made my way through the lounge. I mumbled to myself as I went - the cheek of it! As if I would want anything whatsoever to do with the stinking theatre and all its loathsome artificiality! Their desperation was unpalatable - all they wanted was my cash!

It takes more than a heart-felt appeal and a little flattery to make Payton Edgar whip out his cheque book.

As I made my way through the lounge of the Mayvere I was resolute - I would have nothing whatsoever to do with Gordon Farringdon's miserable production. I stopped at the revolving door, which was busy revolving.

Suddenly, a dishevelled apparition burst from it like a dog from a trap, and before I could move we collided horribly. Almost toppled, I grunted and gasped and complained as loudly as I could. I had dropped my hat, and was horrified to see a filthy boot planted on top. After pulling away the hat I straightened and slammed down my stick, ready to to deliver my finest indignant glare.

My assailant was a familiar face.

Sir Maurice Williams was scowling down at me, rain dripping from his beard. Sir Maurice Williams – one of the most irritating and opinionated thespians I have ever had the misfortune to encounter. Bafflingly considered to be one of the greatest stage actors of our time, the man was a fop, a phoney and a pince-nez wearing fool.

Sir Maurice Williams of all people!

I pulled up my chest and narrowed my eyes. A sly smile melted across his repugnant face, a smile that dripped with noxious insincerity. I could smell alcohol on his breath as he barked in my face like a fussy walrus.

'Well, hello! Who have we here? Mr Edgar again! Oh - bad penny and all that!'

'Excuse me, I must be on my way.'

'Dear Mr Edgar, as puffed up as breakfast corn as usual. Terribly sorry-ish, crashing into you like that. In a hurry - got an important meeting.'

I could contain myself no longer.

'You trod on my homburg!'

'That battered abomination? Kicking it out into the street would be too good for it!'

'How dare you!'

'It doesn't even match that tatty second-hand jacket.'

'I'll have you know that this houndstooth flannel, and entirely bespoke.'

'Oh, yes?'

'Tailored by Ahlers of Savile Row, and by the senior Ahler himself!'

'That what they told you, love.'

I would have muttered something extremely clever and gone on my way had he not blocked my path and chosen to goad me further as he removed his coat. It was all entirely unnecessary.

'Wouldn't expect to see you at the darling Mayvere, Edgar. You do know this is an exclusive joint, don't you? And why I am here, you ask? Yet another West End sell-out beckons - meeting with my director - headlining yet another triumph. So what is a philistine like you doing here in our dolly hotbed of the talented and prosperous?'

Philistine!

'As a matter of fact, Maurice-'

'Sir Maurice!'

'As a matter of fact, Maurice, I was just having a meeting with some very talented and prosperous people who have been begging for my help.'

'Yes, I sure they have, sweets.'

'I have been called to a meeting of a theatrical nature, Maurice, just like you. And following this very successful meeting, I have agreed to invest a considerable amount of money to their cause. I have also consented to act as their… Artistic Director! I take it that you refer to The Taming of the Shrew at the Old Compton? Well, look out for some changes, Maurice, for I am… your new Artistic Director!'

I would have loved to remain on the spot for just a moment to see the shock on his face, but there wasn't time. I turned on my heel and retraced my steps with some urgency, trotting back over to where Rosemary and Farringdon sat. They were a little startled at my re-appearance. Even the glass eye appeared to twinkle.

'I will do it!' I declared in an urgent whisper before Sir Maurice could approach.

'What-what?' grunted Farringdon.

'I will do it - I will invest in your show,' I whispered, moving in a little closer and raising a finger.

'But with one or two conditions…'

And so I was about to embark on a new adventure - a journey into the lights and razzle-dazzle of the West End. Having insisted that - along with my financial support - I should be crowned Artistic Director, Rosemary and her grim husband weren't in a position to refuse, and had accepted the offer swiftly.

Payton Edgar - Artistic Director! The very idea appealed the artisan buried deep inside, and as I lay my head on my pillow that night, I decided to do my very best to enjoy myself. I might grumble about the theatre and the artificiality of it all, but there could be fun to be found in doing something different - and if I could get my own back on Sir Maurice into the bargain, then all the better.

What I didn't know was that I was signing up to a doomed production. A doomed production that would never even make it to the opening night.

I say all this at this early point in the story for no other reason than to peak interest.

A violent disappearance would be the start of it all. Lies, deceit, gossip and scandal would be the derailing of the thing, and then - the very nail in the coffin at the end - horrific, bloody murder.

And I was about to play a starring role in the whole sorry mess.

Part III

In which Payton meets the principle characters

Wanted; efficient secretary for city journalist. Must have typewriter skills and at least two years experience in the field. Would suit female with no family ties.
Contact P. Edgar, Pimlico
P.O Box 2456

The following Monday morning was a foggy one - and change was in the air.

I had gone to bed on Sunday evening as plain old Payton Edgar, renowned restaurant critic and wordsmith, and awoken as Payton Edgar, renowned restaurant critic, wordsmith and - starting that day - Artistic Director.

I had also chosen that Monday as the day to take my first steps towards establishing myself as more than just an independent journalist - it was time for me to employ staff. I had recently had the pleasure of getting to know Harvey Blake, an admirable businessperson and restaurateur of considerable flair, and was offered the use of a private office adjacent to Harvey's, my very favourite restaurant. An office besides the best restaurant in town! Not only that - it came free of charge! It was more than perfect.

I had also received some sage advice - a suggestion that I might obtain a personal assistant. The concept was a sound one, having someone to type up my pieces and deliver to deadlines, to make tea and to jump at my every word. Indeed, now that I had agreed to storm the West End, I would need all the help and support I could get.

I was daydreaming about my perfect secretary at breakfast when something on the kitchen table caught my eye. The jam, a passable blackcurrant, was covered with a cloth gingham cap - a small circle of fabric which clung to the jar with the force of elastic. I lifted it off of the lid, moved my fingers over it thoughtfully, and, coming to a decision, deposited it in my jacket pocket. As I did this, Grace entered the room and greeted me in her cool, calm way. I quickly raised a neatly written card in the air and waved it in her direction.

'Off into town? Have this placed in Positions Vacant at Boots, will you please, my dear? I am branching out!'

She gave me such a sweet smile that I thought I should make a polite enquiry as to her wellbeing, and so I foraged for a smile of my own. 'And how are you this morning?'

'As well as can be expected, thank you,' she replied drily. My aunt's nurse was mostly wonderful, but she could be too sardonic for own good at times. She was a curious creature. The child of an eminent but rather unpleasant couturier, Grace always went to great lengths to displease her fashionista mother - even as far as pumice-stoning my aunt's leathery heels. True to her lineage, however, she had a natural sense of style that one could only admire.

She took my carefully composed advertisement and perused it with interest. Grace was quite content to run little errands such as this, providing I asked politely.

'A secretary?' she continued with a measure of doubt in her tone. She looked up from the card with those disarmingly sharp blue eyes.

I was perhaps just a little on the defence in my reply.

'Yes, a secretary - do I need permission? A secretary, just as any successful businessman requires. I don't know why I haven't thought of it before. Why type up and deliver my pieces myself when I can have someone else do it? I have many strings to my bow, and I need someone-'

'-to help you play!' Grace cut in wearily, and perhaps a little rudely. 'I get it, I get it.'

'I have my delightful new office. No longer will I have to tolerate draughty cold corridors and the thunder of the presses at Fleet Street. All that's needed now is a face - front of house, so to speak.'

'Sensible, I suppose,' Grace nodded, slotting the card into her purse. Her eyes were twinkling as she pulled on her overcoat.

'Taxi to town?' she asked. I shook my head.

'No thank you,' I replied, adding mysteriously, 'I am awaiting collection.'

She didn't enquire further and left rather quickly, somewhat trampling over my enigmatic air.

'The car will pick you up!' Rosemary had said - and indeed it did.

We agreed that the car would come to Pimlico once it had safely delivered the Farringdons and then Sir Maurice to rehearsals, and so it was nearing ten o'clock when I heard the pip-pip of a horn. Ten o'clock in the morning - a most agreeable time for collection. Just enough time to wash, dress, breakfast and even potter around the house a little before the honk of the horn.

I have never before been collected by car and driven to a destination from door to door, but it is a luxury to which one could quickly become accustomed. While the car was impressive, Russell, the driver, was altogether too dark and handsome for his own good. A chauffeur should be white haired, well-mannered and dignified. I hoped that Russell was the man's surname, as private drivers should always be called Fairchild, Worthington, Carstairs or similar, and at least Mr Russell had the ring of the valet about it. Unfortunately, the man was merely being unnecessarily informal and using his first name only.

Despite his cheery greeting I made a point of not chatting, as is correct in such circumstances.

It is not proper for one to fraternise with staff.

The car and driver must have come at considerable expense, and it was only later that discreet enquiries would reveal that both Russell and the vehicle were completing a prepaid contract that was trailing into its final months. Come April, Gordon Farringdon would have to do without this particular luxury.

And it certainly was a luxury. There was something special and splendid about cruising through town in a private car. I ran my fingers appreciatively over the upholstery and then sucked on a lemon sherbet and watched life pass by my window. The day was what Mother would have called a real pea-souper, with thick fog swirling around the crest of each building. The flow of the Thames was barely visible, and the Palace of Westminster loomed up through the smog like Dracula's castle.

The Old Compton Theatre sat proudly on a street corner in the heart of Soho.

I have never particularly enjoyed Soho. Who could love an area that carries an aroma of potato peelings and rotting vegetables by day, and the stench of debauchery by night? Yet it was exhilarating to be driven, wherever the destination, and I have to confess to allowing myself a little shudder of delight as I stepped from the car - once Russell finally got around to opening my door. I stood on the pavement for a minute or so, seemingly collecting myself and adjusting my hat and lapel. In actual fact, I was allowing the eyes that watched to take a good look at Mr Payton Edgar as he left his carriage and entered the theatre with his head held high.

I knew what they would all be thinking - just who was this dapper stranger in theatre-land?

And the dapper stranger came prepared. After attending Pimlico Municipal Library on the wet Sunday afternoon, I had returned with three books; The Theatre and I by Dame Ellen Terry, A History of the stage by S.E.Shepherd and a dog-eared copy of the play itself; The Taming of the Shrew.

I was researched and ready.

Richard Chandler's theatre was smaller and pokier than one might expect, but the place did have a certain historic charm. As instructed, I moved alongside the building until I came to an entrance, over which hung a white box displaying the words stage door. I raised my stick and rapped the brass owl on the panel sharply. It moved a little, and I was surprised to find that it was unlocked and unmanned. Any Tom, Dick or Harry could steal in!

I moved on into the darkness.

The air was unpleasantly musty and damp, and there was no welcoming committee of any sort. Muffled voices became clearer as I made my way along a curiously shaped passageway, and I must have looked something of a clown as I poked my head around the side of the stage and winced under the glaring lights. A small number of people were centre stage, and more still in the darkness of the auditorium, but with the blaze of the lights it was impossible to tell who, or how many.

'Payton, darling!'

For once I was relieved to hear Rosemary's nasal whine as it pierced the darkness. She instructed me to come forth into the light, and I did so with some reluctance. She clapped her hands together.

'Everybody! Everybody! This is Mr Payton Edgar, our generous investor!'

'And…erm - and Artistic Director!' I added, just a little hesitantly. I was keen for this not to be forgotten. Rosemary's disembodied voice continued from somewhere far off.

'Of course. We are all very grateful for your endorsement, Payton, darling. Alex, dear, would you help Mr Edgar through and down to me? I shall take him under my wing.'

A strong hand was clamped on my shoulder and another on my forearm and I was swiftly ushered off stage, down into the cool darkness and then a few feet up a slope. As my eyes adjusted to the gloom, Rosemary flung her arms around me in another forthcoming greeting, and I was soon sitting beside her in the darkness of the sixth row, still blinking flashes of colour from my eyes. As I came to see more, I realised that the whole space was much smaller than anticipated. On top of that, the seats were a little uncomfortable and closely set.

Gordon Farringdon, who kept a spot on the second row, spoke up and resumed whatever nonsense had been happening up on the stage.

'So glad you came,' whispered Rosemary.

'I intend to come every day!' I announced boldly. 'Every day, to every rehearsal.'

Something about sitting at the theatre made me fumble in my pocket and bring out a paper bag.

'Lemon sherbet?'

Rosemary took one, and as we sucked on our sweets she grasped my sleeve and tittered into my ear like an old friend. She proceeded to give commentary on the company in a hoarse whisper.

'Three and a half weeks to opening night, and our cast is pretty tight. Now, let's see… for starters, you know the gentleman at the side with the hat, of course.' I scowled out at Sir Maurice Williams, looming large at one corner of the stage in his scuffed cords and flea-bitten pullover. He had, as usual, that look of confident superiority on his face. I eyed him disapprovingly.

'Sir Maurice is Petruchio, naturally,' explained Rosemary. Petruchio was absent at this point in the scene, and I was to learn that, rather than loiter backstage as most actors might, Sir Maurice preferred to perch stage right (following my extensive research I knew all the terms) and observe his peers with a critical eye, darkly appraising everything he saw. I dare say he considered himself to be the Artistic Director in all but name.

I studied him with an intense dislike as he slipped on a pair of pince-nez and examined his script with narrow-eyed scrutiny.

Despite my research, much of the dialogue was spoken in an entirely alien language. The well-thumbed copy of Shakespeare's 'Shrew' I obtained from the library might as well have been written in Greek. Even the footnotes, supposedly there to make the piece make sense, were often confusing and ambiguous. And yet I had gathered enough information to know that the central part of a cocksure suitor was surely to be played by a virile and masculine actor, not some bearded old fop in a woolly jumper and silly specs.

I said as much.

'Rubbish! Sir Maurice is a dream, and so very versatile. He brings a certain maturity to the part. A Fine actor.'

'A turkey in peacock feathers!' I huffed.

Rosemary continued.

'Now, up front of the stage is our Katherine, Miss Toffee Morrell.'

'Toffee Morrell?'

'Yes.'

'Toffee?'

'Yes.'

'Toffee Morrell?'

'What of it?'

'What sort of a name is Toffee?'

'What sort of a name is Payton, for crying out loud?' Rosemary cleared her throat impatiently and waved a limp wrist. 'These are theatre folk, Payton. Names are names are names…'

I inspected the bespectacled shrew on the stage.

'We inherited her with the venue, you see. She's Dickie Chandler's squeeze.'

'Squeeze?'

'Oh, quite a scandal under wraps, Payton! Once you get used to the age difference they're actually a darling couple. Happened quickly, mind - from pretty acquaintance to fiancee all in a matter of weeks! Dickie's always had a thing for girls like that - bright sparks, you know the sort? Dynamite blondes, all sparkling white teeth and saucer eyes. Yes, so the deal with Dickie was that we got to use this place only if we agreed to have young Toffee in the cast. Dickie insisted she have the title role. Gordy was livid, not being able to properly audition the girl, but in actual fact, as an actress she's not as bad as some of the cast would have you believe. Gordy has a bit of a grizzle about her every now and then - he is entitled to as director, and it's fair to say that she's not particularly liked. General consensus among the company is that she's out for Dickie's cash.'

'Really?'

'And there was a bit of a to-do at the beginning, what with her wearing specs on stage and all, but she's blind as a blindfolded bat without them, and Dickie insisted. Dickie does like to insist! Eventually he and Gordy came to a compromise of sorts. We will be kitting her out with some less obvious wire-framed eyewear for the performances. I'm more fussed about the wig, though. A wig at her age! Don't you think that that's a wig? I'm convinced it is. I know that hairpieces are the thing for some girls these days, but still! You can tell that's synthetic from all the way from row six, can't you?'

She wasn't about to give me time to reply.

'Anyhow, Dickie and the girl are happy together. Wedding bells on the horizon.'

I watched Toffee Morrell as she stormed about the stage in her role as Katherine. She was a tall, svelte young lady with strong golden hair that was pinned back into a marquis style. If it was indeed a wig, it was nowhere near as poor a replica as Rosemary made out. Her face, although heavily painted, was not unsightly, and yet it was difficult to say for sure as at that moment she wore the expression of a thundering elephant that the role required. She had a pair of dark, horn-rimmed glasses perched on her nose. Her voice was deep and thundering, and I decided that I quite admired the girl.

Gordon Farringdon stopped Miss Morrell mid-speech with some grumbling observations. Rosemary continued.

'We'll be having a lovely luncheon with Toffee and Dickie later this week, and you must come too, Payton. Give you a chance to get to know them. Now just behind her, looking a bit lost, we have her sister, Bianca.'

'They are sisters?' I exclaimed despite myself, for they could not have been less alike.

'In the play, Payton darling, in the play! That's Sylvia Pickford. One for the gentlemen, is Sylvia. A bit of a wet weekend, if you ask me, always simpering and sidling up to any man who dares step near enough. A flibbertigibbet, quite frankly, and too soppy for her own good.'

On stage, the small dark-haired girl was cowering as if she were afraid of Miss Morrell. With her glistening eyes and moulded black hair she put one in mine of a poodle, prim and trimmed. Aside the poodle stood a swarthy, handsome young man in tweeds.

'Tony Trace,' said Rosemary, anticipating my thoughts. She rested a claw on my forearm. 'Quite a dashing and promising young buck, our dreamy Lucentio. There's a spark between him and Pickford that's hard to miss.'

I looked at the man. He was indeed handsome. Almost uncomfortably so.

We were distracted from Mr Trace as a rugged man appeared at the side of the stage, massaging his jaw with one hand, screwdriver in the other.

'Oh! Alex Drake, our stage manager, there. Something of a dish too, isn't he? A bear of little brain, though, bless him.'

'A what?'

'Not the brightest bauble on the Christmas tree, darling. He may be a little rough around the edges but those big arms are to die for! And that dark, brooding look! If I were twenty years younger - well! He works here with his sister.'

'His actual sister?' I asked, trying to keep up.

'Mm-mm, his actual sister… flaky little Emma, our understudy and prompt. She has a very poor disposition… a sickly little thing. She'll be back there somewhere, nose in a ball of tissues. Gordon asked me to be prompt when she doesn't turn in. I flatly refused! I have my knitting to do! When poorly Emma is here she can be found slumped in the front row or skulking behind the curtains. There's not much Gordy can do about it - the Drakes came with the building. Alex has worked here for years.'

'It is a small company,' I ventured, to which Rosemary snorted.

'Principle characters today, darling, and for much of this week. There are sixteen in the company, though. A number of lesser-knowns will be hovering about backstage with nothing better to do. Ah! There's one you should know about. The fat thing stepping forth now - that is our Hortensio, Bill Nash. Can't say I'm a fan of his. Bit of a grumpy soul. And don't get too close - breath like a blocked drain.'

I was losing interest somewhat.

'Well I certainly don't need to know everybody's names,' I said as Rosemary produced a cigarillo. She lit it with a deft, practised hand and allowed me to continue. 'Just any titbits of interest on the key players, that's enough.'

At this point the house lights suddenly snapped on and a silver-haired gentleman swept down the aisle towards the stage, slapping his hands together like a performing seal.

'Take five, everybody, please! Take five!' he hollered in a sing-song manner. Gordon Farringdon turned and shot him as much of a thunderous glare as one can with only one eye.

'Not quite yet!'

'Sorry, old chap, but I'm afraid so. Break for tea! I must have words with Toffee!'

Miss Morrell was already stepping down from the stage with an excited grin, forcing Farringdon to concede. He called for a break with a heavy reluctance.

'I take it that that's your friend, dear, dear Dickie?' I whispered. There was a hint of the circus ringmaster about Dickie Chandelier. He held himself high with an exaggerated gait, hands aloft, and was adorned in an unusual green velvet suit with purple collar. His cuffs were purple frills. Edging into old age but well preserved, the care and attention the man paid to his magnificent silver bouffant was admirable.

As he embraced Miss Morrell he beamed like a child in a sweet shop. What was it Rosemary had said - that they made a darling couple? I wasn't so sure. It was like watching a glowing, youthful princess embrace a withered old tortoise, and I felt the sting of disapproval in my gut. I began plotting ways that I might get out of this luncheon Rosemary planned, for watching a tortoise fawning all over a princess would surely be enough to put anyone off their food. I whispered something along these lines to Rosemary, who replied with one of her snorting guffaws.

'Your husband doesn't hide his disapproval,' I added, catching Farringdon's dark glare. Rosemary sighed.

'Yes… there is the issue of creative control. Dickie has the habit of getting involved. No, I am being too kind - he has a habit of taking over. He used to tread the boards himself in days gone by, and rather fancies himself as director too.'

I watched as Chandler slid his arm around the girl's waist and led her away. Down in the second row, Gordon Farringdon, now looking glum and forlorn, stood and made his way up the aisle. He gave a weak smile in our direction and moved along slowly. His fragility was all too apparent.

I pressed Rosemary for some more details.

'It's his prostate gland,' she replied frankly and without a hint of concern while she rummaged in her handbag. 'Gone from a chestnut to a garden plum in a matter of months. He suffers terribly from the dribbles, spends as much time in the lavvy as he does out of it these days. In and out all night, he is. I'm set up in the guest room now.'

Rosemary found what she was looking for - a small hand-mirror, powder and brush. She peered into the mirror and ran the brush over her cheek.

'The specialist said there's nothing they can do, that he'll have maybe a year or so if he's very lucky. Well, he's got some funny ideas, has Gordy. That's what spurred him on to do this. His dream production. This one last hurrah.'

I sensed a hint of disfavour in her tone.

'And what might you call it?'

The enquiry was received with a short purse of the lips.

'A waste of our last days together, Payton - that's what I'd call it. But it's what Gordon wants.'

Suddenly she snapped the mirror closed and grasped my forearm.

'You wanted the key players? Well here's the last of them, our Baptista.'

A figure had appeared on the stage - a rotund, sweaty little man in a black turtle-neck jumper and rolled up trousers. His hair was smoothed over his skull by glistening balm, and his cheeks flushed red. As he called to the company, he waved a bicycle clip in the air.

'I say - sorry I'm late again, peeps. Lost a bike clip en route, had to circle back at Piccadilly.' He glanced at his watch. 'What? Tea break already? Well, I'm just in time then! Kettle on, darlings!'

'Christophe Playfair,' Rosemary whispered tellingly.

'Salutations, Rosie!' he chimed, looking out. 'And who is the new boy? A new face in the crowd, I see!'

'This is Payton,' said Rosemary. 'Our Artistic Director.'

The man hummed loudly.

'I'll be the judge of that! I insist that you come forth to my dressing room immediately, Mr Payton, where I shall pick you over for the good and the bad. I'm in the mood for a good picking. Ooh… just in time for elevenses! I have some of mummy's shortbread back there, you lucky article!'

As he smacked his lips together and leered out at us, I took an instant disliking to the man. Toady would be an apt description. His very manner was dripping with insincerity.

Rosemary lowered her voice. 'You'd better go, Payton.'

'No, I'd rather stay here,' I replied.

'Go on, get it over with,' Rosemary pressed. 'Befriend the natives!'

The man in stage was beckoning me in an exaggerated manner akin to a Macbeth witch, and I spoke softly to Rosemary before moving.

'I've had a re-think. Perhaps I shan't come to rehearsal every day…'

Part IV

In which Payton Edgar learns a horrid new word

Dear Margaret,

My husband belittles my life's work. Ever since university some 25 years ago I have been studying the Vespula Vulgaris - or the Common Wasp, as it is widely known. I have had two volumes on the subject published, but still my husband sees my work as an unimportant and even trivial pastime. He is an accountant, and thinks that money is the be-all and end-all. I take my work very seriously, but he doesn't. I am proud of my work, but he isn't. How can I make him respect what I do?

Mrs G, Ducketts Green

Margaret replies; Unimportant and trivial, you say? I regret to inform you that I cannot side with you on this particular question. Wasps are vile, bothersome irritants - their sole purpose appears to be to ruin picnics and litter bakery shop window displays. Why anyone should need to know more about the nasty creatures, I simply do not know. You could have used your brain and energies on a cure for the common cold or some such scientific brilliance. Instead you chose to look at bugs under a microscope. You have wasted your life and your talents.

It pays to be fastidious and precise when it comes to a cup of tea.

A brew can be a thing of magnificence if prepared correctly. One must take into account the temperature of the water, the condition of the kettle, the brewing time and - in particular - the sweetening thereof. I often add sugar to tea, but only if the circumstances allow it. The desired sweetness of any hot beverage depends upon my disposition at any given moment, the source and quality of the sugar on offer and - most notably - the time of year. As the days grow darker and colder, I find a sweetened beverage to be preferable, and sitting in a cold brick room in a draughty old theatre, I felt that I needed some sugary warmth.

Unfortunately, in this instance I was forced to decline the sugar for I did not trust the yellowing contents of the lidless bowl. I also declined the shortbread, offered in a rusty tin that had once housed bobbins.

Christophe Playfair had whisked me away to his dressing room, a dingy little place furnished with two modest mirrored dressing tables and littered with discarded clothes, hats and shoes. It was clear from the mess and the ripeness of the air that many people changed in this room. Two battered wooden chairs sat aside the dressing tables, towards which Playfair gestured grandly as if they were Hepplewhite treasures. Once settled, the actor simpered over his steaming teacup.

'Payton Edgar! I know that name!'

I smiled modestly. 'You may have come across my work, if you peruse the Clarion.'

'I peruse indeed. Restaurant critic? Pah! My Aunt Clementine knows more about good food - and she's a ninety year-old diabetic.'

'Excuse me?'

'And she lost all her tastebuds drinking scalding hot Bovril as a child.'

'I beg your pardon?'

'Just pulling your leg, duckie!' said Playfair quickly. He blew at the steam rising form his cup. 'Or am I? You gave a particularly favourite eatery of mine a scathing review quite a while back. La Maison Sebastien? You were quite, quite wrong, and for that I shall never forgive you. Their grub's to die for, in particular the pickled herring. Who'd have thought - a restaurant critic who can barely tell duck from fowl? And I'll bet you get all that posh nosh for free? Akin to giving a donkey strawberries, duckie!'

It was impossible to hide my indignation.

'Well - excuse me!'

'Just being deadly honest, that's all,' added Playfair before sipping his tea rather prudishly. 'You'll get used to my little ways. So then, have out with it! Spill it! Tell all!'

'Tell all?'

'Indeed - tell all!'

'I have nothing to tell.'

'Nonsense! Everyone has something to tell. And you can trust me not to pass it on. Five holes up top - eyes, ears, mouth - always keep four well open and the one firmly shut!' He tapped his lips. 'That is my way.'

'I'm so glad.'

'So… who is our natty Artistic Director? From whence have you came?'

I shrugged coldly. 'Pimlico?'

'I refer to your record! The theatrical successes under your belt, or notches on your bedpost, depending on your inclination. Experience, duckie! Theatrical war wounds… any that need licking?'

I watched as he wet his lips in a toady fashion.

'We can exchange information, do a fair trade. Tat for tat, you might say. Come along, you must know a thing or two, working on a daily rag. And prof-theatre is a hotbed of gossip and scandal… the things one hears en passant… I'd shock you 'til your hair curled!'

'I thought you kept your hole shut?'

Playfair sat back in this chair with a faux wounded expression.

'Touché! Of course, just as I know your name, you will certainly have come across mine. Everyone knows of Christophe Playfair.' He raised a finger. 'Christophe, not common-as-muck Christopher! Take special note of the missing consonant. Mummy dropped the "r" because, even as a babe in arms, she knew that I was something special. That said, in this particular production I am but a mere protege, an apprentice, un etudiant. I bend willingly in the presence of his greatness, Sir Maurice Williams. A true king of the art, from whom we can all learn a thing or ten. Television might not want him, but we do! That delightful, velvet tone… a voice at once bold and forceful, and yet somehow sensitively muted. Puts me in mind of my original mentor - for in my fledgling years I was mentored by the one and only Yardley Swain! Yes - Yardley Swain, duckie!'

He sparkled in my direction, searching for a response and when I didn't reply, shot out a string of tuts not unlike a machine gun.

'Yardley Swain! You're of an age, Mr Edgar - you must know the name! Everyone knows the name! An actor of much repute back in the day - a towering titan of the stage. Demon for the Bard!' He waved a dismissive wave. 'Before what happened to him happened, and things turned… a bit sour.'

I wondered what had happened, but wasn't given a second to ask. Playfair brayed a little more about his unbridled talent and experience and went on to spin some tedious yarn about his early days as a jobbing actor - something about climbing in and out of dressing room windows that wasn't really worth the breath he used to tell it. Eventually, he paused in the middle of all his glorifying and I took the opportunity to speak. I posed a carefully crafted question.

'So, despite all your theatre experience, have you ever held down a proper job?'

Playfair's face fell. 'Excuse me?'

'Just being deadly honest, that's all,' I replied.

We each sipped our tea, and then Playfair continued, as if I hadn't said a word.

'So giddy to be a part of all this. A tippetty-top company. I know Dickie Chandelier - such a delightful moniker - of old… yes, we go way, way, way back. A dear, dear, dear, dear chap. Dickie's penchant for serendipity is legend. And then there's Gordon Farringdon, simply an ace of a director - one of the old guard, a true statesman at his craft. Certainly a privilege to star in what is obviously his swan-song. Now… pray tell, have you a vision?'

'A vision?'

'As Artistic Director, duckie! Or is it just a title? A polite way of saying "the money man", so to speak?'

I offered no response, and he continued as if he hadn't been expecting one.

'I should be very interested to know your take on the play, the themes you see as imperative, those particular nuances we might shine a light on. We must have a conference about my character over lunch, if you'd be a dear and pay. I feel that poor Baptista is sometimes incorrectly seen as a peripheral role, a mere plot point, when he could and should have a far stronger presence in the staging of the thing. He is in many ways a protagonist, wouldn't you say?'

I was being tested, and so I smiled a secretive smile and shook my head as if to say "wait and see". I wanted to show the man that I was playing my cards close to my chest. He didn't need to know that, in actual fact, I held no cards. I didn't even want to hold any cards! I had no interest whatsoever about the themes of the stupid play or the point of his boring character.

He went on.

And on.

And on.

And then he slapped my knee playfully and drew me back to the conversation.

'Now, we need to talk about sex, duckie!'

I had no words.

'I feel the need to lay down a few rules, to a fellow male of the species. You will have noticed, I'm sure, the comely faces our production has gathered? Acting is a raw, passionate profession - codpieces and lace bodices, a dangerous but thrilling mix! You are a bachelor, are you not? Well I'll tell you now, the understudy, dear little Miss Drake, and the fair Pickford are bagged – my fancy fillies, and mine only.'

I was somewhat surprised at this, for he didn't seem the sort. Nevertheless, I nodded politely. Playfair wet his lips again with a thick tongue and then cackled a revolting cackle. 'Truly fine specimens - Arcadian deers, r-r-r-ripe for the hunt! But it is my hunt, and mine alone. Remember that, you swine!'

I scoffed openly, and he caught it.

'I know, I know! But the truth of the matter is that while fine fillies might chain themselves to railings or throw themselves under horses, fundamentally when it comes down to the nitty gritty, all they are looking for is a good, strong man to run them down and put them in their place.'

I enjoyed an exaggerated eye-roll, and as he chittered on with boundless idiocy I found myself shivering with revulsion. For a moment I cursed my bad luck, now there were two actorly imbeciles to contend with - first Sir Maurice, and now the vile Playfair!

And then I reminded myself where I was. This wasn't anything to do with luck, this was the theatre, and actorly imbeciles were probably as common here as batter puddings in Yorkshire.

I had listened to Playfair's gibberish for far too long. I stood quickly, thanked him for the tea and made for the door - just as Sir Maurice entered without the courtesy of a knock.

'Just popped in to borrow a glass or two – champers flutes if you have them, treacle? I may have the largest dressing room but it is dreadfully devoid of accoutrements.' He pouted in a matronly fashion. 'I'll wager he's been pumping you for information, Edgar? Well, Christophe, I can save you the time. Mr Edgar has never before had anything whatsoever to do with the theatre, and has absolutely no direction, artistic or otherwise.'

'Do stay a minute, Mo. Mr Edgar was just leaving,' said Playfair slyly. Sir Maurice thrust his face towards mine.

'Well, tootle-pip then! Off you trot!'

Fuming, I slipped out of the door.

However I did not move far away, for just a short way down the gloomy corridor I could hear Sir Maurice's booming roar enough to make out a number of words. As usual, he was bellowing like a town crier. Pulled by the drag of curiosity, I retraced my steps, and may even have been daring enough to put my ear to the door.

Something was said about Fanny Craddock, at which they both laughed. It was a relief to find that they were not talking about me.

And then Sir Maurice raised his tone higher.

'Sherbet lemon sucking fool!'

Well, that could have been me. And then I heard my name amongst some scattered words.

'...mumpsimus old Edgar... bumbling about... stuffy old dandy talks with a plum in his mouth...'

'...nothing but blinking idiots under this bloody roof...'

And then Sir Maurice gave a wail and bellowed proudly. 'Like sand in your pants at Skegness, damn bloviator gets everywhere!'

They laughed, and then Playfair continued, his words a little harder to detect.

'... I would say that... thinks he knows bloody everything...'

'Indeed. Only one word for his type...'

And then I heard a single, clear word repeated, which hit me like a stone.

'Snitty!'

'Oh, yes, duckie! Snitty! Snitty!'

Bellows of laughter pushed my ear from the door and I shuffled away with haste.

Snitty?

The first thing I did upon returning home was to reach for a dictionary.

Grace floated into the lounge and found me flicking through the pages. She was pulling on her overcoat.

'Looking for anything in particular?'

'One word - Snitty.' I slapped a hand down on the book with frustration. 'And it's not here - not a proper word at all. Mmm... it may be a theatrical term. Snitty. What do you make of it?'

For a moment Grace looked a little alarmed, and when she spoke she did so slowly and carefully.

'I would say that, perhaps, it sounds like other words that are ...well, similar. Snobby, or... snotty. That kind of thing?'

'And am I either of those things?' I asked, perhaps too quickly. She bit her lip and then paid unnecessary attention to fluffing up her scarf. I waited for a reply, and when it didn't come, closed the book and stood. It was only as I was halfway out the room that she spoke, and she did so in hushed tones.

'Payton, I feel that I should warn you. Your aunt's not in the best of moods today.'

'When is she?' I replied. 'Is it still over the birthday?'

Only the week before, Grace had made a terrible error of judgement and insisted we do something to mark Aunt Elizabeth's 300th birthday. I tried desperately to talk her out of it - birthdays have never been considered worth celebrating in our family - but the fiery young thing insisted. She had a fruit cake specially made, decorated it with candles and, with balloons in our hands, Grace, Irving and I had entered her bedroom, the two of them singing like children. I was unsurprised to see the scorn on my aunt's face.

'A fruit cake?' she had said as the singing stopped. 'A fruit cake?'

'You adore fruit cake,' said Grace. 'It's your favourite!'

'That's as may be, but don't I warrant something different for a landmark birthday - something tiered, or at least with icing?'

'We bought balloons!' Grace then said perkily, as the woman in the bed grunted.

'Ugh! Rubber bags filled with someone else's breath? What would I want with that?'

After all this, Aunt Elizabeth had sunk into a blue funk that seemed to permeate throughout the house for days.

'No, it's not about the birthday,' Grace replied. 'It's this.' By way of explanation, she turned and retrieved something from the hallway. It was a cat-box and, much to my surprise, an unhappy ginger moggy was cowering inside.

There were two cats under my roof; my dear fat puss Lucille - a fine, stately, clean creature - and Titty, the mangy stray that Aunt Elizabeth claimed as her own. Titty was an unkempt little thing who came and went through her bedroom window as he pleased. And now the poor creature was making unhappy noises from within the basket.

'Off to the vets?' I asked, somewhat obviously.

'Unfortunately not,' replied Grace. 'I'm taking Titty to the cat's home.'

'Does my aunt know?'

'She's the one who's making me do it,' said Grace, making for the door.

'What? Why?'

'Ask her yourself,' came the reply.

And so, pulled by curiosity, I found myself knocking cautiously on Aunt Elizabeth's door. After hearing a grunt from inside, I let myself in.

She was, as usual, sitting up in bed with a black shawl pulled around her shoulders and a thunderous look on her face. She had a tray on her lap and was fingering some striped fabric alongside a small pile of prickly objects. In recent months Aunt Elizabeth had developed a penchant for creating teasel animals, and the room was dotted with queer representations of cats in pantaloons and mice in bonnets. There was even what might have been a camel in felt wellington boots.

It was a curious pastime for one so nefarious.

'Oh, hello, dear Margaret,' she growled. Undeterred, I asked why her feline friend, the only thing in the whole house that she seemed to like, was being taken away in a box. At first she didn't reply, but picked at her blanket sullenly.

'You adore that cat,' I added.

'Not any more. He changed, Payton.'

'Changed?'

'He has taken to sitting on the end of my bed, staring at me. Just sitting there watching, for hours. Staring at me with thin eyes… waiting.'

'Waiting? For what?'

'The number twelve bus, Payton! What do you think he's waiting for?'

'I have absolutely no idea.'

'For me to perish, that's what. Biding his time… waiting for the day when I succumb to all that ails me, so that, as I fade away on my sick bed, he can come forth and chew on my earlobes. He sits there and watches me, day and night. Thin eyes, sharp teeth.' She let out a sob. 'I had a dream he ate my eyelids!'

I stood, speechless. There was nothing to be said, but Aunt Elizabeth had more.

'Poor, forgotten old woman - destined to fester, forever alone. First your dear mother dies and leaves me, then this wretched stroke snatches away my freedom, and now my only true friend turns on me with pointed teeth.'

'You adore that cat,' I said again.

'He had to go,' she said, with a grim finality.

I shook my head. There was no point in arguing the matter, for when Aunt Elizabeth made up her mind, it was final. However, I found I did have a comment to make.

'You will regret it, I fear.'

She raised her bony shoulders.

'And so I am alone. Perhaps it's how I'm meant to be spend my dark winter years. Alone and unloved, with only the sports pages and endless plates of tripe dumped in front of me-'

'You love tripe. You ask for tripe.'

'-endless plates of tripe! The clock ticks. I lie here and see only death, shrouded in swathes of billowing black, death ready and waiting… awaiting my demise…'

She carried on, but I had drifted away to somewhere strange. Visions of the ginger stray gnawing at my aunt's bloody earlobes lingered in the mind. I saw it take sinewy flesh in it's teeth and pull. It was an unwelcome image, and I was distracted for some time.

'…so there it is, laid bare. An old woman's fear. A wretched feeling. Well? Payton? Are you listening?'

I snapped back into the room. 'Beg pardon?'

'What do you have to say on the matter?'

Baffled, and unconcerned. I shrugged. Aunt Elizabeth thinned her dry eyes, and then waved me away.

'You really couldn't care less, could you? Well pooh to you! Standing there gormless in your trumped-up jacket and silly neckerchief! Well, I'm alright - I have my knitting and stitching.' She fingered a pin-cushion. 'And my teasel animals. They don't ignore me. Now get out of my room. I have to finish Grandpa Mouse.'

Part V

In which the Artistic Director offers artistic direction

Dear Margaret,

My elderly father recently suffered a heart attack and is struggling to look after himself. I would like to move Dad into our family home to keep a closer eye on him, however my husband refuses to allow it. He gives no good reason for this, only that we do not have the space. I adore my father, and would love to help him now that he needs me - and we have a beautiful spare room. How can I convince my husband?

Housewife, Chingford

Margaret replies; My dear, unlike your husband I can give you many good reasons why you must never allow an elderly relative to move in and take over your home and your life. What may seem like a sensible solution at the start can only lead to regret and misery. And once you do it, there will be no going back. Costs will amount as they demand frivolities such as food and heating, not to mention medical supplies which never come cheap. Worse, they will also demand your precious time. I suggest that you listen to your husband and consider a convalescent home for your crumbling father. It is wise to keep parasitical relations at arms length.

I had a pleasant surprise the next time I attended The Old Compton for rehearsals, and the surprise involved Rosemary.

First, I was collected at ten o'clock.

Oh - the joys of being collected by car!

I was careful not to be too agreeable or friendly with Russell, and sat in silence with an air of a respectable, professional city gent. It was annoying, therefore, to find that - yet again - the chauffeur failed to take on the air of polite servitude one would expect. He tried to chat a little, and I did my best to shut any conversation down. In the end, he even dared to be a little grumpy and, once we had arrived at our destination, took far too long to heave up out of the driving seat, circle the car and open my door. To make a point, however, I waited with chin high until he did.

I left with a curt word of thanks and entered the theatre, keen to display the confidence and bravado that an Artistic Director must exhibit. I passed through the stage door, said polite good-mornings to the stage hand Alex and then to glass-eyed Farringdon, and breezed on through to my place on the sixth row. Rosemary was already in position, her head bent over something. She was tittering gaily to herself, and it was only as I coughed that she looked up. On her lap sat a copy of The Clarion.

'Good morning - sorry to disturb you.'

'Morning, Payton. I was just enjoying the newspaper.'

'Anything in particular?'

'The agony column, actually.'

I sat. 'Really?'

'Yes, I make a point of reading it. You wouldn't know much about it. I'm sure, but it is the best part of the rag.'

'Is it really?' I replied. She mistook my warm tone for one of irritation.

'Oh, your restaurant guff aside, naturally. But Dr Blythe always tells it like it is. She has a knack for pointing out the ridiculous. Some of the things people write in about beggar belief. Take today's page - a reader writes in about her poor dear ailing father and how she's wants to care for the man, and Margaret says what we are all thinking - relations as parasites! Ha! Classic Margaret!'

Suddenly I felt a warmth towards the woman - a new and not unwelcome feeling.

'I'm glad that you like it.'

She grinned, closed and folded the newspaper. 'You know her, obviously. She seems remarkably forthright, and I should love to meet her. Perhaps you could introduce us?'

'Dr Blythe is a very private person,' I replied carefully. 'Something of an intellectual recluse.'

I was saved from any more questions when Gordon Farringdon slapped his hands together to signal the start of rehearsals.

I sat nestled in the shadows of the stalls with Rosemary knitting fiercely but quietly at my side. Every now and then she paused to light up one of her stinking herbal sticks. I made a performance of wafting away the lingering smoke, but was unsurprised to find that she failed to register my wordless protestations. We endured hours of Sir Maurice Williams spewing gibberish in a ridiculously bogus, booming tone, over and over and over again. Precious little of his prattle made sense. That said, some of the cast found the performance amusing, or at any rate pretended to do so.

I made sure that no laughs came from my corner of the auditorium.

I was just nodding off when a curious lingering silence fell on the room, and I raised my head. Miss Pickford had paused mid-speech. She winced and then straightened.

'Prompt!' grunted Gordon Farringdon from the second row, massaging his brow. 'Bloody prompt!'

There was some backstage scuffling before the hirsute stagehand peered around from behind a curtain, squinting down at a paperback.

'Is it for him - er - you do envy me so…' he stammered. 'Nay then you jest-'

Farringdon let forth a rumble of disapproval from his seat in the second row.

'Where, Mr. Drake, is your sister?'

The young man blinked and lowered his head.

'S'her chest again, sir. Emma's tucked up, I'm afraid. As I said, I'm happy to prompt. She should be back t'morrow, all being well, sir.'

This was followed by a rumble of discontent from the company before Miss Pickford picked up her line and the drivel continued. I shifted in my seat. It seemed like everyone was having an opportunity to be involved except for me - and I was the Artistic Director!

Thankfully, an opportunity to integrate myself revealed itself a while later. Toffee Morrell had been struggling over the delivery of a line for some time, and Sir Maurice had presented suggestions that were nonsensical in the extreme. The girl needed some help. I raised both myself and my voice.

'Er- might I poke forth an idea?'

An unexpectedly chilly silence descended, and all eyes on stage peered out in surprise. It was almost as if they had forgotten my presence! In the second row, Farringdon took a moment to turn, and when he did look back, I noted the absence of a smile.

Nevertheless, I continued, undeterred.

'Only a suggestion. It's just that, when Maurice says am I not wise? and then Miss Morrell, says – what is it? Something about warmth…' I checked Rosemary's script. 'Yes, keep you warm - I wondered exactly what Katherine could mean by this. She may mean his intellect, as is the obvious interpretation, but could she not also step to the fireplace to illustrate heat, and dance around it a little? I think perhaps she is teasing him, and could, well, could even take up a poker and brandish it-'

'A poker?' Sir Maurice thundered.

'A poker?' echoed his little round shadow, the vile Playfair.

'Yes, a poker - as if to suggest that a beating with this may also keep him warm, as she says. It adds a little something else, don't you think?'

Silence.

'And this is supposed to be a comedy,' I added, with all the confidence I could muster. 'It brings a new dimension to the words, wouldn't you say? And perhaps just a soupçon of humour…'

I sat back down, really rather pleased with myself.

Up on the stage, Sir Maurice was glaring out with unrestrained contempt. Farringdon's expression was much the same, and yet when he went to disagree, he was cut short by his wife.

'No, hang on a moment, Gordy, take a breath. I think Payton makes a good point, don't you? It would be funnier. And he is here as Artistic Director – perhaps we can allow him this one intervention?' Rosemary was speaking with a certain intonation that not-so-discreetly said "shut up, we need our funding". Farringdon settled and nodded, and up on stage Toffee Morrell was also nodding enthusiastically. I nodded too.

It was all extremely satisfying.

'Can we add a poker to the prop list then, Alex,' grumbled Farringdon.

They carried on with the play, but all the while Sir Maurice, clearly wrong-footed by my ingenuity, continued to glower unhappily in my direction.

By lunchtime I was squirming with discomfort, for the auditorium seats were somewhat threadbare, and so I was relieved when time for lunch was called. Chandler appeared, smiling happily, his cloud of hair groomed to perfection. We were due to dine at his favourite restaurant in town.

'I was hoping Miss Fudge could join us,' he sang gaily, 'but she has other plans.'

I leaned in to Rosemary.

'Miss Fudge?'

She issued a snort.

'Dickie's front of house - his can-do woman - tickets and sales and accounts and the like. Been with Dickie for eons, akin to something of a wife so far as the business is concerned. You won't see her much, though. She keeps to the box office and the front. In fact, I don't think I've ever seen her out of her box. I presume she does have legs…'

Ahead of us, Richard Chandler slipped an arm around his fiancée and led us outside. It was spattering with rain, and Chandler and Miss Morrell gasped and hurried as if it were sulphuric acid falling from the sky.

The restaurant, Mayfair Gardens, was situated just around the corner from Trafalgar Square. I had never come across the place, but made sure to keep my critic's hat well and truly off and to be on my best behaviour, for Chandler announced that he would foot the bill. In such circumstances, it would have been rude to quibble. The place sounded promising, and Chandler sung its praises as he danced down the street.

Unfortunately, the meal turned out to be something of a disappointment.

The name Mayfair Gardens conjures up visions of a babylon of splendid greenery, exotic flowers and majestic tinkling waterfalls. In reality the place was uncomfortably snug, devoid of splendour or indeed character, and without so much as a pot plant in sight. On top of that, a restaurant situated so close to Trafalgar Square really should be more circumspect about how much of a presence pigeon should have on the menu.

Miss Morrell made a fuss of the old man, tossing aside her menu and insisting that he choose and order food on her behalf. For a while I contemplated her hairline. If it was indeed a falsie she sported, it was a remarkably good one - and stylish too.

Almost everyone at the table plumped for minestrone followed by the spaghetti. Feeling slightly under pressure to fall in with the ordering of broth, I braved the tomato soup, which turned out to be a heartbreakingly weak and flavourless red liquid, and then the lamb, which was stringy and grey. I drew the line at the popular choice for dessert - blancmange. Blancmange? An abomination! The gloopiest, most unappetising combination of sweet slush - not fit for baby food. I sat back and sipped at my wine as I watched my fellow diners slurping down their dessert without complaint. They had enjoyed the pallid spaghetti dish, too.

Toffee Morrell turned out to be something of a bright spark, chatting gaily and punctuating her conversation with tumultuous giggles. She was remarkably thick-skinned, and appeared to be quite unaware that she was unpopular among her fellow cast members. At one point one of the men made a unveiled reference to her pretty face, and as she responded coquettishly I saw Rosemary stiffen.

'You just hang on to it while you've got it, young lady! Age comes to claim us all in the end. With humans, the caterpillar to butterfly thing works the other way around - you just wait!'

It was practically a witch's curse, but the words passed over the young woman without any effect whatsoever, and she continued to titter and chatter. Rosemary leaned in to my ear.

'A tad boisterous today, our Miss Morrell.'

'Mmm. She is a little… unquiet,' I replied.

But I liked her. She had a refreshingly outgoing quality, laughing in all the right places and listening to my speeches with a nod and a smile. Rosemary might have groaned as I detailed the superiority of Savile Row tailoring and rallied against the poor cuts sported by the youth of today, but young Toffee agreed passionately. At one point, she shot me a cheeky wink over her wine, her eyes sparkling behind those horn-rimmed spectacles.

I was, I have to admit, just a little bewitched by the dear young thing, and yet I could see both why Chandler adored her and also why the cast were less charitable. There is often a fine line between adorable and irritating, and Toffee Morrell walked the line with aplomb.

But she made Dickie Chandler a happy man, that much was evident. At every opportunity he clutched Toffee's arm or gently pinched her cheek, gazing down at her with pleasure.

In contrast, Gordon Farringdon was an altogether miserable presence. He endured lunch without speaking a word, and barely touched his food. Dark rings circled his eyes. Between the starter and the main I caught sight of him picking some tablets out of a gilt pill box and attempting to discreetly wash them down with red wine. He looked terribly pale, and as we departed he was noticeably slower than the rest of our company in gathering up his coat and shuffling on out.

Outside, the rain had eased. I made my excuses and managed to wriggle out of an afternoon back in the dark of the stalls. Nobody seemed particularly concerned to see me go, and I resolved to be even more involved as Artistic Director in future. There was surely some more ways in which I could infuriate Sir Maurice or even just irritate that idiot Playfair by way of intervention.

I passed through St James's Park and lingered for a while to watch the noble pelicans. The wind soon picked up, and I headed home feeling quite content - unaware that I was about to receive a terrible, terrible shock.

At first, I didn't notice anything untoward.

I deposited my stick in the wicker umbrella stand, hung up my hat and coat on the brass stag's antlers aside the door, and decided to warm myself with a nice hot cup of camomile tea. It was only as the whistle in the kettle was steaming furiously in the kitchenette that I sensed that something was amiss. I scanned the living room. Something was different – something was… absent.

Back in December I had treated myself to a new briefcase, a delightfully high-quality sky-blue leather affair with charming cream stitching. It only ever contained a number of unimportant papers and the pens which were an unwanted birthday gift from my weekly char-woman, Mrs Montgomery, but it was smart, a joy to look at and pleasant to handle. I kept it slotted aside my lounge chair - but now the case was missing.

I studied the room further. A small blue porcelain vase - one of the few of Mother's processions that had any aesthetic value - was absent from its usual position on the telephone table. And my mantelpiece was almost entirely bare.

We had been burgled!

I must have turned off the gas, for the kettle steadied to silence, but my mind was elsewhere. The mantelpiece, now so very empty, had held my most prized procession.

My antique Tibetan singing bowl.

My mouth went dry. It was as if anything of merit had simply vanished from the room - and the bowl wasn't my only treasure. My fine collection of Mesopotamian pottery came to mind, and I raced along the hallway and up into my chamber at the rear. The pieces were still there, the sharp edged plates and painted tablets mounted and displayed as always. Deceptively valuable, they had clearly looked too humble for this common thief. I barely noted the open window on the far wall, for there was one more thing to check.

The shoebox sat undisturbed under the bed. There were no fingerprints in the fine layer of dust on top, but still I steeled my heart as I lifted the lid. Inside, resting upon a folded velvet cloak, lay my Dresden shepherdess, safely in place. My relief only lasted seconds before I was overcome with anger. I slid the box back under the bed.

My wonderful singing bowl! How hard it had been to purchase and have shipped, and how irreplaceable it was. I could have cried.

I stood in the hall and took in a breath.

And then I did cry, just a little.

My poor, dear, wonderful, beautiful, crimson singing bowl! Bowl and mallet, snatched!

As I returned to the living room, I saw that that the second drawer down in the kitchenette was slightly open. Thieving hands had rifled through the pencils and receipts within, and found the emergency cash which I kept between the dog-eared pages of a 1952 A-to-Z - all thirty-eight pounds gone! It was clear that I had been the victim of a particularly thorough thief.

I steadied myself, for I could feel that familiar acid heat rising from my stomach, and then went to Grace's door, which stood ajar. I craned my neck inside - the room was neat and tidy as ever, and devoid of life. Whether anything had been taken from within I could not have said.

And then, with a start, I was hit by a sober fact - my house was never devoid of life.

Aunt Elizabeth!

She, who never left the house! I was so dismayed over the loss of my bowl, I had quite forgotten! Her door was closed as usual, but what might have happened? What had they done to her?

Suddenly, shock and anger was replaced by fear. I stood at her door, reluctantly touching the knob, my heart pounding. It wasn't that I particularly feared for Aunt Elizabeth, more for what I might find. What if they had attacked her? What if I was to find her lying dead or dying in a pool of blood? My nerves couldn't take it - not to mention my third-favourite Isfahan carpet.

I have never burst into my aunt's room, and even now I was not about to start. I knocked, softly at first and then once or twice with force.

'Get out!' came the usual gruff reply.

Somewhat relieved, I turned the knob and entered. Aunt Elizabeth was sitting up in bed with the Clarion open on her lap as if nothing untoward had occurred. She turned a page loudly and, flattening it with a few violent slaps, snapped curtly.

'What is it, Payton? I'm reading.'

I stood silent - quite, quite tongue tied.

'At least you knocked this time,' she croaked, 'rather than bursting in like a buffalo.'

I took a deep breath before telling her with some disbelief what had happened. Burglars! We had been looted in broad daylight! The vase and the money and my briefcase were missing – and my antique singing bowl was gone! My antique singing bowl! Gone!

Aunt Elizabeth paled as she took in the news. She stared blankly with a lowered jaw as I asked the obvious questions. She was here the whole time. Had she not known? Had she not heard anything?

She stared ahead.

'Well? Didn't you hear anything?' I repeated.

'No, nothing. The only disturbance was you - during my nap, when you rudely burst in.'

'That wasn't me, I have only just got home. It must have been them. They must have found you dozing and left you to it. Not before ransacking the place of my so-very-treasured treasures…'

The old woman rested back onto her plump pillows. 'I-I barely looked up. I thought it was you. I shouted at you to get out.'

And so they had.

Aunt Elizabeth clutched the lace neck of her gown, gasped a little and then peered up from the bed with an unusual expression. There was horror in her eyes.

'Strangers! Criminals, thieves… in my room!' She began to puck at the skin of her neck, coughing as she spoke. 'Filth! Burglars in my bedroom! I could have been murdered! Murdered!'

She went on like this for some time. As she did, I leaned back against the doorframe, a little short of breath.

My poor, poor antique singing bowl, I thought to myself with a heavy heart.

Part VI

In which Payton Edgar mourns his terrible, terrible loss

Dear Margaret,

I have been courting a young man for several months now, and am petrified of kissing. It just seems so silly - touching lips and licking and all that. My boyfriend thinks that petting is romantic and wants to do it all the time, but I won't allow it. Now I feel he is cooling off because of it. How can I overcome my dislike?

Molly, Hackney Downs

Margaret replies; Kissing? Ugh! There is nothing remotely romantic about two people sticking their food-holes together. As far as I am aware, no other living creature on our entire planet thinks that licking tongues to show affection is a good idea. Even dogs , revolting creatures at the best of times, don't do it - so why should we? You are quite right to keep your boyfriend at arms length, and if he cares for you, he will understand. It is a simple matter of hygiene.

A warm peck on the hand or the cheek is more than enough.

The police put on a poor show.

Our terrible crime apparently only warranted one single solitary officer - an egg-headed constable who barely wrote a jot on his pad and who seemed far more concerned over the welfare of my aunt than of my missing treasures. He was under the impression that all that had been purloined was a modest amount of cash and some immaterial nick-nacks. Even a concise lecture on the unique beauty and origin of my singing bowl failed to elicit any kind of empathy. The officer also had the temerity to shake his head in disapproval as he inspected the latch on my bedroom window, as if I had purposely fitted an insufficient lock, simply willing any greedy intruder to pop in. He went on as if I had erected a sign above the window inviting all and sundry inside to take their pick of my goods - as if I was any other commonplace dim-witted homeowner! An unpalatable assertion indeed.

I was only too happy to close the front door behind him.

At the officer's direction I made Aunt Elizabeth a sugary cup of tea. The old thing was - as is her way - entirely consumed by matters of her own welfare, and I was forced to listen as she moaned on and on about the idea of having raiders enter her bedroom. In all honesty, the thought of it made me smile just a little. Surely the most violent and ruthless criminal would still come a cropper if they dared to tackle Aunt Elizabeth during her afternoon nap. The woman was as tough as old boots.

I left her grizzling over her tea and took myself around to Irving's place in search of some tea and sympathy for myself.

Thankfully, Irving cared enough to set down his brush and easel and listen to my tale of woe. I left his house an hour later feeling - while not entirely happy - at least a trifle less discombobulated by this latest turn of events.

I was not in the greatest of temperaments on my next excursion to the West End.

Unfortunately, Russell was - again - in an alarmingly chatty mood. I was not of a mind to converse and, as he blathered on about the patterns of the clouds, I as much as told him so. The unpredictability of the British weather held no interest that morning. My thoughts were beset with the invasion of my humble town house and the pillaging that appeared to be of such little consequence to anyone but myself. If for no other reason than to stop the man yapping, I informed him sharply about the loss of my priceless antique singing bowl and what it meant to me.

'A bowl that sings? Blimey!' he chirped lightly, and I gave my speech about the origins and merits of the missing item with as much fervour as I could muster.

After this, he fell into an understanding silence.

My grim disposition didn't deter me from confessing all to Rosemary at our seat in the stalls. In fact, it was comforting to have a good moan. I was prepared for half-hearted compassion, however she surprised me by demonstrating a previously unseen ability to empathise. I had forgotten - Rosemary always enjoyed a victim. She fussed over me with a welcome sense of drama, and I allowed her to settle me in my seat and to fetch me a strong cup of tea.

'How simply dreadful. Terrible! Shocking! Oh, you poor thing! How absolutely awful!' she bleated over and over, as I sipped on my hot sweet drink. Her concern, however, proved to be short lived, for she was soon distracted by anxious murmurs from her miserable husband four rows down. There was some disquiet bubbling up among the company. Both leads of the piece, Toffee Morrell and the idiot Sir Maurice, had failed to appear. Dickie Chandler swept across the front of the stage in an unbecoming maroon velour suit, announcing in his high tones that he would search out his fiancée immediately.

At that moment, the side doors burst open and a monster entered the auditorium. It consisted of a large heap of clothes, with two spindly legs staggering beneath it. A white hand reached up from within the pile as the person staggered forwards and then dumped the load onto the nearest seat, revealing a new face, and a strange one at that.

'Who's that?'

Rosemary hummed. 'Oh, that's Ethel… I forget her surname. She's the new wardrobe mistress. Something happened to the old one… I forget what. And so Ethel popped up, just at the right time!'

Ethel the wardrobe mistress was cursed with unfortunate features. With tiny beady eyes she had the look of a rodent, and with a hook nose and protruding underbite the look of Judy Punch. Her cheeks had been hastily rouged, and she wore the plainest pinafore dress. A number of tape measures were draped around her neck. She lit up a cigarette and allowed it to hang from the corner of her mouth.

'Measuring up this morning, Mr Farringdon!' she croaked with a smoker's growl.

The director quickly set her onto Miss Pickford and Tony Trace, before turning to his wife.

'Pop and fetch Sir Maurice, darling,' he ordered. 'He's been seen - we might have to eek him out of his dressing room.'

But Rosemary was having none of it. She decided that what I needed was a distraction rather than more sympathy and, snatching away my cup, ordered me to slip backstage to root out Sir Maurice from his dressing room.

I departed with undisguised frostiness.

'The large door with the glittery star on it!' Rosemary said, and it was not difficult to find, although much of the glitter had long since lost its sparkle and fallen to the floor. I rapped politely on the dusty wooden door with the handle of my stick, and from within came a scuffling noise.

'Just a moment!'

This moment turned out to be a good forty-five seconds before I heard the click of a lock. Sir Maurice pulled open the dressing room door. He was not smiling.

'Oh, Edgar, it's only you. Sent you to fetch me, did they? Well, not before my mid-morning pipe you don't.'

Sir Maurice vanished into the room and, with a healthy portion of idle curiosity, I followed on in. It was larger than expected, at least four or five times bigger than Playfair's poky little space. The man stood at his mirror, a pipe in his mouth, fumbling in his baggy cardigan pockets.

'Nice dressing room,' I uttered, although one could not fail to notice the lack of natural light and the musty odour that was rife throughout the building. 'A better size than the others.'

'I suffer mightily with claustrophobia,' Sir Maurice boomed as he lit and puffed noisily at his pipe. 'The crippling fear of enclosure. For every show I insist on inspecting all dressing rooms in the venue and absolutely must have the one with the greatest proportions, for I am hampered by my malady. It is a most unfortunate affliction. I cannot even travel on the wretched tube - I am forced to ply my way with taxi cabs. Many great artists have suffered in such a way - great talent cannot be squeezed into a cubby-hole. It stems from the need to be free to express oneself without walls, without constraint. Like a bird needing space for flight, this is my burden.'

I said nothing, but thought a lot. What a tit! It was difficult to understand how a man so cripplingly dull and idiotic could be so successful in his game.

Sheer luck, undoubtedly.

I turned and gave a start, noticing for the first time that we were not alone in the room. A thin, dark-skinned young man with tight black curls and heavy downcast eyes sat on a corner chair, rolling tobacco into a paper with long thin fingers.

'Oh, hello!' I said breathlessly in alarm. I turned to Sir Maurice. 'Aren't you going to introduce me?'

The actor turned from his reflection, pulled the pipe from between his lips and blew out a perfect ring of smoke.

'No,' he replied with a smirk.

As Sir Maurice turned to rummage through some things on his dressing table, I was left to stand for a minute, the sweet scent of the youth's roll-up curling through the stagnant air and stirring the beginnings of nausea from within my stomach. Suddenly Sir Maurice found what he was looking for - a pen and copy of the script - and then took a long, deep final drag on his pipe, retrieved a tamp and swiftly extinguished it.

'Exactly why are you here, Edgar?'

'To bring you to the stage.'

'I don't mean why are you here in my room, I mean why here, the Old Comp? This is professional theatre, sweetheart, not bloody rep! You don't belong here, in a place of performance, drama and linguistic acrobatics. You are like - oh, how should I put it so you might understand? Like a sticky bun in a biscuit barrel! A dandelion in a bunch of daffs! Is it something to do with fair Rosemary Remembrance? Well, more fool you!' He took a breath and cackled caustically. 'Methinks you have romantic designs on your ex-wife!'

'Absolutely not!' I replied hastily, backing to the doorway.

'Because if you do, you will soon be in with a chance. It won't be long before old Farringdon shuffles off of this mortal coil. I would normally frown upon wanton opportunism, Edgar, but I have to hand it to you, you pick your moments carefully. Sweet Madame Farringdon is a fox, and soon to be widowed fox. Very sly, Mr Edgar, very sly.'

'Ridiculous! I have no such intentions!' I declared fervently.

'Mmm, no. I didn't think so.'

'Well anyway, they want you on stage!' I declared.

I turned on my heel and, in a flash, was out the door and sweeping through the dark corridors, the throaty cackle of Sir Maurice fading behind me.

Snitty!

It hadn't been said, but I heard the word again as if with a whisper in my ear, and I balled my fists.

As I turned a corner I came across Richard Chandler, who was lingering in the doorway of what I took to be Toffee Morrell's changing room. Upon my approach he took a quick step forwards and swiftly closed the door. The man's brow was knitted, his face pale. Something was clearly amiss.

'Is everything alright, Mr Chandler?' I enquired innocently. 'Miss Morrell not coming out?'

He switched on a showy smile. 'Everything's tickey-boo, Mr Edgar. Toffee will be along shortly, I'm sure. All is absolutely tickety-boo!'

I didn't fall for it for a second - something was troubling the man.

'Best get back,' he continued, setting off with a little jump. I was clearly supposed to follow, and I did so for a few steps until he turned the corner. I then doubled back, pulled by an enquiring mind.

I gave a polite knock at the door. When there was no reply, I turned the knob and looked inside.

Miss Morrell's dressing room was in disarray. A chair was upended in the centre of the room and fresh flowers were scattered about the floor amongst the pieces of a broken vase. Pages of script had been thrown against the far wall to form a messy carpet upon the dusty floorboards.

There is an atmosphere within a place in which something untoward has occurred that is difficult to explain but easy to sense - the room was quiet and still, and yet strangely unsettled in the wake of violence.

Something had happened.

I felt a frisson of excitement.

All was certainly not tickety-boo.

Part VII

In which Payton Edgar probes

Dear Margaret,

Our son wants to be an actor. Medicine has always been in our family, and Father and I fully expected our studious boy to follow in the footsteps of his forebears. Last night he shocked us both by declaring that he is going to join an amateur dramatics society and go "on the road". He finds the idea of theatre thrilling - and we are left bereft. How can we steer him onto the correct path?

Mrs K, Maida Hill

Margaret replies; I sympathise greatly. I fear that you will soon lose your studious son as he slaps on the greasepaint and heads into the spotlight. You must nip this in the bud, heed my advice, and you may save him yet. Under the guise of supporting his ridiculous plans, surprise him with a backstage tour at a professional theatre. Once there, make sure he meets with one or two of the thespians within - ideally a leading name. Actors are brash, irritable types, so narcissistic that they will preen and boast and strut, and put any sensible young lad off his ridiculous notion that theatre life is a thrilling life. It is anything but.

Chandler didn't say a word to the company about the mess in his fiancée's dressing room.

As I returned to the auditorium he was spinning some yarn about Miss Morrell needing 'a day to gather her thoughts'. Gordon Farringdon, exceedingly dissatisfied, coughed and spluttered for some minutes over the loss of his leading lady.

'Stop fussing, Gordon!' Chandler spat, showing some impatience. 'Miss Drake can do it today, now please!'

'If she bothers to turn up!' spluttered Farringdon.

'She's here, I've seen her, out back,' Chandler replied. He clapped his hands in a rather authoritarian manner. 'Alex - get your sister out here, pronto!'

As the director went to complain further he was silenced by a flick of the wrist.

'Just get on with it, Gordon!' said Chandler briskly.

A minute or two later, a young lady peered around the curtain, a white face and hand giving her the look of an imp peering from behind a toadstool.

The understudy.

Emma Drake was a small and boyish with a nest of short black hair, and it wasn't hard to read her thoughts upon being summoned - her expression was one of fear mixed with abject hope. Called to the stage in the absence of the leading lady… perhaps she had waited for this moment for some time.

Sir Maurice Williams made his entrance, stage left.

‘So I am to be the understudy’s nanny, am I?’ he bellowed unhappily. ‘I dislike being made to play second fiddle. Toffee taken ill? Well tough titties! I shall go and have words!’

Chandler gave an inpatient gesture.

‘No time for that! Just get on with it! Miss Drake, please step in.’ His manner was abrupt and not unsuspicious, and I watched him for a while. All the sparkle was gone and, as the players did their bit on stage, he stood in the gloom looking sullen. What had happened in that dressing room? I turned to Rosemary.

‘I know that you’re friends, but what do you make of Mr Chandler, really?’

‘How do you mean?’

‘Does he… have a short fuse?’

‘A what?’

‘A temper?’

‘Dickie? A temper? Why do you ask?’

‘Just something I’ve observed. Well? Does he?’

Rosemary clicked her tongue, and spoke carefully. ‘He can be a bit abrasive perhaps - a bit bloody minded even. And we all have our off days. But a temper? What makes you ask that?’

‘Nothing, really,’ I replied vaguely. ‘Just something… observed.’

I made a note that, for all her questions, Rosemary hadn’t denied it.

After a while, Chandler turned and strode up the aisle. I went to speak but Rosemary shushed me sharply and we watched as Emma Drake took up her part.

She was, by all accounts, a surprisingly good replacement for the flighty, showy Toffee Morrell. I would have said that she didn’t look the part, but on stage she had pulled herself up as high she could and was storming about with all the bluster the part required. She seemed to be doing a good enough job, and even the old fool Maurice appeared to enjoy himself.

Christophe Playfair made his presence felt, despite the fact that he had precious few lines to deliver. He enjoyed fiddling about in the background in that horrible turtleneck jumper, rolling his eyes and doing his very best to distract the audience from the developments centre stage. Thing hotted up slightly when there was something of an altercation, as Playfair dared to challenge Gordon Farringdon’s direction.

It was a trifling affair. Farringdon had stopped Miss Drake mid-sentence with a bark. He ordered her to approach an invisible window and fling it up at a certain point in her speech. The understudy hesitated, suddenly dropping the bravado and speaking with a timidity one might expect of an understudy.

‘Really? Because I feel that… well… although they are disagreeing, this is the first time they have… a connection… you see? Turning away from Petruchio… to go all the way over here… would just feel… a bit wrong…to me… I think.’

‘Just do it, Miss Drake!’ Farringdon exclaimed with a stark lack of patience.

This was when Playfair piped up.

‘No, actually, Gordon, if you don’t mind my saying, the dear sweet girl may have a point there. As my old mentor Yardley Swain would say, one should never just plod about the boards mindlessly - one should always have a dramatic objective. We have to ask ourselves what is Petruchio’s objective here? To woo and to conquer. And our Kate? To stand firm and resolute. She would hardly turn away, to show a vulnerable side. And the way they were playing it, so very well, it seems a pity to break up that - yes - connection, as dear, pretty Emma so elegantly puts it.'

Playfair leered in the understudy's direction. She sent him a small, shy thankful smile, which was duly returned with a unbridled predatory grin.

The atmosphere had quickly grown icy. Rosemary sensed the tension and set down her knitting, waiting for her husband to speak. It was one thing taking direction from myself - recognised Artistic Director - but quite another taking direction from the players themselves. I ran my fingers over the smooth curves of my brass owl stick in silent delight. Farringdon suddenly appeared helpless. It was a while before he spoke, and when he did his tone was muted and weary.

'Very well… whatever you say,' he grumbled, adding just loudly enough for us to catch it. 'She's only the bloody understudy, after all.'

We soon broke for lunch, and as everyone milled about, Rosemary pulled at my sleeve.

'What was all that about Dickie?' she asked. 'Why did you ask about his temper? Has he done something to upset you?'

'No… but something has happened… something strange.' I took a moment to weigh things up before deciding to take her into my confidence. I told her in detail about the carnage in Miss Morrell's dressing room, and about Chandler's odd denial. She had the gall to look doubtful, and so there was nothing for it but to take her backstage to show her the evidence. This time I didn't bother to knock on the door, but went straight in.

The room was neat and tidy. The pieces of broken vase were gone, the papers cleared away. Rosemary huffed.

'Oh yes, it's a complete mess, darling!'

'It was, I tell you! Someone has cleaned it up. It can only be your dear Dickie - everyone else was on stage. Why do that?'

'Payton, it's obvious they've had a row. Poor Dickie would be mortified - it's only natural that he'd hide it from all and sundry.'

'A row? Well then - where is she?'

Rosemary rolled her eyes. 'She'll have stormed out. Be back tomorrow, with Dickie shoving a bunch of flowers in her face and all will be forgiven.'

'But there was violence in this room!' I put in.

'Something and nothing! Theatre types are temperamental souls,' said Rosemary as she pulled on her gloves. 'Now, I'm off for lunch with Gordon.'

She left me alone.

She was quite wrong, and I knew it. Something worse than a mere row had happened, and Dickie Chandler was apparently keen to cover it up.

Although I nurtured a bad feeling in my gut, it was still nothing more than a passing concern - a twist of curiosity at some domestic drama unravelling before my eyes. I had no reason to think that Miss Morrell's absence it was any more serious than that.

But it was serious - and something much darker than a mere domestic drama was about to play out… for the leading lady had been taken.

Interval

In which Payton Edgar holds the first round of disappointing interviews

The following Monday I was poised and ready to begin the search for my future right-hand woman.

I enjoyed a stroll around the park in the morning, conjuring up images of my perfect secretary as I went. I then began preparations for the interviews after a pleasing lunch of two hearty luncheon meat sandwiches and a rosy bruise-free apple.

I had received a disappointingly poor response to my carefully composed advertisement, and found only slight potential within. Two applicants were out of the question, one being male (why bother to apply when I had expressly requested a female?) and the other demonstrating a gob-smacking ineptitude for letter writing - all too shocking considering this was an application for the role of private secretary. To this candidate, I penned a sharp rebuff and chuckled to myself indulgently as I popped it in the postbox.

Once I had completed my all-too-short shortlist, I then badgered Irving into joining me.

'An interview needs a panel!' I insisted. 'One must outnumber the applicant in order to create the necessary hierarchy. You needn't say much, or even say anything at all. I shall make the introductions, I shall ask the questions, I shall make the decisions. But it is essential that I have a panel.'

His enthusiasm for helping out a dear friend left a lot to be desired, and so I made sure to add some softer words of encouragement. Sometimes my friend needed a little buttering up. 'I shall be in dire need of your input, Irving. You are, more often than not, a sound judge of character. You can help me separate the bad eggs from the good, so to speak.'

And so he reluctantly agreed. It was good to have an excuse to prize him from his paint-spattered studio, which was becoming ever more stuffy and prison-like at my every visit. On top of that, I enjoyed showing off my new place of work.

Ah, my darling new office! So much more pleasing than the poky old cupboard I used to have at Fleet Street. It was also beautifully positioned - close enough to Harvey's restaurant for convenience, but far enough removed not to be able to hear nor smell the kitchens. The office came readily furnished with clean red brick walls, shining varnished floorboards, two sturdy desks and a number of fashionable chairs. I only needed to add a few touches to make the place my own – a scattering of hardy houseplants, a discreetly quiet carriage clock and two of Irving's jollier paintings for the walls. Upon entry, a visitor found themselves in a neat reception area, where a lovely mahogany desk sat just waiting for my underling to take her place. To the right there was a short corridor that led down to my office. We shared lavatorial facilities with the restaurant, but this was perhaps the only disadvantage in an otherwise perfect set-up.

I scheduled the two successful applicants for one and two o'clock interviews respectively. The first was a Mrs Phyllis Fawcett of Islington, to be followed by Miss Elaine Daniels of Potters Bar.

I would interview from behind my desk, naturally, and spent some time setting things up to my satisfaction. The typewriter was set aside, my pens tidied in their little pot, and the blinds angled so as to cast enough light into the room while maintaining privacy from the street outside. I positioned Irving an arms reach to my left and ever so slightly behind of my chair, and instructed him to lift his shoulders and consider his posture, for he had a habit of slumping. As I did so, my clock chimed once.

Mrs Fawcett was late.

I spent the empty minutes waiting for our first candidate ruminating over my tragic loss - my poor antique singing bowl. Lost and vulnerable, destined to be manhandled by ignorant cretins. My missing treasure.

Irving, not even bothering to hide his boredom at the subject, offered only a little, somewhat economic sympathy. For one supposedly coherent with the arts, he sometimes demonstrated remarkably scant regard for exquisite ornamentations.

Mrs Fawcett was unacceptably late - eight and a half minutes late, to be precise. No amount of clucking about how unreliable the bus service was would excuse the fact that first impressions had not been good. I gave her a short lecture on the importance of punctuality as she flapped her umbrella and dripped water across my beautiful boards. Entirely ignorant of this scolding, she pulled off her raincoat and began chattering away like an imperious, over-familiar domestic.

It was obvious that Mrs Fawcett was not the person I was looking for.

I watched her with disapproval. She was mousey, sloppily dressed and had the shrivelled and puckered lips of a heavy smoker. As if this wasn't enough evidence, she also reeked of tobacco. On top of that, she chittered like a caged bird, barely letting me get a word in edgeways. I went through the motions from behind my desk, asking wearily why the woman wanted the job and enquiring politely as to her credentials, but the whole exchange was entirely futile. I was only too happy to have Irving usher her back out into the downpour outside. Once she had gone, I raised the blinds and opened the window just a crack, to air the room.

Irving listened politely to the reasons for not employing the woman, and offered no observation of his own. He knew that my mind was made up, and the candidate was unsatisfactory. Punctuality was a requirement - and a non-smoker essential.

Regrettably, Miss Daniels of Potters Bar fared little better.

Punctual, but equally as rain-soaked, Miss Daniels was altogether smarter and less candid than her predecessor. She was, however, just as unsuitable for the position in other ways, not least by being much younger - certainly far too young to be the experienced hand I was in search of. Sitting in the interview chair was a very modern type of girl with hooped earrings and a tall, wild black perm - a young person who exuded a youthful confidence in her every sentence. She was a perky thing, and she kept her saucer-like eyes fixed on mine throughout the interview in a manner which was just a little unsettling. I could picture her in a spotlight on stage, with hair piled high, wailing into a microphone about being Bobby's girl or some such notion.

I suspect that the very best secretaries are, first and foremost, rather drab creatures. When one has a secretary, one expects her to adopt a degree of subservience. A good assistant must display a willingness to perform as instructed without question, and to perform any required tasks to a very high standard. One expects maturity, loyalty and unconditional respect. When I informed Miss Daniels of this, she wrinkled her nose and spoke out thoughtlessly.

'Well, I'll type up yer stuff and answer the 'phone for yer, if that's all you mean.'

I laced my fingers together, placed them on the desk and leaned in.

'No, Miss Daniels, that is not all I mean.'

I let her go without fanfare and took a few minutes to mull over the applicants. A great disappointment indeed. Irving conceded to my criticism of the first applicant, but had the cheek to question my issues with the second. Indeed, he appeared to think that Miss Daniels was an entirely suitable candidate. He used the work bubbly.

'Precisely! Far too perky! And did you see her nails? Painted talons! How could one manipulate a paperclip with those?' I shook my head. 'And she was much too young! A girl like that - well! - there will be boys hanging outside the door by the second week, an extra half hour taken for lunch here and there, and then she'll abandon ship for a baby within a year. I do not want a woman of childbearing age, Irving. No, my secretary must be mature, and functional. Her nails must be short. She should wear spectacles, be bookish...'

A fresh image popped into my mind.

'Yes, spectacles! She absolutely must wear spectacles!'

Irving suggested I re-consider my advert, and I agreed wholeheartedly. Perhaps I had been a little too vague about my requirements.

I put pen to paper.

Wanted; efficient female secretary for city journalist. Must have typewriter skills and at least four years' experience in the field. Would suit quiet, mature and refined female with no current or planned family ties. Short nails preferred. Punctuality essential. Non-smokers only. Must wear spectacles.

Contact P. Edgar, Pimlico
P.O. Box 2456

Act II

Part I

In which Payton Edgar is asked the wrong questions

Dear Margaret,

My daughter is ten, and struggles terribly with spelling. It has never been a strength of mine either, but my daughter is even worse that I ever was. She thinks she is doing well, then puts the letters in all the wrong places. She makes the most atrocious mistakes, and it takes her forever to construct a sentence. She also finds it hard to read and sometimes gets terribly frustrated about it all. What is wrong with her?

Yvonne P, Woolwich

Margaret replies; I can diagnose exactly what is wrong with your child - she is slow - and you cannot necessarily blame yourself for having reared a slow child. One wouldn't expect every child to be a budding poet or wordsmith. It takes all sorts to fill the world, including those who are more backwards than forwards. Gentle encouragement and reassurance are the ways to go, and - if lucky - your little girl could even grow up to be a very pleasant (if a little incompetent) shop assistant.

I had hoped for a hot breakfast of grilled peppered tomatoes and vinegar poached eggs, but was disappointed to find that Grace had locked herself away in her bathroom. Instead, I made myself some toast, opting for strawberry jam and the very best salted butter (I kept the unsalted, standard stuff for Aunt Elizabeth, who didn't know good butter from bad). The jam jar came with one of the gingham cloth covers that had started catching my eye. Funny how I had never noticed them before. I lifted it off the lid and examined it carefully before slipping it into my jacket pocket.

I had my reasons.

I polished off my toast and was sipping on sugary tea when Grace breezed into the room in suspiciously high spirits. She whistled a little as she gathered her things to go into town. After a minute or two I couldn't tolerate her chirruping any more, and said as much. I could be honest with Grace - she returned honesty with honesty. She even laughed a little.

'A dozen apologies, Payton. It must be terribly irksome to see someone so happy, I'm sure.'

She buttoned her coat.

'Going somewhere nice?' I enquired politely.

'I have a date!'

'With a man?' I asked, a little warily. I noticed that the collar of her blouse was silk and her face was painted, albeit modestly.

'Indeed with a man. Is that so unusual? Your aunt put me on to it, actually.'

'Aunt Elizabeth fixed you up with a man?'

'Hardly. But she had words, said I'd been on the shelf for too long. Good wine left un-drunk turns to vinegar, she said. And she had a point. So I took the plunge.' Grace clutched her purse tightly. 'I met him only yesterday, at Mr Spence's house. We're to breakfast together.'

'One of Irving's friends?' I asked, unable to hide my displeasure. Irving had an increasing number of youthful, beatnik types that came and went at all hours - unwashed, arty souls who spent eternity discussing matters of politics, freedom, creativity and philosophy in a cloud of swirling smoke.

I posed a considered question. 'And what does this young man do? What is his profession?'

Her smile vanished.

'He is… between jobs, I believe.'

I was unsurprised.

'And his name?'

She hesitated.

'Spoon.'

'Spoon?'

'A nickname… because, well, his face is rather wide, like when you look into a spoon.'

'I see. He sounds like one to treasure.'

Sensing my disapproval, Grace quickly changed the subject.

'Have you looked in on your aunt recently?'

'No.'

'I am concerned for her. She's not been the same since the burglary.'

'Mmm. I've not been the same, either.'

'If you don't mind my saying, your bowl that was taken really wasn't all that. You'd get the same two-a-penny down the Portobello Road Market.'

I shuddered and refused to dignify this with a reply. She went on.

'Still, she brightened up a bit when Mr Spence popped by yesterday.'

'Irving was here?' I asked, surprised. This was news to me.

Grace nodded, her blonde curls bobbing as she did so.

'Yes, while you were out at the park, fattening squirrels or whatever it is you do out there. He came especially to see Elizabeth.'

'He never said!'

Irving had been known to visit my aunt on the odd occasion - there was a peculiar mutual fondness there for reasons which were entirely unknown. I mulled this over. Perhaps I too should poke my nose around the door. I left Grace gathering her things, stamped down the hallway and rapped on my aunt's bedroom door.

'Keep out!' came the standard reply. I entered gingerly.

'What do you want?' Aunt Elizabeth snapped. She was propped up in bed amongst cream sheets, a skeletal hand raised to her sternum, clutching at her black shawl. The air was heady with carbolic soap and lavender. On her lap was a tray with teasels and scraps of fabric piled high.

'I hear that Mr Spence visited yesterday,' I began carefully.

'So what if he did?' Aunt Elizabeth croaked. 'At least there's one person on this street who cares enough to try and soothe my tortured soul.'

'To soothe your what?'

Grace appeared behind me. 'Well, I'm off out, so you'll have to stop in, Payton.'

'I beg your pardon?'

'You'll need to stay in. Your aunt wants someone in the house at all times, so you'll have to stay here while I am out.' This was said in a matter-of-fact tone as if it were the most normal request in the world. Grace continued. 'I'm off out for breakfast, then I'll collect your weekday sundries on the way home.'

'To stay in?' I uttered in disbelief. The old woman had never before stipulated where I should and should not be. Grace tilted her head and thinned those inscrutable eyes.

'You do know how shaken she has been by this whole burglary thing, don't you?'

'Of course I know!' I replied. 'My poor unique singing bowl! I am still beside myself!'

'It'll just help her to know someone is in the house, for the next few days or weeks at least. I can't be here all day and all night.'

'She has always been absolutely fine by herself,' I put in. 'She has her books, and those rancid teasel abominations-'

'I am here, you know!' Aunt Elizabeth piped up from the bed. 'And Grace is quite right - I will absolutely not be left alone in this house. Never again. Never!'

'Well I can't stay!' I stated, without compromise.

'Do you actually have anything to do this morning, Payton?' asked Grace pointedly.

'As a matter of fact I do! I have vital business at the Old Compton theatre. I am waiting for my car as we speak.'

'Well… perhaps you can call Enid and see if she can sit in,' suggested Grace.

There was a ring on the doorbell and as Grace went off to answer it, I returned my attention to the old woman in bed.

'How on earth could miserable old Enid Smith protect you from a hardened criminal? That shrivelled mouse would be about as effective a guard dog as a piece of fluff from the carpet! She couldn't challenge an intruder - all she ever seems to do is shuffle about and grunt like a pig.'

As if by magic, I heard Enid Smiths familiar croak from the hallway. The miserable thing then padded through the house without removal of headscarf nor raincoat, clutching a shoulder bag to her chest as if it contained the most priceless of treasures. As was her way, she acknowledged my presence with a grunt.

'Did you bring it?' Aunt Elizabeth asked.

Another grunt. Enid fumbled in her massive bag and produced a tatty cribbage box, shooting me a shifty sidewards glance.

'Cribbage?' I groaned. I have an opinion on this sort of thing. Card and board games are, in my opinion, a pastime of the most cretinous of minds. It is simply baffling how some grown adults enjoyed playing like children - and cribbage was the worst of them. I said something along these lines only to receive a snort from the woman in the bed.

'Enid and I are going to enjoy a game,' she said firmly.

I was instantly suspicious.

'Enjoy a game? But you loathe games! Come to think of it - you loathe enjoyment!'

'Just scat! You can both leave now that Enid is here,' Aunt Elizabeth announced. 'Go on - shoo!'

I thought about saying something, for there was certainly something suspicious going on. However, Grace was gently nudging me out when a horn sounded outside.

'Ah! There is my car, right on time.'

There was still no sign of Toffee Morrell at the Old Compton.

Rosemary leaned in and hungrily gave me her account of the latest happenings. Emma Drake was getting on well in the part, and all the players apparently carried on as if Miss Morrell and her girlish sparkle was just a distant memory. A new leading lady had brought the production a fresh energy - a fresh broom giving a clean sweep.

'And - guess what? Sir Maurice has also been visited by a burglar.'

'No!'

'Well, it was a near miss by all accounts,' whispered Rosemary. 'Happened yesterday. Although Sir Maurice was here rehearsing at the time, there was a young man back at his house, and so the thief was frightened off before anything could be taken. I can't think who the young man might be - his son?'

'No,' I replied cautiously. 'Not his son…'

'Well anyway, another burglary - quite a coincidence.! Sir Maurice said-'

Gordon Farringdon turned and shushed his wife. I considered this news. Two burglaries. A coincidence? A remarkable one, if it were.

I spent a dull few hours watching the stage while sucking on lemon sherbets, with Rosemary knitting efficiently at my side. Tony Trace and little Sylvia Pickford took centre stage for much of the time. She was as wet as a wet weekend in Bognor, but he had some appeal - dashingly handsome with a gentlemanly, smooth delivery that garnered attention. As their scene ended and Sir Maurice took to the stage, I kept my eyes on Pickford and Trace as they moved aside to share a few words in a dark corner. Suddenly, the actress leaned in and presented him with an amusingly clumsy kiss. I think I was the only person to see it. Miss Pickford had taken the initiative, only for Trace to push back, thrusting a hand between them. He shook his head and said some words.

I chuckled to myself quietly as Miss Pickford covered her mouth with a hand as if to stifle a sob. She fled across the rear of the stage, head bowed.

On stage, Sir Maurice was prancing about in the most irritating of fashions, and I soon tired of it all. Still, I let him carry on, uninterrupted. I was biding my time until the opportunity arose to demean or humiliate him in some way of another. Something would occur - it was only a matter of time.

Snitty indeed!

Suddenly, I noticed Dickie Chandler loitering in the darkness of the aisle. I watched him with some scrutiny, and then - much to my surprise - he turned, fixed me with a glare and beckoned me over. He moved up the aisle towards the rear, and I was given no choice but to follow.

At the back of the auditorium a narrow doorway led through to the theatre bar. It was an unappealing little room with a faux Regency air. There was just enough space for a short, basic bar and several tiny round tables, which sat in crimson velvet surroundings. The air inside was thick, not unlike the backroom in a church. As I entered, Chandler was behind the bar tipping scotch clumsily into a cut glass tumbler. He was a funny looking, dandy of a man, and with his frilly cuffs and loose cravat he put me in mind of a silver Beau Brummell.

'Drink?' he asked sharply.

I politely declined. I might have been smiling, but inside I gathered my wits for a confrontation. I made up my mind to challenge the man over the missing actress, the mess in her dressing room and his odd, suspicious behaviour. It might be a difficult conversation, but I have always valued honesty, and something should be said. I wondered how I might start my interrogation.

He fixed me with a glare.

'What happened in that dressing room, Mr Edgar?'

Somewhat wrong-footed, I stammered a little.

'In the… b-beg pardon?'

'I know you know about it - the mess in Toffee's room. I saw you look in there. What's going on? Where is she? Mmm?'

To my shame I continued to stammer and stutter, quite dumbfounded. He was asking me the questions that I should have been asking him!

'What happened in that room?' he continued.

I struggled to find words.

'These are my questions!' I said, perhaps a little feebly.

'You need to tell me what's going on, Edgar! I've seen you skulking around, giving me dark looks, like you where chewing on a vinegary wasp. You obviously know something, so tell me!'

I tried to look innocent, but it was hard in the face of such passionate accusations. He paused and took a long drink before continuing along the same, unpalatable lines. 'What have I done to upset you, and where, Mr Edgar, is my fiancee?'

I steadied myself.

'Excuse me, Mr Chandler, but I find your accusatory tone offensive in the extreme. You have been watching me? Well, I have been watching you, and all I see is an exceedingly suspicious soul and an empty dressing room where something untoward occurred. Yes, I saw inside the room – all the mess, the broken vase. And I think you tidied it all up fairly quickly. There has clearly been some upset, but I have absolutely nothing to do with it, and I am incensed - and offended - that you think I might have.'

At this he took in a deep breath, and then deflated before my very eyes. His look was suddenly nothing short of helpless.

'In all honesty, Mr Edgar, I really don't have a clue what's happened. I did go back and tidy the room, but only because I was scared that tongues would wag. Some around here feast on gossip, and I couldn't let that happen. Now I'm just grasping at straws, trying to understand what's happened to my girl. Where is she? I am lost… quite lost.' His shoulders slumped. 'Please don't say anything to anybody. I haven't seen Toffee since the end of last week. There was something wrong, thinking back, but I just can't put my finger on what it was. She was in a strange mood - all the sunshine had gone. Most unlike her.'

He stopped, mindlessly tapping a finger against his glass. I couldn't find anything to say. Eventually he continued, with a statement which was less than convincing.

'She'll be back soon. She will.'

I cleared my throat. It was time to probe a little.

'Did she take anything with her?' I asked.

'How do you mean?'

'Well, did she pack a case? Take some things…'

He shook his head. 'All her clothes and bits and bobs are still there, untouched. Everything I've bought her. All her trinkets…'

'Did she take any money, or items of monetary value?'

Chandler straightened. 'Certainly not! You are implying that she has left me and run off with the silver?'

'We have to consider every possibility.'

'Well quash the thought immediately! Toffee was no thief, she was a dear girl. A dear girl who simply wouldn't leave me like this. She was loving the play, loving our time together… loving everything. She had it all.'

It was true. She seemed very happy and content at our lunch together. For the first time, the thought crossed my mind that the girl might not have run. Not voluntarily, anyhow.

Suddenly Dickie Chandler sat up and smiled a forced, tired smile.

'Yes - she will turn up, and all will be well again. When she is ready.'

He drained his glass.

There was only one thing to say to this.

'Of course she will. She'll turn up. When she is ready.'

Part II

In which Beryl Baxter senses blood in the water

Dear Margaret,

Every morning I catch the train from Clapham Junction into town, and have fallen in love with a man in the very last carriage. We have only spoken once, mere passing comments on how we both wore green scarves and had a copy of The Clarion tucked under our right arms, but he is exceedingly handsome and I am plucking up courage to talk to him again. Any advice on how I can break the ice?

Anita, Clapham

Margaret replies; In your full letter you make a point of asking me not to disclose certain facts about yourself, and I rather think you are trying to use me as messenger. This is not the lonely hearts column! One detail you ask me to withhold is the trifling fact that you are already married, albeit unhappily. And so I shall take this opportunity to address the exceedingly handsome man in the final carriage with the green scarf and The Clarion under his arm; the woman that eyeballs you so hungrily every morning is taken! I suggest you do your best to avoid a sticky situation and travel in an alternative carriage or even on an alternative route from now on.

I was starting to get used to the ways of the theatre, and was learning how to navigate the pomp and hysteria of it all. As I entered the auditorium, I greeted the company with as much gusto and fanfare as I could muster, sparkling as if I belonged.

As was his way, Gordon Farringdon issued a grumble from behind a broadsheet and I followed in the direction of Rosemary's shrill 'morning!'. There was only Alex Drake and a small handful of actors milling about the stage.

'Starting late again?' I observed keenly as Rosemary beckoned me over. As I approached, I noticed that her eyes were twinkling - and that there was a distinct tenseness in the air.

'Best keep your head down and out the way today, Payton,' she whispered urgently. 'It's all a bit taut. Sir Maurice is refusing to come out of his dressing room for some as yet unknown reason, and old Hortensio has the beginnings of flu. It'll mainly be Bianca and Lucentio scenes today.'

Miss Pickford and Tony Trace appeared on the stage with a few others, and Farringdon snapped down his newspaper. 'Finally!' he shouted. 'Right then, let's crack on. Back to Act Three now. Miss Pickford, could you take off those dark glasses please, it would be nice to see your eyes. Tony, try to avoid that cockney twang today, as discussed.'

Pickford removed her glasses and Trace cast over a grim look.

'Has Miss Morrell finally made an appearance?' I asked Rosemary in a whisper, anticipating the reply.

'Not a peep! It's been long enough now. Everyone's very sad for poor Dickie, naturally, but general consensus is that she's done a bunk. Playfair told me there'd been something of an upset.'

'An upset?'

'Well, pinch of salt and all that – he really is the most dreadful gossip - but he claims to have heard raised voices before she went. He thinks the romance of the year is over and that she's done a flit, permanently. Have to say - I'm inclined to agree.' She pulled up her knitting needles but wasn't about to knit. 'Not that it causes that much of a headache for the show. Little Emma Drake's proven herself to be a most capable replacement. Even Sir Maurice sang her praises yesterday - he'd rather have Drake than Toffee. He never liked the fact that his Katherine needed to wear specs, never mind that the girl had very little to do with the theatre before this. He said that while Toffee's Katherine was cartoonish at best, little Emma's take is a force of nature, and on another level entirely. I shouldn't be surprised if Sir Maurice petitions for Emma to stay, even if Toffee does make a re-appearance. The change in her is phenomenal - she used to skulk about like a drudge, but now she's got the title role, she's here on time every day and is much more committed. She carries this on, she'll go far.'

I mulled this over. The unpromising understudy blossoms unexpectedly in a star role; it was a theatrical parable that apparently had some grounding in reality.

On stage, Pickford and Trace were in keen embrace, and I watched closely. It was clear even from back in row six that there was genuine adoration in young Silvia's eyes. Trace, on the other hand, was merely playing a part. Christophe Playfair appeared from the theatre bar, slithered down the aisle to the second row and placed himself near the director. After a minute he glanced over his shoulder, grinned an artificial grin and gave a slow nod in my direction, his sweaty brow and beady eyes flashing in the shadows. Even wordless in the dark the man was an unctuous creep.

My stomach rumbled, and I longed for lunchtime.

Little did I know, I was about to be hi-jacked.

Beryl Baxter never did anything by accident.

The self-professed Queen of the Society Columns was more than a Clarion colleague, she was a dear friend, and I knew her well enough to know that when she just "bumped into" someone, there was probably a reason.

It was lunchtime. I was stepping out of the stage door whilst fixing on my hat, and was barely given time to draw breath before a familiar voice called out.

'Coo-ee, Payton! Coo-ee! It's me!'

Across the road, Beryl was waving frantically. I was always pleased to see my friend, even though she was wildly rambunctious at the best of times, and I steeled myself for an onslaught as she tottered across the road in a pair of shoes daringly high for a woman of her age and breadth. Beryl was a handsome woman who made her generous proportions ever more generous by the massive fur coats she wore with aplomb. Today, her wig of choice was a light chestnut hue, drawn up from her scalp in an all-too-youthful haystack style. Heavy gold earrings pulled at her lobes.

'Fancy bumping into you, dear-heart!'

'Yes, fancy,' I replied in my driest of tones. 'How are you, Beryl?'

'We were just out for a spot of lunch - you simply must join us!'

It was only then that I noticed that she was not alone. Two steps behind her stood a small, pale little man in a light grey suit, with sunken pink cheeks and a lost expression on his face.

'Payton, this is Mr Pinkerton, my fiancee.' She slapped my shoulder. 'Yes, I'm doing it again, dear-heart! Pinkerton, this is Mr Edgar, that dear friend from The Clarion I was telling you about.'

Pinkerton and I might have said something to each other had Beryl not chattered on. 'I don't know about you, darlings, but I am hungry as a diamond without a carat! We'll shimmy along to Bruno's Trattoria on Dean Street. Have you eaten there, Payton? No? I'm shocked! You'll simply adore it - you must review it! Bruno always has a plum table for dearest Beryl.'

And so off we went. Pallid little Mr Pinkerton soon dropped behind, and I lowered my voice.

'Pinkerton? Correct me if I'm wrong, but I seem to recall that was the name of your divorce lawyer? For divorce number three?'

'The very same! It's only natural that a girl should, at some point, marry her divorce lawyer. Cuts out the middle man down the line, so to speak. Pinkerton is a valuable resource.'

'A nice way to describe your betrothed.'

'Ha! I proposed to him at New Year - I'm so frightfully modern. Never seen a man look so petrified as poor Pinkerton.'

'I also recall that you said he was something of a wet fish.'

'Oh, the wettest, Payton! But he's a rich fish. Rich, quiet and does what he's told - something of an improvement on the last three.' She was quite right - Pinkerton didn't utter a word that afternoon, and seemed content to follow her around with an obedient devotion akin to the most loyal of dogs.

'Have you a solicitor, Payton?'

'You know that I have.'

'Not still Crack, surely?'

I bristled. My solicitor, one Mr Crack of Marylebone-based Hammond, Hammond, Hammond, Hammond and Crack, was an unimpressive and somewhat ineffective soul - but I had promised dusty old Hammond, just before his passing, that I would retain their services, and I am never one to break a promise. I said as much, and Beryl snorted.

'Well, I can certainly recommend Pinkerton over that wet mop Crack!'

I cast an eye backwards. 'Your man's hardly a dynamo, Beryl.'

'Oh, you'd be surprised!' she replied a little loudly. I was nauseated to find her looking up at me with raised eyebrows and suggestive eyes. 'Oh, yes! Never judge a book by its cover, dear-heart.'

At the restaurant, Beryl flirted outrageously with the swarthy maitre-de, and we landed a choice seat in the window.

'Pinkerton! Go and wash your hands!' said Beryl firmly. He departed.

We exchanged some words about the menu, but Beryl was much more interested in The Taming of the Shrew.

'I nearly fell off my perch when I learned that you were involved in the production, but there you are, bold as brass, launching yourself out of the stage door like a seasoned pro! A Dickie Chandelier piece, no less! Everybody makes out he's an effervescent master of the arts… bit of a dullard dandy, if you ask me. Never any dirt there… is there? So what brought you in? Something of the money man, I hear…'

'I have a hand in the financing of the thing, yes. They also insisted that I take on the role of Artistic Director, no less!'

'Artistic Director? So what does that mean, then?'

'It means I get to nitpick and make Sir Maurice's life a nightmare.'

'I see. And how is the old fossil doing? Can be a bit of an uppity grump.'

'Indeed - the uppitiest and grumpiest. And entirely miscast, to boot.' I was about to continue, but stopped myself. 'Beryl - this… meeting, this meal… I take it that I am talking off the record?'

'Oh, my giddy aunt, no! I don't do off-the-record, Payton - you should know that! What you tell me will be in print before you can say please-don't-put-this-in-print! What else I am here for, dear-heart, if not to cull a little ripe gossip? What about Sylvia Pickford? Some paint her as a notorious beauty - bit of a wide-eyed spook, if you ask me. Do darling Beryl a favour and spill. Between you and me, my gossip well has been running irritatingly dry of late, and I'm eagerly searching for this week's hot topic. I simply refuse to lead with the Queen's new hat and brooch combination - again.'

Her frankness was refreshing. She went on, gesticulating wildly.

'And besides, I already know what you think of Sir Maurice, and I will print something anyway - it might as well be your truth, as much as anyone else's!'

She had a point. But still, I remained indignant.

'Beryl, you know I am a discreet soul. I am offended that you come running to me for gossip and scandal.'

'Don't be offended, darling!' She fingered her wig. 'I come to you for gossip alone, not scandal.'

'There is a difference?'

She took a breath, and then spoke to me as if I was something of an idiot.

'Gossip is the juice that keeps my column chugging along. Indeed, my every waking moment is spent knee deep in water, panning for glistening nuggets of gossip. I make sure to mix with the titans of tittle-tattle! This lunchtime, I am merely out panning. But scandal - well! Scandal is gold bullion, the top prize, jackpot - and something I hardly expect from the likes of you!' She shot out a hand. 'No offence!'

I wasn't given time to take any, for her fiancee returned.

'Pinkerton, sit!' Beryl ordered. 'Peruse the menu!'

Pinkerton sat and perused the menu.

'So! Farringdon's Shrew - a troubled production, by all accounts!'

'Troubled?' I replied. 'Really? Where did you hear that?'

A sharp cackle burst from her lips. 'Just launching in with that as an opening gambit, dear-heart. All big-deal productions like this are troubled in one way or another. So tell me - is it one way - or another?'

I went to speak candidly, and then stopped myself again. Pinkerton was watching with blinking eyes. I leaned in to Beryl's ear.

'Is he listening? Does he have to hear all this?'

She roared.

'Payton, you could be telling me state secrets or the combination number to the vault of the crown jewels, he wouldn't bat an eyelid! He is entirely devoid of care or emotion!' She nudged a knuckle into the poor man's hollow cheek and pinched a little skin. 'Entirely benign, aren't you, my little pencil-stub?'

Pinkerton allowed his face to be manipulated, and remained mute. It was all very strange.

Well... alright then,' I said. 'But I won't tell you anything that might jeopardise the production.'

'Naturally!' She sat forward. 'There are, however, one or two... issues?'

I nodded keenly. Beryl sat bolt upright and breathed in noisily as if shaking off a thrill.

'Ooh! I smell blood in the water!' she exclaimed hungrily.

I sat forward, licked my lips, and told her what I knew.

I returned from lunch with Beryl refreshed and with new energy.

Before I could take my place in the sixth row, however, I was called aside by Dickie Chandler. He beckoned me into the theatre bar, which was quickly becoming our retreat, a place to share secrets.

The man was in a state of befuddlement. His eyes were red-rimmed, and his once magnificent, wavy bouffant had a distinct limpness about it. He sat heavily behind a little round table, his left hand finding a tumbler of whisky. Before drinking however, he stopped and remembered his manners. 'Would you like to sit? Would you like a drink?'

I sat with a shake of the head.

'And how are you?' he continued vaguely.

'I am fine, thank you, Mr Chandler,' I replied.

'Please, call me Dickie.'

'I am fine, but you, quite clearly, are not. Is something amiss... Dickie?'

He swallowed. 'Yes.'

'You have found her?'

'In a manner of speaking.' He pulled a brown padded envelope from his pocket and slid it across the table. A wrinkled hand lingered over it protectively. It had been opened hastily without the use of a knife. He lowered his voice.

'If I show you this, it must go no further. Absolutely confidential.'

'Of course,' I was quick to reply and to repeat. 'Of course.'

'It's absurd. Quite, quite absurd.'

He drew back his paw and I took up the envelope hurriedly. There was something hard inside, and also a single slip of paper. I pulled the paper out, unfolded it, and read.

It was a ransom note.

'They have got Toffee,' said Chandler after a gulp of whisky. 'They want cash.' His voice cracked. 'Cash for her life!'

The short note, carelessly penned in scruffy capitals, stated that Chandler would need to issue £5000 if he wanted to see his fiancée alive again. He was to do nothing for the time being but gather the cash, as details were to follow. Something slipped part way out of the envelope and I helped it out. It was a dark pair of horn-rimmed spectacles.

'Toffee's glasses. She can barely see without them.' Chandler's voice was wavering. 'They have her, Mr Edgar. Blind and bound! And they will kill her!'

He let out a quick, painful sob.

'Well, you must go the the police!' I said sensibly, only to find myself on the receiving end of a dark look.

'Then they would certainly kill her! They say quite clearly that I must do nothing. So that is what I will do - nothing. For now. They are just giving me time to gather my assets. You mustn't say anything about this… to anyone.'

'And can you afford the £5000?'

Chandler chomped on his dentures. 'I can… cash in on an investment or two.'

I watched him with some pity. Over the table was a jittery, tortured man, fiddling nervously with a beer mat. And then - for just a second - I wondered if it were an act. Had Chandler done away with his fiancee, then this bold play might be enough to account for his innocence.

I shook off the idea, and decided to trust the man - for the time being. He reached out a hand in appeal.

'Please - you mustn't say anything?' he said again.

'You can count on me,' I reassured him firmly. 'I am the very soul of discretion.'

Part III

In which Payton Edgar denies everything

Beryl Baxter's Whispers, February 2nd 1964

Ahoy mateys! All aboard the good ship Baxter as we up-anchor and set sail for the West End and a brand-spanking new production of Taming Of The Shrew. The vessel launches under the watchful eye of Captain Dickie Chandelier. My theatrical spies tell me that there have been a number of looming waves to choppy the water, not least being the mysterious vanishing of the leading lady, Miss Toffee Morrell! A production lives and dies on its central performers, and this leading lady appears to have gone overboard and is lost at sea!

Oh, Buoy!

But! - I hear you cry - what of the company? Well, as my spy reliably informs, the crew is nothing but a rabble of shameful amateur pirates. But hie! Admiral Sir Maurice Williams has enlisted... surely he can steady the storm and keep things afloat? Well, Beryl has it on good authority that the old salty sea-dog is woefully miscast as the cocky male lead, and is ready to sink the ship entirely with a truly ripe performance.

Cheeky!

And then we have pretty, celebrated Miss Sylvia Pickford, who has cast out her net to haul in fellow star, the dashing Mr Tony Trace... only to find nothing but a couple of flailing tiddlers within! Well shiver-me-timbers! Pickford joins the ranks of hundreds of Trace's fawning admirers who have found their hauls sadly wanting. Makes you wonder what he is holding out for...

Saucy!

And so Beryl Baxter sends commiserations to Dickie Chandelier's motley crew, and we end this voyage with one simple piece of advice for the cast - abandon ship, darlings - abandon ship!

I was greeted by sour faces at the stage door on the following Monday morning.

Sir Maurice and the toad Playfair were standing at either side of the door like a couple of particularly mordant Chinese lions, each scowling grimly upon my approach.

'Ey-up! Here comes Fanny Craddock!'

'Here she comes!'

I raised my chin and ignored their rudeness, and would have gone straight inside had Sir Maurice not blocked my path. He lifted a copy of the clarion.

'You're for it, Edgar! We take it that this is your work?'

I was quick to reply, with a truth.

'I don't know to what you are referring!'

At this, he thrust the folded paper under my nose, forcing me to grab a hold of it.

'Page twelve, society rubbish.'

I only needed to skim the piece to get the gist. It seemed that Beryl had been especially candid. I prayed that my cheeks wouldn't flame and shoved the paper back where it came from.

'Nothing to do with me!' I announced, moving quickly into the gloom. They called after me.

'Gordon's livid!'

'You're for it, Fanny! In the soup without a ladle!'

I moved on forcefully. Before entering the auditorium, however, I stopped, took a deep breath, and lifted my chin. As I stepped into the light all heads turned. It felt almost as though they were lying in wait for my arrival. Much of the company was on stage, and in the second row, Gordon Farringdon leapt up with surprising agility. He was indeed livid.

'Mr Edgar, about time! Come forth - step into the light! I hope you have an excuse for this!'

He too was clutching a Clarion.

'Well? Speak!'

I adopted my most innocent mien and, with raised shoulders, held out my palms beseechingly. I too could act, when necessary. From my position, centre stage, it was surprising how easily my voice travelled.

'I assure you, Mr Farringdon, I had absolutely nothing to do with that nonsense! I am offended - and deeply wounded - that you think I should have anything to do with it whatsoever!'

'You work for the Clarion, do you not?'

'Many people work for the Clarion,' I replied swiftly.

'And yet only one of them is also a part of our company. Rosemary tells me you are pals with that serpent-headed gossip monger!'

I peered into the darkness. Thank you Rosemary!

At that point, Sylvia Pickford appeared from the wings in a raincoat. She didn't need to clutch a copy of the paper for us to see that she had read it - her eyes were red from crying. Nobody spoke. Her lip trembled remarkably, and then she set her eyes on Tony Trace across the stage. With a sob, she turned and ran.

'Oh, wonderful! Just wonderful!' Farringdon growled. He glared his glass-eyed glare. 'This is your doing, Edgar!'

'Mr Farringdon, how many times must I say that I am entirely innocent? Yes, I am acquainted with Beryl Baxter, but that is all. If you persist in seeing only the worst in me - well, there is nothing I can do but withdraw myself from the company, and withdraw my support, also.'

I referred to support of the financial kind, and he knew it. Rosemary spoke up from her seat.

'I think we should give him the benefit of the doubt, Gordy. Why should Payton wish to harm a project in which he's financially invested? Baxter will easily have found our cast list and made a few presumptions. Wild speculation is what she does best.'

Her husband grumbled.

I was then allowed to move to my place at Rosemary's side. I leaned close to her ear.

'Thank you for that.'

She sniffed. 'Why did you do it, Payton?'

'Excuse me?'

'I had to say all that clap-trap to calm the waters with Gordy, but I don't believe a word of it. I know Baxter's type, and I know you. She'll have squeezed you for gossip like a snake to a mongoose. Now shut up and suck on a sherbet lemon.'

I sat back, seething. It took me a while to calm my racing heart, and when I did I made a silent pact to myself. It seemed that whatever I said was misconstrued as gossip or tittle-tattle, and so from this moment on, I would firmly button my lip. Absolute discretion would be my modus operandi.

A short while later, Dickie Chandler appeared, and he swept up the aisle with a gloomy look on his face. He gave no recognition or greeting, and disappeared into the back.

'Poor Dickie,' said Rosemary.

'Mmm,' I replied.

'He's under such strain…'

'You don't know the half of it,' I uttered mindlessly.

'Oh, I do, Payton. I know too much! So much on his shoulders. We talked about it all at the weekend. The money… the demands… all of it…'

'Demands? What do you mean?'

'Toffee, and all that money. Dickie may be well off, but even his affluence has limits.'

I gasped. It seemed that Chandler had taken someone else into his confidence!

'What do you know about that?'

She shook me off. 'Nothing. It's private. Nothing to do with you, certainly. I shouldn't have said…'

I wasn't about to be put off that easily.

'You know about the demands?'

'I shouldn't have said!' Rosemary squeaked. 'It's none of your business.'

'But it is!' I said, triumphantly. 'I know all about it. He showed me the ransom letter.'

'Ransom letter?'

'What a relief! I have been fit to burst, desperate for someone to talk to about it!'

'Ransom letter?' Rosemary gasped. 'I was talking about the demands Toffee made before she disappeared, running up an extortionate bill for all those fancy De Groot frocks and kitten heels she bought. What's this about a ransom letter?'

Oops!

I back-pedalled furiously.

'Nothing… I've got it wrong… cross wires! Nothing at all.' I lifted a finger. 'Forget I said anything!'

Mercifully, a break was called, and I hurriedly left Rosemary's side.

I was unsurprised to find Dickie Chandler alone in the saloon bar. I was also unsurprised that it was not quite lunchtime and yet he already had a drink. What did surprise me, however, was that he looked genuinely pleased to see me.

'To be honest, you are the only person I trust, Mr Edgar, and the only person I can talk to about all this. I am thankful for your ear, and for your discretion.'

My mouth went dry.

He took out the note and Miss Morrell's glasses. 'I can't stop looking at them. She's blind without them.' Bloodshot eyes peered up at me, beseechingly. 'Where is she?'

I took the glasses and inspected them, as if they might offer a clue.

'You haven't heard anything else?'

'No, but they have her, and I dread to think what they're doing to the poor girl. She can be effervescent, boisterous even, but deep down she's not really made of strong stuff. A dear, fluffy thing. And she's used to the finer things and being looked after, not being snatched and held like a prisoner in a cell. She-'

Suddenly he stopped, straightened and changed his face.

'Anyway, Mr Edgar, thats enough chit-chat about the weather, dire though it has been.'

'What?'

I looked around. Rosemary was standing in the doorway.

'Oh! Yes, the weather,' I continued, trying to sound as natural as possible. 'Simply dreadful.'

As if he could hide what had happened, Chandler grabbed the note and spectacles and shoved them into the envelope.

'Everything's fine here, Rosemary,' he stammered unconvincingly with a flick of his wrist. 'Are you off out for lunch? Have a good one.'

I have known Rosemary long enough to know that she was not one to take orders, nor to act with discretion. This was a woman who had once decorated a simple box-room with leopard print wallpaper. She wasn't to be dismissed so easily. Before we knew it she was at my side and extending a painted claw out to her friend.

'What's that you've got there, Dickie? And what's this Payton told me about a ransom note? Mmm?'

Chandler's face dropped a mile and his eyes met mine. I could hardly deny I had said anything, and instead offered up my palms.

'She… worked it out,' I said, perhaps a little weakly.

Rosemary clicked her fingers.

'Come on! Let's see that letter!'

Chandler hummed and stammered a little. Standing over us with a schoolmarmish authority, Rosemary snatched the letter and read it with pursed lips. She took a moment to think and then folded it back into the envelope, tutting as if disapproval was the natural response to such a revelation.

'This affair needs a woman's touch,' she announced.

'Please keep your voice down!' I said with some authority. 'This must be kept strictly under wraps. Dickie wouldn't want every Tom, Dick and…Rosemary knowing about this.'

'What rot!' Rosemary spat. 'You must tell everyone, Dickie! Shout it from the rooftops, put everyone on their guard! And go to the police immediately!'

'Never!' Chandler cried.

'It might be prudent to report it,' I said carefully. 'Miss Morrell is in danger.'

'I can't! I mustn't! They will kill her if I set the police onto it - they say as much. No, I must do as instructed, and await their next move. I have made steps to get the cash.'

I was overcome by doubt.

'Mr Chandler… Dickie, while your apprehension is understandable, this is a very delicate situation, requiring tact and consideration. The police are surely used to managing situations like this. You need to let the professionals help. It's the best way.'

His eyes met mine, and he appeared to be listening. He crumpled.

'Do you think so?'

'I do indeed. We can't-'

'You know what, Payton? Perhaps Dickie is right!' Rosemary declared, bulldozing her way in just as I was about to make the man see sense. She pulled a stool to the table, sat and continued in a low, conspiratorial tone. 'This is an ugly business. Toffee may be in even more danger if they get wind we have involved anyone outside of our little circle. We could be dealing with very dangerous criminals - dangerous, bloodthirsty animals.'

I examined her face. She was enjoying this.

'Go against their wishes and before you know it, you'll have a severed ear in the post. Or a finger. We've all seen those films!'

Chandler paled, but I was having none of it.

'Rosemary, please! This is not one of those films!'

'You are quite right, Payton. This is real - and serious.' She reached out and tookChandler's hand. 'We must be tread carefully, Dickie, do as they say and get her back safely - all in one piece. That's the most important thing.'

Rosemary was attempting to take charge, and I didn't like it. Chandler nodded in agreement. He took a few deep breaths and then spoke softly.

'Please, both of you, respect my wishes - this must go no further. Not even Miss Fudge should know.' He lifted a finger in Rosemary's direction. 'And not Gordon either. I must act discreetly, and calmly, and get my girl back. You're to say nothing, either of you.'

'Alright. But let us help you,' Rosemary put in.

'You already are,' said Chandler. 'This is my business, and I'd like it to stay that way.' He looked down at the spectacles, sadly.

'I can't bear to look at these.'

He sipped them into his top pocket and we were about to leave when the ugly little wardrobe mistress appeared, a box in her hands and a cigarette in the corner of her mouth.

'Expecting a delivery, Mr Chandler? Here you are - left at the box office overnight. Miss Fudge asked me to pass it on.'

Chandler struggled to find words.

'Thank you... Mrs Damp...'

She padded away.

It was a paper parcel about the size of a small shoebox. Chandler placed it in the centre of the table and we all stared down at it in horror. The parcel displayed no postmarks, only Chandler's name and that of the theatre in bold ink, scrappily written.

For a moment, we all held our breath.

'Expecting a parcel?' I asked slowly, hoping that Chandler would say something about his sister sending a brand new pair of wingtips or some such thing. But, of course, he shook his head.

'It's from them!' whispered Rosemary, rather unnecessarily.

'Why a box?' I asked, sensibly. 'Surely we are only expecting some details... instructions...'

'A severed ear!' said Rosemary wildly. 'A finger! Or worse!'

'That's not helping!'

'Well, you open it then, Payton.'

When I hesitated, she continued. 'No? Afraid of what you'll find?'

Chandler found his tongue. 'I - I just can't touch it. I can't bear to think...'

'Oh, give it here!' said Rosemary sharply. She pulled the box towards her and tore at the paper deftly, with little regard for her manicured nails. As she did, Chandler took in a deep breath and closed his eyes. The man was terrified. What was he expecting - a severed head?

He would not have been far wrong.

It was indeed a box that had once held shoes, and after the paper was set aside Rosemary flicked off the lid and dug in a hand. We could all see what it was before she lifted it up. Golden locks of hair sprung up between her fingers, and Chandler let out a horrified gasp.

'She's been s-scalped!' he stammered.

Rosemary unceremoniously took up the hair and dumped it aside on the table, instantly revealing large flecks of what looked like blood dotted here and there within the acrylic strands of the marquise-style piece.

'It's her wig, Dickie, that is all,' said Rosemary before giving me a conspiratorial glare and whispering triumphantly. 'I told you so!'

'A wig?' Chandler gasped. 'But there's blood on it!'

'Fake blood, I'm sure.' She examined it closely. 'Or perhaps not. Pigs blood? Surely you knew that Toffee wore a hairpiece, Dickie?'

He shook his head.

'It was obvious!'

'I had no idea. I never had reason to think it might be. We had... we hadn't...'

What they had or hadn't done went unsaid, as Rosemary produced a folded sheet of paper. She read it agonisingly slowly to herself, before turning it to Chandler and I.

amazon.co.uk

A gift note from Liv Maddocks:

Enjoy reading this and stay sane during lockdown! See you soon. Love Liv. From: LivvieM

Gift note included with **Payton Edgar's Performance: Payton Edgar Mysteries Book 4**

It read;

£5000 CASH. BROWN PAPER PARCEL. THIS THURSDAY 7PM. COME ALONE, DROP AND LEAVE. PLACE BESIDE WASTE BIN, SOUTH END OF BLUE BRIDGE, ST JAMES'S PARK

MORRELL WILL BE RELEASED THIRTY MINUTES LATER ON THESE TERMS ONLY.

'Well, there is it - what I must do,' said Chandler, setting his hands on the tabletop. 'I have three days to get the cash, and I will do as they say.'

Rosemary nodded. 'Thursday at seven Gordon will be at his club meeting, I am free to help.'

'Club?' I asked.

'Gordon belongs to the Whitehall Gentleman's Bridge Club.'

'Never heard of it.'

'I'm not surprised - it's a Gentleman's Union,' said Rosemary, as I were something else entirely. 'All terribly exclusive. You won't ever have been invited, but you can imagine what it's like - crusty old majors dribbling into their broadsheets and gibbering on about their hunting days over a pint of scotch. Stalwarts of the British Empire and all that. Anyway, that's by-the-by. I'll be free - I'll come with you, Dickie.'

'No. I must do this alone. Without you, or Mr Edgar - or the police.'

Chandler was nodding gently, resigned, as if the deal was already done. I studied the shoe box thoughtfully and then held a hand out.

'May I just have a brief look at the letter, Mr Chandler?'

'As I've just said-'

'I don't mean the words, I mean the paper itself. Just a glance at the back of it.'

Chandler unfolded the paper and held it up. I examined it briefly. There was a neat tear in the top left hand corner, where it had once been pulled through staples.

Curious.

'There's something about this...' I found myself saying as I fingered the corner.

'There is something about it, all right - something downright evil!' Rosemary snapped. I turned to her with a question.

'Rosemary, do you have a copy of the script?'

'The script?'

'Yes, the script.'

She gave a grumble. 'It's in two sections.'

'The second set, I think.'

She fumbled in her sizeable bag, an unappealing woven-fabric accessory which would have been better placed around the neck of a horse, eventually pulling out a bundle of papers. I keenly inspected the pages. It was just as I thought - the last few pages were blank sheets. I tore one away.

'Payton!' Rosemary screeched, snatching back her script.

‘It’s alright, there’s nothing on it; the last few pages are entirely blank. Mr Chandler, might I offer some insight? It seems that our foe has been somewhat negligent.’

‘How so?’

I drew in a breath. It was time to shine.

‘We have on the table a couple of rather damning clues.’

Chandler was looking at me perplexedly. Rosemary was doing her best to appear nonchalant.

Enjoying the moment, I went on at my leisure.

‘My first observation; the demands are hand delivered. Which perhaps means nothing in itself, besides the avoidance of a postmark, but then – the second point - a time is picked for the exchange which is comfortably outside of rehearsal hours. Third; that shoe box is from Smith and Horton, which - if I am not mistaken - is more of a theatrical costumier than your average shoe shop. Am I correct?’

‘Smith and Horton? On the Tottenham Court road, yes,’ said Chandler.

‘What are you twittering on about, Payton?’ said Rosemary, annoyingly. She was being tirelessly dense. I placed a finger on the blank paper.

‘My final observation; this paper probably comes from the back of a script for The Taming Of The Shrew. If you look, the paper is of poor quality and yellowing a little at the edges. And look at the torn corner here, where the paper has been pulled through staples - identical to the paper used for your ransom note, Mr Chandler. Very sloppy.’

The man was still looking at me blankly.

‘Don’t you see? I may be wrong of course, but all this suggests that - just perhaps - your kidnapper hails from here… from this theatre… from this production…’

Now I had their attention.

I leaned in closer.

‘A reasonable hypothesis? He is most probably one of us.’

Part IV

In which Payton Edgar hears of a hoo-ha

Dear Margaret,

My sister's husband makes romantic passes at me when we go caravanning. We live on the same street, and he keeps his distance at home, but twice a year we go on holiday together to a campsite, the men drink and he always finds a way to get me alone. My sister's husband is not unattractive, and I have found myself secretly anticipating his overtures. What can I do to make this stop?

Mrs G, Walton-on-Thames

Margaret replies; First things first - stop going on holiday together. Rather an obvious answer to your quandary, but one you seem willing to over look. It is clear that you enjoy this attention and have no intention of "making it stop", as you put it. I think the best way to end this is to get it all out in the open. Allow me to help. I suggest that you, Mrs Clarissa G of Little Paddocks, Walton-on-Thames, tell your sister, Nadia, all about Norman's exploits on your holidays in Priddy, Somerset. Honesty is, after all, the best policy.

The following day I had a mid-morning appointment with Mr. Rees.

Rees is a coiffeur of the highest order who has, for decades, been beavering away in a cupboard-sized booth set far back from the pavement in dear Charlotte Street. It was Rees who introduced me to Bream's Scalp Tonic, a tincture that not only stimulates the growth of follicles but also adds moisture to the skin - a boon to an exposed crown.

Rees is quite the most efficient and talented barber that I have ever lent my scalp. I feared for the day when he would hang up his scissors - a day not far away, for the man was even older than the faded sketches of moustachioed men forever displayed in his window. Despite his longevity, he possessed a remarkably steady hand and a deftness with a blade that was unrivalled in the entire city.

On top of that, Rees respects discretion and keeps idle chatter to a minimum.

I left his establishment feeling - as usual - reinvigorated and ready for action. After the bizarreness of the kidnapping, attending the Old Compton had become a far more appealing notion and I hurried just a little in anticipation.

I arrived at the theatre at a quarter to one to find Rosemary finishing off her honey sandwiches. I had forgotten about her penchant for honey. How the woman maintained a stick-like frame while guzzling a half dozen thick and dripping honey sandwiches at lunchtimes was a mystery. I have never been a fan of the stuff, and even though she wrapped up the brown paper carefully, the heady, nectarous aroma hung stagnantly in the air for quite a while.

There was no action on stage whatsoever. As she wrapped her package, I said a friendly hello.

'And where have you been?' was the matronly retort. I lifted a hand to my temple.

'I have been at the barbers.'

Rosemary squinted and examined my head.

'Really? Thought you'd have given that up long since.'

I leaned over and whispered.

'Any news on the… situation?'

She gave an expression of remorse. 'Not a sausage! Diddly-squat!' I joined her in a disdainful frown. 'But thank goodness you're here - other happenings have been happening and I'm bursting with it! Sit down and gird your loins!'

I sat at her side, listening keenly as she updated me with the latest news, and as I did a sudden realisation dawned and I found myself momentarily distracted. Rosemary's tone was urgent, and we were each sat with knees turned towards one another, with one arm across our middle and a hand raised to a cheek. Gone was the prickly ex-wife I had avoided all these years, and in her place was a companion - a confidante. Suddenly I heard Irving's cutting tone. I knew exactly how he would describe us.

Like fishwives at a bus stop.

And he would have been right. Our kidnap secret brought us closer together, and I listened to Rosemary's account of the latest with all the interest of a bloodhound to the scent of a fleeing fox.

'Well - where to begin! Things started slowly, and then Sir Maurice finally pitched up mid-morning, with Miss Drake at his side. The sullen little thing has been glued to the man for days! Something of a protege, he has been regaling her with wild stories and offering sage advice!'

Wild stories and sage advice? Trite observations and hackneyed musings would be nearer the mark. I uttered something along these lines.

'Well, whatever you say, they are thick as thieves. Poor taken Toffee is nothing but a dim and distant memory! It's quite shocking, really - the Drake girl was dreadful as an understudy, all nervous ticks and sniffly colds. Now she takes to the stage like she owns it - and the men all love it.'

'And you?'

'I just can't warm to her, although I don't know why. Well, anyway - then came the hoo-ha…'

'Ooh! A hoo-ha!' I parroted, hungrily. 'What hoo-ha?'

'Little Miss Pickford had one of her spells. She was in the midst of a piece with Tony when all of a sudden, she exploded with a loud gasp and collapsed onto that wooden chair! It was a painfully theatrical faint and you might have been forgiven for thinking it was simply a part of the play. A minute later she was leaning forward in her seat and sobbing loudly with her head in her hands. It was a pitiful display - and we all sat watching - nobody knew quite what to do. Well, of course she must have been mortified that nobody rushed to her aid!'

'Indeed!'

'Well, after a dreadfully awkward hiatus, Mr Trace stepped over to her with the most insincere look of concern I have ever seen. She was putting it all on, of course, just to get that young man's arm around her shoulder - and it worked. Gordy was having none of it! Trace suggested they take another break - said that Miss Pickford was under a lot of personal strain, whatever that meant. Well! Gordon blew a gasket!'

In my head I heard Gordon Farringdon's distinctly bovine bleat.

'He insisted that they carry on. Break early for lunch, Trace said. Not a chance, said Gordon, and good for him! Then Miss Pickford upped and stormed off the stage without so much as a by-your-leave! Gordon called after her - and then Christophe Playfair stepped up to put his two pennies worth in! Well, of course, that was the worst thing that could have happened.'

She stopped.

'I have a little confession here, Payton.'

'Confess away...'

'Well, I don't like to speak ill of people...'

'Go on...'

'I just don't like him - Mr Playfair.'

'In that, you are certainly not alone.'

'There's something... unpalatable about his way, how he holds himself, and he's just a-'

She stopped again. I pressed forth.

'Go on - say it...'

After a short pause, she said it.

'A slithering creep.'

'Oh, yes! The very worst type! A poisonous toad, if ever there was one.'

'And those horrible turtle-necked jerseys he wears...'

'Don't hold back, Rosemary, dear!'

'Well... he makes my skin crawl! Not a pleasant person.'

'I concur wholeheartedly.'

'So, Mr Playfair spoke up and insisted they give the girl time to dry her eyes - and Gordon exploded! You stay out of this! he shouted. You should worry more about your pantomime performance than about telling folks what to do. This is all Gordon speaking. And then he said - this show only has one director, and that is me!'

I shook my head. 'Well, I never did!'

Rosemary huffed.

'Good for Gordy, I say - needs to pull rank, been a long time coming. That Pickford girl's a rum sort. A simpering flibbertigibbet! I warned him about her, but he went ahead and hired her anyway. She thinks of nothing but men, fashion and money!'

'I dare say!'

'Thereby hangs a tale, Payton. I've been asking about, and little Miss P's done this before. Her silly little fainting episodes are all about getting male attention, I'm quite convinced of it. It'll be all over her rent again, looking for a handsome face with a fat wallet. Do you know, at the start of all this she had the nerve to request an advance on her pay? An advance! Gordon put her into place, I can tell you. Can't pay the rent, and yet I know for a fact she keeps a rather desirable Park Lane apartment. And she can keep herself well stocked with the most fashionable shoes, fine stockings and those dreadful garish chiffon scarves she so likes to wear!'

'Really!'

'So, we have Mr Playfair with a face sourer than last week's milk, Tony Trace huffing and puffing on stage and Miss P. locked in her dressing room. As if that wasn't enough, Sir Maurice then plays up something rotten!'

'Plays up?'

'Takes centre stage and tells poor Gordon - to his face - that Beryl Baxter had it right! That he is helming a troubled production! Says he's never known anything like it - petty squabbles, unprofessional conduct and all that. All out of nowhere!'

Hardly out of nowhere. Sir Maurice must have sensed the spotlight lingering elsewhere and felt the urge to fling himself into it.

'And as if that weren't enough, there was suddenly the loudest crash - everybody leapt in the air! I nearly dropped a stitch! The backdrop of Paduan fields had come loose from the fittings and tumbled down. Poor Gordy, it felt like everything was falling apart - it was all terribly symbolic. Well he called out Alex and shouted him down, telling him to do his job properly. Well! How that young brute glowered! I'd call Gordy brave if it wasn't so unfair.'

'And what did Mr Drake have to say about that?'

'He wasn't given a chance, Payton. Sir Maurice had a hissy-fit, threw his arms up and declared the production doomed - literally falling apart at the seams.'

'Of course he did.'

Rosemary tutted and sighed.

'So at that, Gordon set off in a huff and everybody vanished! And here we sit, staring at an empty stage. But I can't help thinking that Sir Maurice had a point. This production's been beset with complications, disagreements and - well, at risk of sounding a bit batty - bad spirits.'

I chuckled at this.

'I didn't have you down as the spiritual sort, Rosemary.'

She popped a cigarillo between her lips, passed me a box of matches and allowed me to light it. After a deep draw on the stinking thing, she continued with a growl.

'It's just a feeling in my gut. And with the disappearance of Miss Morrell.... well! And it's only a matter of weeks to opening night. I think it's all a stress that Gordon could do without.'

'You think it's too much for him?'

'Undoubtedly. But I really shouldn't say...'

'Go on,' I said. 'Unburden yourself.'

'Well... perhaps with all this upset he should call it all off, spend his last days doing something a little less... trying. Watching him struggling to keep this thing afloat is like...well, watching a lame sheepdog herding cattle.'

'You think he's too tired?'

‘I just don’t think he’s got the - how to put it? The edge that’s needed for all this. Or the energy.’

‘Oh, haven’t I?’

We both jumped. Gordon Farringdon was standing tall in the aisle, with thin accusing eyes - one real, one glass - fixed on his wife. She squirmed in her seat.

‘Lame sheepdog, am I?’ he grumbled.

‘Gordy, I… I didn’t mean-’

‘Don’t bother to explain. I’ve had enough of your opinions, Rosemary. I’ve had enough of everyone’s opinions. We’ll talk about this later. Right now, I have cattle to herd!’

On stage, cast members began to position themselves.

‘You’ve talked it through, Gordon! You’ve sorted it all out!’ Rosemary exclaimed approvingly through wisps of smoke. He waved a dismissive hand.

‘Miss Drake did. She’s been peacekeeping, saying some sensible things to those that need to hear it. Even Pickford is back in line. And about time!’ He turned and moved to his place on the second row.

On stage, Sylvia Pickford appeared, dry eyed and resolute, and took her place by Trace. Miss Drake appeared alongside Sir Maurice, both smiling calmly. The leading lady had indeed worked wonders, and the rehearsals recommenced as if nothing untoward had occurred.

‘Theatre folk!’ Rosemary said with a tut. ‘So fickle!’

She finished her smoke, gathered up her knitting and shook her head.

‘Oh dear. I have some making up to do tonight, Payton!’ This was said almost with relish. I wondered what this might entail - might she feel the need to share some secrets to pacify the man? I wondered to myself how long it would before she broke confidence and gossiped to her husband all about Chandler’s kidnapping turmoil.

Some people found it very difficult to keep private affairs private, and Rosemary was, amongst other things, the most dreadful gossip.

Part V

In which Payton Edgar receives an evening visitor

Dear Margaret,

I am a 16 year old with a crush on the girl next door. We are working towards our exams and sometimes study together. She has lived next door for a year, and I know that she likes me, but I cannot summon up the confidence to ask her to a dance. I worry terribly that I'm ugly, but my mum says I'm not bad looking. But still I am so scared that she'll say "no" and I won't be able to live with the embarrassment. What should I do?

16 year old, Croydon

Margaret replies; First things first - what is a 16 year old lad in the middle of exams doing wasting his time writing letters to a daily rag's Agony Aunt? Get on with your revision! There'll be plenty of time to court girls once you are older, so knuckle down and focus on your studies. And of course your mother tells you that you're handsome - she is a mother and mother's see beyond the pimples and imperfections. You could be a monster and she would still sing your praises.

I was surprised to find that I stayed all the way to the end of rehearsals that evening. I almost enjoyed it.

Almost.

As things wound down and everybody milled about the place, I said goodnight to Rosemary, pulled on my coat and made my way down the aisle. As I went, I passed by Tony Trace, who was exchanging words with the wardrobe mistress.

'…and all I wore for that particular part was a loincloth and a smile, not much for the wardrobe mistress to get her teeth into. Not that I'm one to complain, Ethel. Some actors are much more content in a codpiece…'

The unsightly little seamstress was gazing up into his eyes in a dreamy fashion. I wondered how exhausting it must be for the man to constantly have adoring eyes beaming up in his direction.

I left them to it, mounted the stage and passed over the boards. As I went, a hurried movement caught my eye. The lightly sketched backdrop showing the bountiful fields of Padua was illuminated, revealing two shadows lurking behind. I caught hushed whispers - apparently the shadows were having a disagreement. I surrendered to curiosity and took a minor detour. At the very rear of the stage I found Emma Drake and her brother, mid-spat. The leading lady's thunder was gone and she was staring at her shoes, deflated and forlorn. Alex Drake had raised a dirty finger. I was slightly too far away to catch any words, but they were certainly having a disagreement of some sort or other.

Suddenly Miss Drake saw me standing there, raised her shoulders, forced a smile and gave a little wave. Her brother only glowered in my direction. I returned the wave and quickly moved on.

It was pelting with rain outside, and so I loitered for a while in the doorway. After a minute, Sylvia Pickford appeared at my side and looked up at the dark clouds with dismay. We exchanged some words about the weather and then she lifted her chin up in my direction. Her manner was warm and considered, and she whined as she spoke.

'Oh, Mr Edgar, I do wonder… you are a dark horse.'

'I am?'

'Oh yes. You keep your cards close to your chest, I can see that. Well composed, I believe is the term. Measured.'

'And that is a good thing?'

'Oh, yes, sweetie! Girls adore quiet, clever sorts.'

'Is that so?'

'Oh, yes. Still waters run deep.'

I had the sudden realisation that I was being charmed. She went on.

'You don't say very much… for an Artistic Director. Are you perhaps a little shy?'

'Certainly not!'

'Well, that's good. I would be interested to hear more of your views on Gordon's direction. He is often so set in his terribly old-fashioned ways, when I think we could be doing something different… something more contemporary with the whole thing, wouldn't you say? Sir Maurice thinks so. He does his best to bring a bit of vigour to the set, but your voice added to the mix would be most welcome.'

I felt a little sorry for Farringdon. It seemed that nobody appreciated his direction. The actress was blinking up at me with large innocent eyes, and I couldn't help but smile.

Our exchange was interrupted by the toad Playfair, who lurked up behind and boomed loudly.

'Budge up, my lovelies!'

'Blimey, Christophe! My heart hit my head!' Pickford squeaked, effortlessly throwing her attentions in his direction. 'Are you ready? Still up for a drink or two?'

'Or five! Yes, of course, treacle… oh, yes.' His reply was a little distracted, and Miss Pickford caught it.

'What is it, Chrissie?'

Playfair cleared his throat, frowning. 'Nothing, kitten. It's just… something I've seen… something not quite right. Mmm…'

'Been looking in the mirror again?' Pickford squealed.

'Silence, you rude tart! Well, never mind all that - come along then!'

He thrusted an overlarge pink umbrella in between us, opened it out and took Miss Pickford's arm. I watched as they moved through the rain, and huffed a little to myself. I was about to move out into the rain myself when Emma Drake appeared at my side, buttoning her mac. She looked a little surprised to see me, and blushed a little.

'Gosh! The rain!'

'Indeed,' I replied.

'Quite something!'

'Indeed,' I said again, my vocabulary failing somewhat. She nodded a farewell and I watched as she went over to a red bicycle, unchained it from a railing and rode away. I wished I could ride quickly away. I hadn't planned for a downpour, and rather regretted my choice of footwear.

Much to my surprise, Rosemary appeared on my doorstep that night.

She arrived under the guise of needing to discuss ideas about recent events, but I suspect that it was both a perfect excuse to get away from her pallid, glass-eyed bookmark of a husband and an opportunity to nosey in on my private affairs.

I was none too pleased. As much as I had enjoyed a gossip earlier, I had certainly taken my daily dose of Rosemary, and my evenings were my own. The knock at the door came at eight-fourteen precisely. I noted the exact time as I had peered at my watch and grumbled, for eight-fourteen in the evening was certainly not a suitable time of day impromptu house calls of any nature. She immediately got off to a bad start by telling me off and prying shamelessly.

'You took your time answering the door!'

'Naturally. One isn't prepared for visitors at this hour.'

'Well, I jumped in a taxi, I simply couldn't wait until tomorrow. Stuff to say.'

'You could have called,' I replied dryly.

'You never answer the phone, Payton.'

She barged through and eyeballed my furnishings. 'Oh! Well, this is nice enough. Neat and tidy. Very you. Nice area, too - though not a patch on Chelsea. But I'm sure it's good enough for your needs.' She approached my sideboard. 'Well this is delightful!'

'Isn't it just.'

I waited for it - and it came.

'We have one like it. Ours is just a bit more antique and in far better condition.'

'How kind of you to say. Why are you here?'

'And you have a piano!' she exclaimed, brazenly running a finger over the keys. 'A baby grand, no less! I had no idea you played.'

'I don't.'

She pretended to flick dust from her fingers. 'So I see. So what… you just sit and look at it?'

'Pretty much, yes. Why are you here, Rosemary?'

'My brain's been buzzing! I've been thinking… and have come up with a sensational theory that I simply must share. Also, I needed some fresh air. Gordon's under a cloud - I tried to win him over, but he can't see past the end of his nose. Between you and me, Payton…'

She hesitated.

'Yes?'

'I think he's losing the plot a little. This play and all the pressure, with his illness, well-' she faded into thought. It took her a frustrating minute to find the words she needed. 'He's… he's got his mind fixed on some wild treatment, for his… condition.'

'Treatment? I thought that there was no...' I skirted around the words I needed - and failed in finding them. 'You told me that it was all very... thumbs down.'

'I know, I know. We've seen enough doctors to tell us there is no treatment, no cure. And then - unbeknownst to me - Gordy takes himself to this outrageously pricey quack on Harley Street, recommended by a friend from his damned Bridge Club. Didn't breathe a word about it until afterwards, and this quack suggested a treatment - in Tunisia, of all places! Smoking herbal pipes and the laying of hot stones or some such clap-trap. According to Gordy they practically guaranteed a cure. Absolute tripe - and costly tripe, to boot. Extremely costly. He can't afford it. We can't afford it. And anyway, even if we could, it's a wild goose chase.'

'Oh, dear.'

'But I think he'll try anything. Tells me that some other club member, Nathaniel something-or-other, double barrelled name I forget, will stump up half the cash. I've never heard of the man. I don't know what to do! I don't want our last few months together to be wasted trekking backwards and forwards to Tunisia, of all places!'

'Of course not.'

I pondered over what the might mean. We had a missing actress, held to ransom, and someone desperate for cash - Gordon Farringdon. Perhaps not such a coincidence.

Rosemary was still talking when Grace appeared from the hallway. She paused in the doorway, looking very fresh in a mauve blouse and navy skirt. Her hair had recently been set in curls and she looked, as ever, very presentable.

'And who is this?' Rosemary chirped. 'A cigarette girl?'

I was momentarily lost for words.

'Oh, don't bother, Payton!' Rosemary tutted and glided across the room. 'Good evening, dear. I am Rosemary Farringdon. Pleasure to meet you.'

'Grace. Grace Kemp,' Grace replied with a smile. She paused, and then continued with a glint in her eye. 'Ah! Rosemary? As in-?'

'That's right, I am the ex-Mrs Edgar. What's he been saying about me?'

'Nothing.'

'No, he wouldn't dare. Well, that's all centuries ago now. More water under the bridge than fills the Thames.' Rosemary turned to me, her eyes rolling. 'So, Payton, you dark horse! You never said anything about this dear young thing sharing your roof! I thought you were cagey about your domestic situation, and now I see why. You bad, bad boy!'

I felt the swell of heat in my stomach, and stammered out something or other, only to have it shouted down by one of Rosemary's explosive snorts.

'Pah! I'm pulling your leg, darling! Look at the girl! You'd have to live in a castle to catch a girl like this, not to mention quite a different, well - visual set up!' She waved her hand around her face in circles and turned back to Grace, speaking as if she were a vase on the mantlepiece. 'A presentable young specimen like this must have a young husband to match, right?'

'Sadly not,' Grace replied sweetly. 'Well, there is someone, but... well, early days yet.'

'Just you set down your terms up front, dear. Show him who's boss. But please satisfy my curiosity - what is a treasure like you doing Chez Edgar?'

Grace wet her lips. 'I am the resident nursemaid, to Mr Edgar's aunt.'

Rosemary froze, and I enjoyed watching the look of incredulity melt over her face. 'Your Aunt Elizabeth? Elizabeth? Old Lady Dry Bones! She is…. here? She is… alive?'

I gave a sullen nod.

'You said your mother passed on, but I never thought about her other half. I just assumed they'd both pop off together! Why, she must be a hundred-and-twelve, if she's a day. And living under your roof, Payton!'

I detected some sympathy in her tone.

'Would you like to say hello?' Grace asked, not entirely innocently. 'I'm pretty sure she's still awake.'

Rosemary gasped.

'To face the Gorgon? No fear! In fact, I have the sudden urge to flee. If I didn't have a burning theory to share, that is.' She took my sleeve and let me forcedly to my lounge chair and, once we were seated, issued an order to poor Grace in the doorway.

'Some sherry would be nice, dear. A generous nip - cream if you have it.'

I caught the flicker of indignation in Grace's eye. She swallowed and replied slowly and carefully. 'It would be an honour to serve you. Port, Payton?'

'Just a small one, please,' I replied, daringly. Rosemary watched her go.

'Starchy,' she said, by way of observation. 'Well - you'll be needing that drink when I tell you my theory.'

'Oh, yes?'

' I don't know why we've not seen it before, Payton. We've been duped!'

'Duped?'

'Had! Conned! Taken for a ride by a slight of hand!' She sat back in her seat triumphantly. 'What would you say if I suggested that this isn't a kidnapping at all!'

'I would be lost for words,' I replied, unimpressed.

'I thought you might!'

'And if it's not a kidnapping - then what is it?'

'Murder, Payton! We are talking about murder!'

Grace returned and set down our drinks.

'Kidnapping? Murder? I thought you were doing Taming Of The Shrew?'

'Off stage, my dear,' Rosemary purred dismissively. She took a haughty sip of Aunt Elizabeth's best sherry, pulled a face and then glanced up at Grace, who was hovering with interest. 'You may leave now, thank you.'

While she may have appeared calm and made her way to the door, I saw the irritation behind Grace's smile. 'Goodnight, then.'

'Good night, Grace,' I replied. 'And thank you so much for the drinks.'

There was a demonic look on Rosemary's face, and after waiting for the girl to go, she leaned over and slapped my knee.

'Richard Chandler. Richard Chandler!'

'Your friend, Dickie? ' I put in with a raised eyebrow. 'Dear, dear Dickie?'

Rosemary took a breath, and continued cautiously. 'I know him well. And I've always liked and trusted him. But you asked me about him, about his temperament? And I wasn't quite forthcoming. It's true, there's always been something about the man… something unspoken.'

'Unspoken?'

'Gordy and I, we never speak of how he treated his wife, Una.'

'Dickie was married?'

'Unhappily. Only lasted a year or so and this was a good - gosh! - twenty, twenty-five years ago. Una was a bombastic thing, sturdy and forthright. She's the reason he's stuck to pretty but flighty sorts over the years - having been poisoned by a rotten marriage. They had one of those relationships that thrives on squabbles and disagreements. Being Dickie's friend we, naturally, took his side when the milk turned sour. But the way he treated her… bullying, pig headed and, well, I hesitate to use the word, but there was a little… violence involved.'

'Violence?'

'I don't want to go into details, but it's the truth. Dickie drank too much, back in the day, even more than he does now. Una was a fiery, physical sort, and he kind of rose to the challenge. I'm not saying that he laid a finger on her as such, if anything it was Una that would do the slapping, but he was very bullish and… temperamental in those days. And so when you questioned me about him, you set me thinking. I do feel a little guilty but, well, when you think about it, we only have his word for it that Toffee was kidnapped.'

'That and the evidence of a scuffle in her dressing room, the posted spectacles, blood-stained wig and ransom note!'

'All things that Dickie has been sure to share with you, Payton. Ever thought for a minute that you might be nothing more than a stooge? You are a gullible sort. We know that they argued-'

'Says Playfair!'

'Granted - but what if it was more than simple argument? What if that scuffle in her dressing room ended in murder? What might a man do? Dispose of the body, deny all knowledge and then act shocked when a ransom note appears! It makes a horrible kind of sense, Payton. If you ask me, it's the only thing that makes sense! And why does he insist we aren't involved with the exchange at St James's Park? Because there will be no exchange. And he has been shoddy, you said so yourself, sending the note with a page from the script and using the familiar shoebox. It really does make sense!'

I thought this over, and came to a conclusion.

'I can't say that it hadn't crossed my mind already, Rosemary. But I can't see dear Dickie as a murderer.'

'Why not?'

While I struggled to reply in any detail, for I had nothing more than intuition, I did my best. 'I just don't think he did it. I can't see him as a cold-hearted killer. The way he holds himself, the way he dresses. His hairstyle is far too neat - too considered.'

I found myself on the receiving end of a black look.

'His hair? What does his hair have to do with it?'

'I simply can't see dear Dickie Chandler being quite so cunning. Besides, he is visibly shaken by all this, Rosemary. Shaken, and scared. No, I'm inclined to believe him.'

'Payton, darling - these are theatre people! They'll pull the wool over your eyes as good as look at you! And Dickie can act up just as good as the rest of them, mark my words!'

She finished her drink.

'I say we watch him carefully over the next few days. I don't want it to be Dickie… but I just can't shake the feeling. We should be prepared for the possibility.'

I laughed a little and she cocked her head.

'What? What is it?'

'Just what you've said before, about your darling friendship with dear, dear Dickie…'

'Well?'

'If this is the way you treat your dear, dear friends, it makes me wonder how you might treat your enemies.'

Part VI

In which Payton Edgar nails Jimmy The Dip

Dear Margaret,

I need some womanly advice. I am a forty year old man who has been married for five years. A few years ago I had a brief affair with a secretary at work. I felt terrible about it, finished the affair and confessed to my wife. She took it badly, but said she forgave me. However, ever since then she has been convinced I am having affairs with every woman I know. Her jealousy has soured our marriage. There is a new girl at work who is attractive, fun and single. She is everything my wife isn't. My wife is so convinced we're having an affair that I feel I might as well go ahead. Would this be a mistake?

Mr T, Putney

Margaret replies; Your transparency bores me. You are writing to me purely to gain consent to cheat on your wife once again - and I will most certainly not give my permission. That said, a leopard never changes its spots, and if you don't cheat with this pretty newcomer, I am certain that there will be another pretty newcomer to take her place. And so, in a rare moment of resignation, I will advise you to ignore anything that I might say and just get on with it. Go on! Mistakes won't make themselves!

Wednesday was another wet one, and I had Russell collect me just after ten.

I was dressed and ready a little earlier than usual, and so spent some time organising my cupboards and making sure all the cup handles were turned to the right and all labels on the tins and jars faced outwards. I noticed that, like the jams, the marmalade had a gingham cloth cap stretched across it. I pulled it off and looked at it thoughtfully, before depositing it in my jacket pocket.

The car horn sounded outside. It was perhaps the first morning since the break-in that I had not passed the empty mantelpiece in my living room with a sharp pang of grief for my singing bowl. There were other things on my mind.

Sitting in the back of my ride, I gazed out at the miserable Londoners plodding through the puddles outside - the many faceless dark shapes, pushing themselves against the wind. Was I wise to be getting myself involved in all this theatrical nonsense, with missing persons and ransom notes? All I ever wanted was a quiet life, and yet it seemed that whichever way I turned there was some shady felonious soul up to no good. I was distracted from my thoughts when - much to my chagrin - Russell piped up in his unprofessionally chirpy manner as we passed by Hyde Park Corner.

'Had any luck retrieving your stolen goods then, Mr. Edgar?'

I replied in the negative.

'Pity. That there red bowl you told me about had me thinking. You said it was a singing bowl - how exactly do you make a bowl sing?'

I stared at the back of his head. Was this sarcasm?

'I would need to have it with me to demonstrate,' I replied curtly. 'The experience cannot be explained - it has to be heard.'

'Yeah, but… a bowl singing? It don't do it on its own, does it? What helps it to work?'

'A mallet.'

'Yeah, but how does it work? Really? How?'

'Please,' I replied wearily, 'I am still sore. I do not wish to discuss it.'

Thankfully, he didn't press on with any further questions. I stared at his neck and his inexcusably scruffy hairline, which tickled the collar of his chauffeur's jacket. He was rough around the edges - hardly the type to have an interest in trinkets and antiquities. Why should a domestic driver care about the properties of a singing bowl?

I cast this thought aside for a moment and returned my gaze to the wretched people on the street. Not one of them could possibly understand the beauty of an antique singing bowl. A minute later my thoughts wandered back to the driver in the front seat - there was something niggling on my mind. I posed myself the question once again.

Why should he care?

Unless, perhaps, he had one in his procession. One that he couldn't get to sing.

And then another thought sprang into mind - it was notable that the burglary happened in daylight. How did our thief know I would be out of the house at the time of the robbery? Possibly because he had driven me elsewhere? It was the same for Sir Maurice - a broad daylight break-in while the actor was at rehearsal. And Sir Maurice also had Russell drive him in every morning. And then the final, revolutionary question presented itself - how did he know that my bowl was red? He had just said it was red! I was certain that I'd never mentioned the colour, and if I had, I would have most definitely described it as crimson!

And that scruffy hairline!

I was now glaring with anger at the back of his head as these clues all slotted into place. My heart pounded - I knew it to be true, and that I must raise the alarm.

It was just before Piccadilly that I made my move. I had searched the streets for some minutes until I saw just what I was looking for up ahead; a filthy blue police box.

I cleared my throat.

'Russell, please pull over at the corner there, I need to make an urgent purchase of some lemon sherbets and this morning's Clarion.'

The driver duly did as he was told and, careful to hide my true intentions, I thanked him kindly. I watched as he slumped a little in the front seat and pulled out a newspaper of his own. I was only too glad to get out of the car and away, and I headed towards the corner shop with some haste. At the door I made as if to enter, quickly casting a look back to the car. Russell was behind the newspaper. Once I was certain that I was out of his line of vision I hastened my step, letting out a little giggle as I went - it was actually quite exciting. I carefully ducked aside and headed for the police box with some haste.

Once inside, I made the call.

It had been a dramatic morning, and I didn't get to the theatre until well after two. As I arrived, the company was enjoying another of their many, frequent breaks.

I passed by Ethel Damp, who stood with a mouthful of pins fussing over Sylvia Pickford. Again I was struck by the wardrobe mistress's Punch-like visage, her heavily rouged cheeks only adding to the look. She was helping Miss Pickford into an unbecoming frilly blue dress.

'Dmmmm Bmmmm mmm mmmm, mmm!'

'Beg pardon, Ethel?'

The pins were spat out.

'Don't breathe in so, Miss Pickford!'

'I am not breathing in, Ethel, this is my frame. I am naturally svelte.'

'Carry that on and you'll go bluer than your frock, dearie! You have to be able to get your words out on stage! Arms up, Tubby!'

I moved on. Gordon Farringdon was in his usual place in the second row, and his wife was at his side. I made a bee-line for the couple, and without preamble explained how I had exposed a thief, and had Russell the chauffeur arrested with quiet flair on the corner of Sackville Street. It was a fun tale to tell - one of exemplary deduction and bravery. Russell was, I informed them with some satisfaction, nothing more than an opportunistic thief. He would surely be put away for years.

I had expected some form of congratulatory response at this revelation, perhaps even a dose of admiration or thanks. However, Rosemary merely sat mute with surprise as her husband grumbled in his usual way.

'Are you telling me that I now have no driver?'

The man could not have been less appreciative. I steeled my energies. Rosemary was looking strangely despondent.

'Your Mr Russell was a notorious thief! Notorious! He unravelled in the most sensational way. He was well known to the plods - real name James Kipp, known as Jimmy The Dip back in the day, so proliferate was his pickpocketing. Has been known to befriend old ladies in order to scarper with their silverware. And now, fresh from release at Her Majesties pleasure, the man blagged his way as a private driver, with a perfect plan. Once he knows that his affluent victim is elsewhere, he swoops in to grab the loot. You've been hoodwinked!'

Rosemary was barely listening. 'What a shame!' she cooed. 'I took quite a fancy to Russell.'

'The man was a godsend,' Farringdon put in.

'The man was a crook!' I was quick to add. 'A nasty piece of work. You could be a little more grateful! First me, then Sir Maurice - you would probably have been next!'

Gordon Farringdon frowned an impressive frown.

'Mr. Edgar, I can barely get myself out of the house of a morning. How am I meant to get in to Soho every day without my driver, mmm? All the way from

Chelsea! What am I supposed to do? Walk all the way? I need door-to-door delivery. Heavens! How am I to get home today?'

'I'm sure the agency will come up with a new driver,' said Rosemary softly.

'And what am I to do in the meantime?' replied her husband. 'Fly?'

'Gordon, we'll find a way-' Rosemary added. She turned and gave notion that I should leave them be, and I did so with some reluctance. Where were my plaudits? I was – yet again – a hero! A fighter of justice! I had done the right thing, acting with integrity in the name of fair play. I was merely been upholding the law of our land. Miserable old cyclops Gordon Farringdon had no right to treat me with such contempt. He had, very quickly, become my least favourite person under the theatre roof - and there was quite some competition.

Well then, I thought to myself, he could crawl home as far as I cared.

Back in the sixth row, I seethed silently as rehearsals resumed. Now that the culprit had been apprehended, I dared to hope that I might get my singing bowl back again - to polish it and place it back where it belonged, in pride of place on my mantelpiece. I glared at the back of Gordon Farringdon's head. How ungrateful he was! And so very selfish.

After some time Rosemary returned to her place in the sixth row. She offered up a wry smile and pulled out her knitting. She was using particularly gaudy pink wool.

I sat upright and tried to pull myself together.

Feigning interest in the play as best I could, I perched in the dark and watched the players with scrutiny. I had already exposed one criminal that morning – could I do so to another? One of the people under this roof was, somehow or other, involved in the disappearance of Toffee Morrell, I was sure of it. And yet there were no guilty faces amongst the company - everyone seemed quite enthralled by the job at hand. I began to daydream a little. I was getting quite adept at solving crimes and wheedling out bad eggs - perhaps there was something in this. As much as I loved writing my columns, perhaps there was another calling that shouldn't be ignored.

Perhaps.

Payton Edgar; Private Investigator.

Payton Edgar; Chief of Police.

Payton Edgar; Lord Mayor of London Town!

I was so caught up in thoughts of criminality and recompense that when Sir Maurice said something and all heads turned in my direction, I was caught horribly off guard.

It was the abrupt silence in the room that wrenched me from my reverie. Gordon Farringdon had also turned, his eyebrows raised and the whites of his eyes - one genuine, one artificial - shining in the darkness.

'Well, Edgar?' he panted, clearly peeved about something or other. 'What say you?'

'Beg pardon?' I uttered, quite foxed. Sir Maurice shuffled to the edge of the stage.

'Hello? Earth to Mr Edgar! Are you with us? I should think we are in need of the wise musings of our so very useful Artistic Director on this particular subject.'

His high-toned and condescending manner was breathtakingly galling. Playfair was at his side, smirking keenly.

'I'll explain again, Mr Edgar,' Sir Maurice went on. 'It seems we are drawn in our opinions and stumbling on interpretation. "I'll bring mine action on the proudest he, that stops my way in Padua," and so on. Is our man particularly concerned of matters of litigation and practicality, or does Petruchio have some emotional investment when he says this piece? And how might we stage the thing, to bring it some life?'

I stared at him blankly. He issued a repulsive guffaw.

'Tongue-tied, Mr Edgar? You must understand that we actors thrive upon bold direction.' He turned to his fellow players and brayed. 'Well! I can't say I'm surprised. It appears that our Artistic Director has no direction whatsoever - artistic or otherwise!'

I tensed.

Snitty!

A number of titters disseminated around the stage. The rancid fool was smirking the very worse kind of smirk, and my heart was racing so fast that I barely heard what Farringdon was saying as he blethered on about the stupid play and its stupid characters. As action on stage resumed, Sir Maurice slipped on his pince-nez, thinned his eyes along with his smile and smouldered in my direction like the slyest of cats. A superior grin lingered upon his mug for a long while.

He will regret turning me into a laughing stock, I thought to myself. I would never - ever - forget such a public shaming.

Eventually, Farringdon called a halt for a break and the company relaxed. The rain kept most people from venturing out into the streets. I had missed lunch but, for once, wasn't hungry. I remained, arms folded, in my seat. I may even have been sulking a little. Sir Maurice took himself away to his dressing room as was his way, but most of the other players dithered about the stage. Slimy Playfair was in an officious mood as usual, and enjoyed holding court over the room. He sat cross legged near the edge of the stage pulling fluff from his pullover as he bored everybody to tears with yet another anecdote about his misspent youth.

Miss Pickford, messing with a thermos, went on to say something or other about Carnaby Street fashions and the raising of hemlines, to which Emma Drake laughed over her biscuits.

'I can't say I've noticed that, but I'm sure that my brother has! Skirts can never be too short, eh, Alex?'

Alex Drake grunted and glowered from the corner of the auditorium. The man was akin to a caveman. One could easily picture him sharpening flints at the fireside or skinning a rabbit to make a new pair of moccasins. Playfair raised a finger in the understudy's direction.

'You speak of observation! It is most important, my dear girl, to remain observant at all times. Not only when it comes to fashion, but in all things. One never knows when one may learn something to ones advantage, simply by keeping the eyes open...'

He paused meaningfully before continuing.

'For example, I was hanging around like bad smell after rehearsal yesterday, just for a few minutes, had a devil finding my bicycle clips. So there I was, minding my own business, and guess what? I witnessed the most interesting thing… right there, backstage… by the splendid, sprawling trees of Padua.'

'What was it, Playfair?'

This was Dickie, speaking up from the gloom of the aisle. Heads turned in his direction. Nobody had noticed that he was lurking in the shadows. Perhaps he had been watching as I had, trying to ferret out the weasel in our midst.

Playfair cracked his knuckles.

'Oh, I am never one to gossip, Dickie, darling. Ill deeds are doubled with an evil word, and all that. It was nothing that important, really, just something - well - something rather interesting. Not your usual tidbit of gossip, more of a healthy dollop of scandal. Such a dolly word; scandal. What does it really mean? An immoral act, set to disgrace and shame? Well, this is something that a certain someone would probably be far happier if I didn't say. Disgrace and shame indeed! And they say lightening doesn't strike twice! On the contrary, it appears that some people are magnets to a scandal. Two stormers in one lifetime! Unheard of!'

It was curious speech, and one that was taken in with a distinct lack of patience by an unwilling audience.

'Oh, do button up, Chrissie!' said Miss Pickford playfully.

'Less of your rubbish, Playfair!' brayed Tony Trace.

Thick-skinned as ever, Playfair ploughed on regardless.

'All I want to say is that last night I witnessed scandal of the most unpalatable kind. Sinful is the only word for it. And truth will out! Devilish behaviour!' He hummed a little, and then chuckled. 'Hell is indeed empty, for the devils are here.'

Gordon Farringdon made a meal of getting up from the second row and trooping up the aisle. Within the blink of a glass eye, Rosemary pushed past and was at his side. Playfair carried on his chatter when, a halfway up the aisle, Farringdon stopped and turned, overcome by impatience.

'Oh, riddle-me-ree! Enough of your puzzles, Playfair. What scandal? What are you talking about?'

The actor got to his feet and drew in a breath, puffing himself up with his own self-importance.

'Let's just say - they know who they are.'

And with that, Playfair headed backstage, having had the effect he clearly intended. He had left us all wondering.

A while later, I overheard a conversation that irritated me beyond belief. Rosemary was sitting with her husband in the quiet of the bar. I would have gone on my way, but hushed voices beckoned me closer, and I listened a little. In my defence, one of the first things I heard was my name, so I was therefore fully entitled to eavesdrop.

'We've got to let Edgar go! The man's a liability!' said Farringdon.

'Oh, don't be so melodramatic!' his wife huffed.

'He is a curse! First bringing us into disrepute with a vicious slaying in the Clarion, and now denying us a driver. He serves no purpose. We've got to let him go.'

'No purpose?'

'You can tell him - we simply don't need him.'

'Not this late in the day. He would be furious.'

'Fury… yes. The man seems to spend his life in a perpetual state of fury.'

'Now then, he's not that bad!' said Rosemary, almost kindly.

'He's worse! I can hardly find the words…'

'I'm sure you'll try, Gordy.'

I was shocked by what came next, as Gordon Farringdon picked his words.

'Insipid… and sly…'

No!

'…cruel and cowardly!'

Never!

I stood agog, waiting for Rosemary to leap to my defence.

I was to be left waiting. All she seemed to care about was money.

'What would we do without his funding, Gordy? This is your dream. You need him!'

'Not any more, I don't.'

'Of course you do!'

'Circumstances have changed, Rosemary. I have some… unexpected capital coming in…'

'This from Mr Nathaniel whatsisname at your club?'

'No, a new source…'

'Oh? What source?'

Interesting…

'A private financial matter, my dear. All you need to know is that I have a fair slab coming my way, and we can drop that prancing dandy like a hot brick!'

'You will do no such thing! Payton has been a dear friend to me since he joined the company, and I won't see him hurt! What's done is done - ousting him won't bring Russell back nor unwrite Baxter's piece in the Clarion.'

Farringdon grumbled.

'Grumble all you like!' Rosemary snapped. 'I have spoken!'

They appeared about to move and so I slipped away. Although I was mildly appeased by Rosemary's kind comments, my stomach was still aflame over Gordon Farringdon's ill-chosen words.

Words I would never forget.

Part VII

In which Payton Edgar receives a violent shock

Dear Margaret,

My best friend has the worst table manners imaginable. She thinks nothing of chewing noisily, speaking with her mouth open or helping herself to the lion's share. Much of her food winds up on the tablecloth. She has a confidence I will never have, and I daren't bring it up as I don't want to ruin our friendship. But it is extremely distracting, and frequently embarrassing.

How can I broach the subject without upsetting my friend?

Vera, Maida Vale

Margaret replies; I feel for you! Poor table manners are - in my opinion - to be ranked alongside whistling nostrils, body odour and the wearing of pince-nez. You ask how you can avoid upsetting your friend - I question why you should care? She clearly thinks nothing of upsetting you. I suggest you hold a mirror up to your friend and show her her habits. And I do not mean this as an airy-fairy metaphor - I mean literally holding a mirror up to her when you next dine. She'll think twice after spotting a guzzling pig in her reflection.

That evening Irving and I went out for supper.

In a rare moment of poor judgement I had allowed my friend to select the venue - a friendly gesture that proved to be a terrible mistake. I was horrified to discover that our chosen eatery was not one of Irving's steadfast preferences, but was in fact a recommendation from one of his bohemian, artsy friends. The minute I clapped eyes on the place I knew we were in for a bad night, for it was all far too contemporary. Bafflingly named Kensington Stash, the pop music blaring from a gramophone behind the bar was loud enough to arouse the dead, and when I asked for the volume to be altered they did so with undisguised contempt.

The biggest disappointment, however, was the unruly nature of the service staff.

A restaurant can live or die by the appearance, approach and attitude of the waiters and waitresses it employs, and the Kensington Stash died a grim death so far as this was concerned. Our unnamed waiter, his shirt untucked, rattled off the specials as if it was the most uninspired list in the world. As we ordered he raised an eyebrow at our choices as if we were making the very worst selection possible. He also failed to bring the table water I had sharply requested.

I was already disquieted by all this, when Irving decided he was in the mood for an argument. All he wanted to talk about was Aunt Elizabeth. He was under the impression that somehow she was the victim in recent events, as if he had forgotten that it was only my prized possessions that had been nabbed in the burglary - nobody wanted to steal her tatty white-elephant-stall knick knacks or those horrible teasel animal abominations! All my aunt had done was lay in bed dozing, just as she did day in, day out.

'And that's exactly my point,' said Irving. 'She feels frightened and vulnerable. She just needs to feel safe in her home-'

'My home!'

'- and it's not too much to ask. Have you taken any action since the burglary-'

'Action? I'll say! I have collared the burglar!'

'I mean anything to fortify your house any more - to make Elizabeth feel more safe. Changed the window locks, perhaps?'

He may have had a point, but Payton Edgar is never one to be patronised into action. I muttered something vague and swiftly changed the subject. I fancied having a grumble about Sir Maurice Williams. Had I been expecting Irving to show any empathy, I was to be disappointed. Not only was my friend an expert on Aunt Elizabeth's suffering, he appeared to know everything about life at the Old Compton as well.

'Actors, Payton! This is what you get if you choose to mix with actors.'

'Oh, what do you know of it?'

'Enough. You know I quite like the theatre-'

'Pah! You wouldn't if you had to sit there, day after day after day!'

'You just have to be a bit more charitable, Payton, if-'

'Charitable!'

'-allow me to finish. You have to be a bit more charitable if you are to understand actors. It's a strange life, quite unlike any other job. Hard to get work, never knowing where the next cheque is coming from. A dog-eat-dog world of audition after audition…'

'They choose to do it, Irving, nobody is forcing them. And what do you know about it?'

'I have had a few actorly friends, over the years. Good, honest people…'

'Honest? Quite the reverse! In my experience, actors are as false off stage as they are on. A lifetime of pretending to be someone else takes its toll, and they quite lose themselves.'

'Mmm. It is the nature of the beast, I suppose.'

'Enough about all that!' I snapped, folding my arms. 'Is there any avenue of conversation in which you are not an expert, Irving? Perhaps you'd like to lecture me on Neapolitan tailoring, or London's finest eateries?'

Our main course came at just the right time. We ate in silence.

The food was, annoyingly, quite good, and I begrudgingly allowed a compliment to pass my lips as we set down our knives and forks. Unfortunately, however, I left the venue with a bitter taste in the mouth following an altercation with our upstart of a waiter. After checking the bill, I set down the exact payment upon a blue and white checked saucer. Our waiter lifted the saucer and passed his hands over the cash, frowning, and dared to fix me with an accusatory glare.

'That's all? No tip for me?'

I returned his glare and held it for a moment.

'Never boil woollens,' I replied, unsmiling.

I took up my hat and left.

I received a violent shock upon returning home.

I had only just stepped over the threshold and barely pulled off my hat when Grace appeared from the kitchenette. She was a little breathless and her eyes danced with anxiety. In her hand she brandished my shiny copper milk pan. She spoke urgently, in a throaty whisper.

'Payton! Thank God you're home! Someone's in the house! There's noises out back!'

'Someone's in the house?' I echoed doubtfully.

'A burglar! It's happening again! They're at the back, in your bedroom!' I had never - ever - seen Grace rattled, and it didn't suit her. She stammered on. 'I... I heard him... or them... moving around, going through your things...'

'Mmm - it'll be Aunt Elizabeth sneaking around on one of her meddling missions. I've told you before that she wanders when we are out. It explains the teaspoons in her handbag-'

'No, it's not her, I'm certain. I've only just got home, when I heard the noise-'

'Er - excuse me! You said we weren't to leave her alone!'

'I only nipped out to the corner for some matches - she was fast asleep. I was back in minutes - that's when I heard the noises from the back. They're in your bedroom!'

'It could be Lucille,' I suggested sensibly.

By way of reply, Grace pointed to the fat cat innocently dozing in a furry pile upon my lounge chair. 'I tell you, there's someone back there!'

Only then did I feel alarm. Thieves in my bedroom?

My Dresden Shepherdess!

I should have been frightened, but I am a brave soul at heart. Something like anger fuelled my fire, and I tossed my hat aside. There came a clattering from the rear of the house.

'See! You hear that? Someone's there!' Grace was panting. It was most unlike her to be so ruffled.

I took the milk pan from her grasp.

'We'll see about that! Get on the phone and call the police immediately!'

Grace probably said something sensible to warn me as I made my way through to the hallway, but her concern fell on deaf ears. I had tackled one house-breaker already, and I was fit to take on another one. Nobody steals from Payton Edgar. Nobody!

As I silently padded towards my room, I raised the pan, my weapon primed. I really was being terribly brave, and, in retrospect, didn't stop to think that I might be harmed or putting myself in any danger. All I could think about was my treasure under the bed and the pain of losing my singing bowl.

That said, I did hesitate for a moment at my door before peering carefully inside.

There was no burglar within. The room lay empty. My window, however, was open a little - had I left it that way?

A sudden movement made me cry out - a ginger beast shot out from under the bed and past my ankles. That rancid ginger cat!

It pelted down the hallway, scooting past Grace as she appeared at the other end.

'Titty?' She breathed, relieved. 'How did he-?'

I let out a breath in relief and lowered the pan.

'I keep a crack in my window sometimes, probably forced his way through, or else Aunt Elizabeth let him in. You must catch the flea-bitten thing and this time take it to a cat's home far across the city!'

We stood in the corridor for a moment, each gathering breath after the excitement. And then we both laughed a little. From inside Aunt Elizabeth's room there came a shout.

'I know you're out there!'

'She's awake then,' said Grace, smiling.

'Hmmph! I bet that she had something to do with the reappearance of that rancid moggy!'

In normal circumstances I would knock on my aunt's door. But that evening, with the fear of another burglary and with adrenaline pumping though my veins, I merely grabbed the doorknob and entered.

It was a terrible mistake.

I barely got a word out before a loud noise stopped me in my tracks. The sound was akin to a car backfiring in the dingy little room - a deafeningly sharp crack which bounced off the walls. I dropped the pan. It took me a stunned moment to see what had happened, and I noted two things.

Firstly, my Aunt Elizabeth was wide awake, sitting bolt upright in her bed with eyes closed fast and arms stretched out in front of her. Secondly, she held something - shaking nervously in her grip was a smoking revolver.

And then before I could say a word, I felt a warm, wet sensation across my neck. Lifting my hand to my head, I touched the warmth lightly and looked at my fingers. Bright red blood wet my fingertips. I began to feel the warmth of my blood cascading down my collar. The room swayed, the lights dimmed.

I had been shot!

Part VIII

In which Payton Edgar bleeds

'You… you shot me!'

It took Aunt Elizabeth a moment to open her eyes, and when she did they were wide, almost crazed. The revolver was still pointed in my direction, but wavered in her weak grasp as she stuttered and gasped.

'I… I was… '

'You shot me in the head!'

Again I pressed my hand to my ear and lowered it to stare at the glistening crimson blood on my fingers.

'You… shot…me.'

I felt faint. As my knees quivered, Grace moved quickly to my side.

'Put that down, Elizabeth!' she ordered, reaching a hand out towards the woman in the bed. The gun tumbled onto the eiderdown. Grace turned and helped me to sit. Had I realised that it was my aunt's commode that she pulled up behind me I would have thought twice, but I sat as instructed, faint and in shock. Before I knew it a rose-scented hand towel was pressed against my face.

I couldn't take my eyes off the assassin in the bed. I watched as her look of astonishment was quickly replaced by one of relief, and then contempt.

'What were you doing, sneaking around? Bursting into my room like that!' She scowled at Grace. 'And where were you? I called out but you weren't there!'

Grace didn't reply. She wasn't about to confess that she had popped out for matches. Instead, she moved my hand gently and took the towel in her hands.

'Let me have a look, Payton.'

'You shot me!'

I felt it was worth saying again. Aunt Elizabeth huffed.

'I thought you were a burglar,' she said in a very matter-of-fact way.

'I live here!'

'You were creeping around! I heard noises!'

'Yes, noises made by your flea-ridden friend!'

'You should be more careful!'

'It was the cat that was the intruder-'

'-bumbling about like an oaf! Bursting into my room, uninvited!'

Did she not grasp what she had done?

'You shot me!' I said again.

'It's not too bad, actually,' said Grace quietly. She was a very patient and kind nurse, the sort you feel safe with. 'Just your ear, and only nicked a bit I think.'

'So much blood!' I cried.

'Ears bleed a lot,' she replied simply, as if this were common knowledge. I pointed at the gun lying innocently on the bed.

'Where did you get that? Eh? Where?'

'I needed it,' Aunt Elizabeth said defiantly. 'Enid brought it over. It's her husband's old service revolver.'

'Enid Smith?' I said, as things became clear. 'In the cribbage box!'

Grace was pressing the towel at my head with some force.

'I needed protection!' Aunt Elizabeth screeched. 'I am not safe here!'

Before I knew it, I pushed Grace aside and was on my feet. I would have said something, but I had no words. Instead, I snatched the revolver from the bed and made for the door.

'Payton, wait!' Grace pleaded, the blood stained towel in her grasp.

'Gracie, don't go! I need you!' Aunt Elizabeth croaked.

'See to her,' I said, and left the room, clutching the gun.

A minute later I was in my bathroom, holding the thing to my chest, and seething. I dropped it into my little silver bin and tied up the liner. I would take it out and toss it into a dustbin - somewhere Aunt Elizabeth could never find it.

My ear flamed with heat, and my neck was horribly warm and tight with quickly drying blood. My heart was pounding. I looked into the mirror and studied my bloodstained face and neck with bubbling rage. The shirt was certainly ruined, never mind the damage done to my Houndstooth suit. I wet a flannel and did my best to mop away the blood and then inspected the wound closely. Grace was right - the bullet had, thankfully, only nicked my ear. But there was a wound, and a small middle part of the ear was missing.

I sobbed a little, casting my eyes down shamefully.

An imperfection!

Part IX

In which Payton Edgar enjoys some wild, unrestrained speculation

Dear Margaret,

I have been married for over 30 years now. My husband is a well respected Chief Executive, who works in The City. He is a good father to our two children, and I would describe our marriage as a happy one. My problem is that I have twice walked into my husband's room to find him wearing my make-up and trying on one of my floral dresses.

What should I do?

Name withheld, Camberwell

Margaret replies; Knock.

The following morning I set out early to avoid having to talk to anyone at home.

Without a car calling to collect, I found that I wasn't in any particular hurry to get to rehearsals, and spent some time indulging in a little light shopping along Bond Street. It was another foggy and heavily cast day - perfect for moseying about town. I have aways found shopping to be a balm during stressful periods, and this expedition was no exception. I purchased a few choice items - a set of two burgundy velvet cushion covers for the living room and an impressive new italic-nib fountain pen. I also treated myself to a black leather belt from Liberty - I refused to do as Irving suggested, take up a skewer and create new notches in my old one.

On something of a spending spree, I spent some delightful minutes pondering whether to get myself a fine new Homburg, but eventually turned away from the hats and congratulated myself for my restraint.

Of course, I could never tell Rosemary that I had been shot at close range by my decrepit old aunt. She would undoubtedly find something humorous in this most horrific turn of events, and so I said nothing and spared myself the mockery. As it was, it was a disappointingly small wound I sustained to my right ear, which was covered by an equally unimpressive Elastoplast. Either Rosemary didn't notice the plaster, or didn't care to question it.

It was the day of the drop-off - the day in which Dickie Chandler would exchange cash for the love of his life. Rosemary and I barely bothered with any of the action onstage, and instead whispered keenly to each other in the darkness of the sixth row. She was thrilled at the mystery of it all.

'You really think it's one of this lot?' she asked keenly.

'I do.' I waved a hand towards the stage. 'Or, at the very least, someone here knows something. The question is, who… and what?' I moved in a little closer. I was ready for this. 'Let's partake in some wild, unrestrained speculation!'

'Let's indeed! Well, I've been mulling over our conversation about Dickie. You were quite right, I was being a bad friend. He may have an edge, but to mastermind an elaborate kidnapping plot? Not sure it's really his style.'

'You may be right.'

'And that's what's so infuriating about all this - who's style is it? I don't know who would go to all the bother of taking Toffee and calling a ransom. I can't see any of them doing it.'

'Really? All it takes is a little imagination, and the will to answer the most pertinent questions. For me, the most pressing question would be who stands to benefit the most from the vanishing of Toffee Morrell? To which I would answer - our new leading lady, Miss Drake.'

'Emma?'

'What do we know about her? Only that she appears to be an accomplished actress, one who has certainly benefited greatly from Morrell's disappearance, with the lead role in her lap.'

'Well, yes, but that's taking it a bit far, isn't it, just to get a part in a play? And besides, this was a violent act, Payton, and little Emma's got the frame of a ten year old! She doesn't have the physical strength to grab the girl, surely?'

'Well then, if we follow down that path and it is physical strength that's needed then we can rule out poodle-haired Pickford too.'

Rosemary sighed. 'Perhaps, but there's something I just don't fancy about Miss P. Men might fall for her little girl lost act, but I don't. I have seen her in a tantrum, and believe me, Payton, it wasn't pretty. She puts on this act, you see, little Miss Fluff-head, all spoony-eyed and innocent and forever on the verge of being overcome with the vapours. Most unattractive, really. She's not a woman's woman. Stronger women see through girls like her.'

'Really?'

'I've never trusted her. And she loathed Toffee, come to think of it. Green-eyed jealousy - that's what it was. And we know how that can turn out.'

'Perhaps, but she wasn't the only one who disliked the girl.'

'Pickford could possibly overpower Toffee in a fit of rage,' Rosemary continued. 'She's tougher than she looks, and she hasn't shown an ounce of care for her disappearance!'

'A salient point,' I put in. 'But there are others in the company, more suspicious types, who have stronger motives for the kidnapping…'

'I know who you are referring to, Payton, and it won't wash! You have had it in for Sir Maurice since day one. The man is a legend, and a gentleman-'

'The man is a buffoon!'

'But he wouldn't dare jeopardise the production, Payton. He lives and breathes the theatre!'

'Only because television wouldn't have the likes of him! And let's not forget that this crime is all about financial gain. Sir Maurice complains about money all the time. The man's got holes in his pockets, sponging off others, expecting a free ride from all and sundry. "Do you recognise the profession?" he preens wherever he goes, expecting a hand-out. You must have heard him.'

'True…'

'A parasite! That's what he is!'

I paused for breath.

Snitty!

'Just because you don't like the man, Payton dear-'

'And with good reason, Rosemary, dear! Add to that the fact that he is large and very long-limbed, and could easily have snatched up little Miss Morrell.'

'I can't see it, myself.'

'Mmm. Unfortunately, I agree with you. When I said that there was someone, it was not Sir Maurice that I had in mind.'

'But you just said-'

'Only because you goaded me! Sir Maurice, in my opinion, does not have the gutzpah to turn to such a crime, much as he might like to pocket the cash. Spineless, really. No, there is someone else in the company – someone who we haven't considered.'

Rosemary bit on her lip.

'Tony Trace?'

I shrugged. It was fun to be evasive.

'Lovely Tony? Rubbish, Payton! What would Tony want with kidnapping Toffee? He would never-'

'I note that you are quick to stand up for him.'

'Tony lives for the theatre, just like Sir Maurice. He wouldn't put the production in danger, I'm certain of it. Such a fine young specimen!'

'You are too easily distracted, Rosemary. Far too dashing for his own good, Trace. He has shifty eyes.'

'Shifty eyes do not a kidnapper make!' Rosemary sang. She took out a cigarillo, passed me a matchbook and allowed me to light her up. This little pantomime of hers was beginning to irritate, but I bit my tongue and did as I was bid.

'What about Christophe?'

'Playfair? Mmm. I'd refer back to my comments on Sir Maurice. Equally as unimaginative, and far too fey and ineffectual to turn to violent crime.'

Rosemary shivered.

'He gives me the creeps.'

'And yet, he does seem to know something…'

'How so?'

'You were there, yesterday - what he said to the company - some riddle about seeing something he shouldn't have. All that about scandal and lightening striking twice.'

'You think he might have… what? Witnessed the kidnapping?'

'It's a possibility.'

'We should ask him!'

'And make complete idiots of ourselves? Not to mention breaking Dickies confidence?'

At the side of the stage, a shadow lingered.

'Now,' I declared, 'what about Alex Drake? He certainly has the physical strength you're looking for.'

‘Oh, those arms!’ Rosemary trilled. ‘But nothing going on upstairs. Far too much of a Dim Tim to mastermind a kidnapping plot, surely?’

‘Mmm, while I’m inclined to agree, although I should point out that whoever is behind it can hardly be a master criminal, can they? The whole enterprise smacks of theatrical amateurism, with the girl’s tokens being sent in the post like that. But we haven’t finished - there is one person we haven’t mentioned, and I’m afraid we should. My prime suspect.’

‘Who?’

Along with our enthusiasm, our volume also increased, and Rosemary had raised her voice just a little too much. It took a cough and a stern glare from her husband for us to quieten. Rosemary, never one to give up, mouthed “who?”, to which I mouthed “who is left?” following by a sharp jab in the direction of her miserable husband in the second row.

‘No!’ Rosemary hollered angrily, at which Farringdon turned and spat out another shush.

I gesticulated that we should leave, and so I took Rosemary and her anger out to lunch.

Rosemary had never really seen the point of restaurants.

Honey sandwiches and the odd olive in a martini aside, the woman saw food as an unappealing necessity and sometimes even a minor inconvenience. The way she would pick at her plate like an especially fussy chicken was unappealing, to say the least. She would usually hold a look of distaste on her face before even putting a fork to her mouth, and when she did eat, it was without trace of any pleasure whatsoever. Nevertheless, she found something enjoyable in the act of restauranting, and we revisited Mayfair Gardens, if only for convenience sake. I ordered a large glass of what turned out to be a disappointingly sub-par Claret and, with some reluctance, plumped for the rump steak. Rosemary surprised me by ordering the pork belly.

We picked up the conversation where we had left off.

‘Your prime suspect!’ said Rosemary sarcastically. ‘Gordon? Payton! How dare you!’

‘The question has to be asked. Nobody should be exempt from scrutiny.’

My wine arrived, and I sampled it with the utmost care and attention. Rosemary waited impatiently until our waiter moved on.

‘Well I insist that we rule out poor Gordy here and now. The very idea is ridiculous!’

‘I don’t see why. He never liked the girl, did he? Pretty much thought she was ruining his show, I do believe. On top of that, he took me on board due to a dire financial situation, and now - suddenly - he says he’s got some money coming his way.’

‘Oh.’

‘I heard him say it, Rosemary. Where is this capital coming from?’

She hesitated.

‘I don’t know.’

‘You… don’t know?’

'He has an aunt - Aunt Gert - far up north. She has been gravely ill, perhaps she has died.'

'That sounds a bit flimsy, if you don't mind my saying. You are his wife - and you haven't wondered?'

'Gordon doesn't like to talk about finances, he never has. He has very specific opinions about the whole thing. As his wife, I am kept far away from the accounts. Besides, it's not really my thing.'

'Rubbish! You dissect every bill, marking every penny! Or at least, you used to.'

'Gordon doesn't think finance is a woman's job. He holds the purse strings. But he can't have anything to do with all this. I've been with him practically all the time.'

'Have you? Well then, we can certainly rule him out. I take it that he was with you after rehearsal the day Toffee was taken, and that he remained with you all evening?'

Rosemary fell suspiciously silent.

'Well, was he?'

'Gordon has been at his guild in Westminster a lot recently.'

'Ah, yes - his guild.'

'He loves that bloody club. Cigar-smoking dullards… bridge and buckets of whisky. That's where he was that night.'

'And that's where he is going tonight?'

'Yes. So he can't have anything to do with it.'

Her obstinacy was irritating, and I would have said more, had our food not arrived. My steak looked - and tasted - very average. Eventually, after poking wearily at the meat on her plate as if it might spring back to life, Rosemary spoke.

'I think you and I should accompany Dickie to the drop-off tonight.'

'He won't have it,' I replied.

She huffed impatiently.

'Well, I am lost. I guess all we can do is to wait and see what happens. Dickie might not let us go with him, but I'll wait at his place for him to return.'

Dickie Chandler's apartment building was not far from the Old Compton. We had passed it when going out for lunch. Rosemary continued, ignoring her food.

'He'll need someone when it's all over. You can join me.'

'No, I won't.'

'Why not?'

'I have other things to do.'

'Really?'

When I failed to reply, she pressed further.

'What, exactly?'

'Nothing important,' I lied. 'I'll go home, have tea, read a book with the cat.'

'Go home?' said Rosemary in a horribly sneering tone. 'Have tea with the cat? Very helpful, I don't think.'

'Where is it written that I have to be helpful?'

I didn't care what she thought - I had settled upon a secret plan. As a suspect, Rosemary's ailing husband ticked many boxes. He had been against Toffee's casting from the start. He was a desperate man who appeared to be clawing for cash to hand over to some quack. Supposedly heading to a Gentleman's club at the time of the ransom drop-off – the closed ranks of such an establishment would be the perfect alibi. The man had every reason and opportunity to take the girl, and to fleece his old friend Chandler for the funds he required.

And to top all that, there were those those horrible things he said about me! Insipid and sly! Cruel and cowardly! Words I would never forget - and ones that he would come to regret.

My plan was to follow Farringdon after rehearsals. I simply didn't like nor trust the man - and had grown evermore certain that he was involved in all this… somehow.

One should never trust a man with a thirst for cash, a stormy temperament and a glass eye.

Part X

In which Payton Edgar peeps

Dear Margaret,

My younger sister and I have had the most horrible row. Our mother died late last year, and what little money she did have she left to me in her will, with no mention of my sister - who always had a stormy relationship with Mother. My sister is a creative soul who writes poetry for a living and has little income. She can be irritable and flighty, and now she refuses to speak to me. How can I win her over?

Jenny, Purley

Margaret replies; Why would you want to win her over? She is clearly a miserable piece of work. Your dead mother had worked that out, and obviously expected that you would too. And poetry? A pastime for uninspired, egocentric types who don't have the imagination or talent to write a proper song. You should enjoy your inheritance without a second thought - and for your sister, a poem;

Your mother didn't like you,
She much preferred Jenny,
And it's all your own fault,
You're left without a penny,
Poetry's an inutile hobby,
A waste of everybody's time,
You need to get a proper job,
And herein ends my rhyme.

As the end of rehearsals grew nearer, I took a moment to scrutinise the cast.

Nobody seemed particularly distracted. Nobody peered anxiously at the clock or hurried to get away. Nobody seemed to be aware that a life-changing deal was about to take place. Everybody milled about uselessly as if it was any other day. Only Dickie Chandler looked ill at ease, planted in the corner of the auditorium with folded arms. As rehearsals finished I approached him cautiously and did my very best to say a few supportive words.

'This will all be over in a few hours,' he replied firmly.

'I certainly hope so,' I said, kindly. I felt I should say more.

'Are you… really sure about this? It's not to late to go to-'

'Absolutely certain. They will get what they want, and so will I. Within a few hours Toffee will be back where she belongs, and this will be over.'

'I do hope so,' I replied, and was a little surprised to find that I meant it.

I watched as Rosemary said farewell to her husband and then stampeded purposely in our direction. She had one of those prickly, no-nonsense looks on her face.

'Right, Dickie, back to yours. I'll bunker down for the evening, but if you change your mind, just say the word and I'll come with you. If not, I'll be waiting on your sofa with a hot pot of tea, ready for your return.'

Chandler allowed the corners of his mouth to lift. 'How kind.'

'Not coming, Payton?'

'No, Rosemary. As I said, I have other things to do.'

'Oh, do as you like!' came the exasperated reply. I watched them go, and followed on slowly.

Once outside, I found a corner beside a post box where one could hide, but also see both the stage door and the main entrance to the theatre. I leaned on my stick and waited.

Emma Drake appeared, without her brother. She went over to her bicycle, which was chained to a railing, untethered it and rode away. Ethel Damp was next out the stage door. She pulled tight an unappealing pink and green raincoat, threw a cigarette into her mouth, lit it and loitered in the doorway for the entirety of her smoke. She then cast it aside and retreated back inside. Why should a wardrobe mistress work such long hours, I wondered, only to be distracted by more movement at the stage door as Tony Trace stepped out onto the street. Moving quickly and with purpose, he headed towards the heart of Soho. Miss Pickford then appeared, almost immediately. She pulled up her collar and followed purposely in his wake.

A minute later, the toad Playfair slithered out. He lingered in the doorway, with a cigarette hanging in the corner of his mouth. There was an unusual, questioning expression on his face. I could see that he was deep in thought, and perhaps even somewhat troubled. Then, as if coming to a decision, he crushed the cigarette under foot and returned back inside.

He was up to something, that much was clear.

I waited a further four minutes and then was rewarded for my patience when Gordon Farringdon finally left the building, turning swiftly and trotting along the pavement with suspicious ease. Wherever he was heading, he certainly had more spring in his step than ever before. I checked my watch. It was exactly a half past past six - thirty minutes until Chandler was to drop off his package.

I began my pursuit.

I am surprisingly good at discreet surveillance. It is a useful skill - the ability to blend into the scenery and to keep the distance necessary so as not to arouse suspicion while not losing track of ones suspect. I found my skill tested somewhat as we headed south in the direction of St James's Park, for Farringdon occasionally stopped, turned and looked furtively around. I made certain not to be spotted. It was evident that I was on to something - his very demeanour was achingly suspicious - and I felt the flutter of a thrill as I followed.

I didn't have to tail this particular suspect for long, however. Certainly not as long as I had expected. Just as we headed alongside Trafalgar Square, where I was convinced we would take a right turn somewhere along the way, Farringdon vanished, and it took me a good minute or two to locate him again. He had crossed The Strand and and was at the corner of Northumberland Street. I hastened, and then, just as I gained a comfortable distance, he disappeared again.

Slowly, cautiously, I carried onwards. It would be horrible to bump into the man, to be forced to try and explain my presence to an angry eye. Thankfully, I soon found him - he had turned into a doorway, where his gleaming bonce was illuminated by a warm yellow light shining from an open door. He stepped inside. I took a breath and then moved carefully on, to study the building. A silver plaque shone in the lamplight.

Whitehall Gentleman's Club, est. 1845. Strictly members only.

Disappointing was hardly the word. It seemed that Farringdon could indeed be scratched from our suspect list. And yet, as I plodded slowly away, a niggling doubt began to creep up my spine. I had done my best to be discreet, but what if he had spotted me following him in the shadows? What if this was exactly what he hoped I would do, provide an alibi to his whereabouts while he slipped out of a rear door to collect his bounty? I looked at my watch - a quarter to seven.

It was certainly possible.

I doubled back and brought myself up on tip-toe so that I could peer into the high window aside the door. The brightly-lit hallway within was devoid of life. The wallpaper, which may once have been red, was a faded rose. Numerous tasselled light-shades adorned the length of the right-hand wall, and the lush carpet beneath was a fine royal blue with a gold line where the carpet met the wall. At the far end of the room, a sturdy oak door stood firm. What was behind that door?

Back on my heels, I moved past the main entrance and, much to my delight, found a gateway a few strides along - something of a tradesman's entrance. A long alleyway stretched down the length of the building. I gathered up strength and made my way along the wall.

Each window cast a block of golden light out over the passageway, and I was careful to stop only in the darkness. Here the windows were also rather high, but with some effort I was able to see the rose wallpaper inside as I followed on down. I soon came to a larger window which gave a fine view of the lounges of Whitehall Gentleman's Club. A roaring fire danced upon the far wall. Sturdy armchairs and a small number of fine-tailored men with papers and pipes dotted the room. There were enough books to fill a couple of libraries lined upon many creaking shelves, dusty and unread. A heavy cloud of smoke hung low in the room, curling through the dense air. Although the room contained a number of pallid dullards, I couldn't see Gordon Farringdon anywhere.

Satisfied of his absence, I moved further down the alleyway and came to a smaller, higher window. I was seriously straining my brogues with all this pirouetting. This room was cosier, the walls a more vibrant red. It was darker too.

I had found Farringdon. He was perched on a claret-red velvet banquette, and I saw immediately that there was something very different about the man. It took me a moment to place exactly what it was - he was smiling. I had never before seen an ounce of a grin on that ashen visage. The smile made him look younger, youthful even. He was beaming up at a waitress as she leaned in to deliver a drink.

But she was not delivering a drink! She was leaning in to whisper something in his ear.

But she was not whispering in his ear! She was kissing his neck!

Golden hair fell down onto his shoulder, and a pale hairy hand moved up and across her back. It was then that I noticed that the young lady had neglected to put on a blouse - she was naked from the waist up!

Alarmed, I re-evaluated the room.

Across from Farringdon, a youthful blonde was bouncing entirely topless on another gentleman's knee, laughing gaily. I gasped, horrified. Besides her a rotund old gent was being pulled through a doorway by his tie. I shifted my gaze back to Farringdon, and I may have watched for a while.

Eventually I could take no more - I had certainly seen more nipples and fleshy curves in those few minutes than I have in a lifetime, and I lowered myself back to the ground. Suddenly, someone shouted from the darkness of the alley.

'Oy! We've got a peeper!'

I almost leapt out of my skin.

'Oy! You!'

A figure in filthy white overalls appeared from a steamy kitchen at the rear of the building. He approached menacingly, growling like a dog.

'Oy! Peeper!'

'Excuse me! I wasn't peeping!'

'Yeah, right! This is a private club! Gentlemen only!'

'Pah! A gentleman's club!' I parroted in scornful disbelief, stepping backwards.

'That's right, a gentleman's club, not a perverts free-for-all! Get out of it!'

He was advancing quickly, and his bark was harsh. I turned and fled, just as heavy rain began to fall.

At twelve minutes past seven I entered St James's Park.

The rain had steadied a little, and I trotted cautiously through the puddles. Whatever would happen at the drop-off surely would have happened by now. A little further along I caught sight of Dickie Chandler loitering behind some bushes, and came up behind him.

'What's the latest, Chandler?' I asked. The poor man jumped out of his socks.

'Oh, Edgar! I told you not to come!'

'Well I have and here I am. What's going on?'

'Absolutely nothing!'

'Nothing?'

'I dropped the package off at five to, and there it's sat for all this time. I couldn't help myself, I pretended to leave and then hid here. It's still there, at the end of the bridge.'

I looked out to where the blue bridge stretched over the water, and at one end I could just make out the corner of a brown paper parcel.

'Why wouldn't they collect it?' asked Chandler with a squeak.

'Well, perhaps they suspect that you are still here, watching.'

'Why would they think that?'

'Because you are still here watching!' I replied with a smidgeon of impatience. 'I found you, why wouldn't they?'

We stood for a minute, cowering behind the bush like lemons, and then I came to a decision.

'What you must do now is pass by the parcel again, make sure you're seen, then head away over the open track, where any watching kidnapper can see you go. Take yourself home. I will make a play to go this way, double back and find a good spot to watch. I'll see who comes for the parcel.'

'Are you sure that's wise?'

'Wiser than both of us crouching here,' I replied. 'Trust me. Now, off you go - I'll meet you back at your apartment.'

Chandler mulled this over for a moment, then nodded. I watched as he made his way out towards the bridge and then away across the green. I also pretended to saunter away, only to find a new spot adjacent to a holly bush. I turned my attentions to the parcel.

I waited… and waited.

The package was still there.

Nothing happened.

After another fifteen long minutes I gave up, came out of hiding and went to collect the parcel myself.

I had barely taken my finger off the doorbell when Rosemary answered, flinging the door open all too dramatically.

'What's happened?' she gasped, hungrily. She could see the parcel under my arm.

'May I come in?'

I was let in. One had to scale a heavily polished wooden staircase to get into Dickie Chandler's flat, but once at the top you were greeted with an impressive open-plan living room and kitchen. The place had a pleasing, warm air that put one in mind of dark evenings at Christmastime. Impressive antique knick-knacks were dotted here and there, and everything was ornate and considered, from the billowing velvet curtains to the lush golden dado rail. There were a couple of posters for West-End plays mounted on the walls that I could give or take, and the sofa was a poppy-patterned mistake, but apart from that it was a captivating space.

Dickie Chandler was slumped in an armchair, drink in hand, and his expression was what I can only describe as haunted. He saw the package, and let his eyes drop.

'Nothing doing, then?'

'I'm afraid not. I gave it a good long while.'

'Are you saying that absolutely nothing happened, Payton?' Rosemary stammered, as if the lack of drama was all my fault. 'Nothing at all? Surely you saw something… or someone?'

Only your husband cavorting with a topless strumpet, I thought to myself. It took me a moment to gather my thoughts.

'Something didn't go to plan tonight,' I said, perhaps a little obviously. 'Why go to all the trouble of the demands and then not collect the bounty?'

'So, we are at a dead end,' said Rosemary. I could sense her simmering impatience, and when neither Chandler nor I responded, she voiced our thoughts. This latest development raised countless questions. 'Now what are we supposed to think? Where were they? Why not collect the cash? Does this mean Toffee's still tied up in some basement somewhere?'

Chandler let out a muted sob.

And then Rosemary asked the most pertinent question.

'What do we do now?'

'There is nothing we can do!' Chandler shouted, rather startling us both. 'Absolutely nothing! All we can do is wait and see what happens.'

There was a detectable air of despair radiating from Chandler's corner. Then, Rosemary spoke up.

'Oh dear, oh dear,' she sighed. 'What a terrible anti-climax!'

I felt I should say something.

'An anti-climax indeed. Something must have happened…something didn't do to plan tonight. But what?'

The answer was murder

Part XI

In which Aunt Elizabeth has something to say

Dear Margaret,

I have a problem with my friend that you may consider petty, but which bothers me greatly. She is so noisy. She has a very loud voice which sets everybody on edge, and even when we are sharing secrets over a cup of tea I can see other people looking over disapprovingly. She crashes about like a bull in a china shop. I have discreetly asked her to keep her voice down or to temper her manner, but she rarely does. It seems such a small thing to break a friendship over, but I am timid, and it bothers me more and more each day. What can I do?

Violet, Kensington

Margaret replies; Too small a thing to break a friendship over, Violet? I think not! I cannot abide loud, brash sorts who think that what they have to say is so important that they announce it loudly to all. I dare say she wears wild colours and irritatingly loud heeled shoes too? Is she, by any chance, American? Whatever the case, terminate your friendship immediately and seek to find a quieter, more harmonious friendship elsewhere.

After the damp squib of the cash drop off, I returned to Clarendon Street feeling strangely perturbed. One's home should feel like a comfortable retreat - a fortress or sanctuary, a place of safety. After the break in, and with Aunt Elizabeth brandishing a firearm, I only felt… unsettled.

All I wanted to do was go straight to bed, but Grace had other ideas. We exchanged pleasantries, but as I moved in the direction of my bedroom she blocked my path, and it was clear that from the look on her face that I was about to be badgered.

'Payton, your aunt needs to see you,' she said firmly. She had her arms folded and grim look on her face. 'Your aunt needs to see you,' she said again.

'It's late, Grace, and I have had an extremely testing day. I am going to bed.'

'It's only a quarter past nine, and she is still wide awake. I will not let you into your bedroom until you have seen her.'

'Please let me pass. I am exhausted. I-'

'Payton, go and see Elizabeth!'

Suddenly enraged by her belligerence, I almost stamped my foot! Instead I raised an involuntary hand up to my ear. 'No! I refuse to go! She hurt me.'

'Yes, and she is hurting too.'

'She shot me!' I said. It was worth pointing out again and again.

'Yes, I know, and she needs to talk to you about it.'

'Let me past!'

'No!' Grace shouted - she actually shouted! Those blue eyes were ice cold and uncompromising. She really was a force to be reckoned with. 'Now, I will repeat myself, but only once. I hope that, this time, you hear me. I will not let you through this door until you have gone and seen your aunt.'

I knocked sheepishly on Aunt Elizabeth's door. When I thought I heard a word inside, I made sure to speak loudly and clearly.

'This is Payton, Coming in now… please lay down your arms!'

I entered. Aunt Elizabeth was sitting up in bed with a queer look on her face. It was the absence of a frown. Not quite a smile - there were precious few teeth on display - but the corners of her mouth had certainly raised, ever so slightly. I studied her features with some alarm. There was definitely a trace of something not unlike warmness in that expression. She was trying very hard, I could see.

'Payton, I'm glad you are here. Come in, shut the door.'

Shut the door? She always insisted I keep the door ajar upon visiting, but when I hesitated she repeated her order, a little sharply.

I shut the door.

'Pull up that chair.'

This was all very new, this - what was the word - hospitality? A trifle suspicious, I pulled a chair near and sat.

'Closer.'

'This is quite close enough, thank you,' I replied.

'How is your ear?'

I lifted my hand to my head.

'Healing.'

'Good. I wanted to see you… to talk. There are a few things that need to be said.' She took in a deep breath. 'What happened, with Enid's revolver… I am sorry. That's it - sorry. It was a shock for me, too - after those rogues broke in… the terror of it all. I let fear take over. It took a hold of me, and I didn't think about what I was doing. All I wanted to do was to protect myself.'

'You could have killed me!'

'I am aware of that. I have been… so aware of that. The what ifs have plagued my every waking thought. When you could have been seriously hurt, or worse… I realised that you had to know… to know some truths. I've barely slept.'

I scoffed and spluttered - I couldn't help myself.

She went on, a little louder.

'If you'd died, without knowing… the things you need to know…' She rested back in bed. 'I don't think I could live with myself.'

I spoke out firmly, keen to put an end to all this melodramatic gibberish.

'Let's just forget about it. Put it all behind us. There's no need to be quite so theatrical, really.'

Suddenly she let her caring face drop, just for a second, and continued with an ounce of spite in her tone. 'I am simply being honest, Payton. That's why I needed to see you - to be honest. There is something I have to say, something that should have been said… years ago.'

'You really don't have to say anything.'

She cleared her throat. 'It concerns your mother.'

Suddenly, and with a pang of panic, I became painfully aware that she had demanded my presence and made me sit by her bed for a reason. And not a comfortable or easy reason. She had apparently come to a decision and was about to make a disclosure of some sort.

A disclosure!

I wanted to run a mile.

'There is nothing you can say about my mother that would interest me,' I replied, as casually as I could. Winifred Edgar was a sharp-tongued, spiky soul who left this world largely unmourned, so far as I was concerned.

'There are things... things that you don't know about your mother...'

Pink spots appeared at Aunt Elizabeth's cheeks. This confessional was taking its toll, and her expression was now one of profound discomfort.

'I'm sure there are,' I uttered, curtly.

'Secrets... oh, secrets!'

'Well, that's what's so lovely about secrets, they are usually happy to remain just that.'

'Do you know the damage that scandal can do to a family?' she asked, seemingly out of thin air.

'I certainly do not!'

'Yes, and you've Winifred to thank for that.'

She was looking at me... meaningfully.

'Well, alright then,' I said with false cheer. 'It's been lovely talking. I'm off - goodnight.'

I would have got up quickly, had a cold bony hand not suddenly settled over mine.

Aunt Elizabeth was reaching out - and touching me.

I don't think we had ever touched before. Her fingers were ice cold. I stared down at our hands, too shocked to flinch.

'You mustn't judge your mother harshly. What you don't know is... she was so young when she fell pregnant, so innocent and fun loving. A party girl, footloose and fancy free. Flighty... a flapper! She didn't want a child. All she wanted to do was to raise a glass and to have fun.'

'Fun? Mother?' I let out a rasping laugh. 'Mother was no more fun loving than I am... Sudanese!' It was the first thing that popped into my head.

'I am not talking about Winifred, Payton. I am talking about your... real mother.'

'My - my what?'

'Your real mother. Your real mother, who wasn't ready for motherhood. Winnie was the sensible one, the level-headed one. Without question she took you on as her own, so that your mother, your... real mother, could-'

'Stop saying that! My real mother! My real mother was Winifred Edgar!'

'No, Payton, not so.' Aunt Elizabeth drew in another horribly deep breath. 'Winnie and her husband took you on as their own because they had money and they could cope... when her sister couldn't.'

'What?'

'I was young, foolish. I was the flapper. I was the party girl. There was no question of coping myself, unmarried - I wasn't even courting. I was just young and silly, and - well - there was simply no question of keeping it. The disgrace would have all been much too much! The whisperings, the gossip, the scandal of it all would have torn apart the family. The mere whiff of it would have killed grandmama outright...'

'Scandal?'

'Oh, there's nothing worse! If it wasn't for my sister, the scandal would have broken our poor parents and torn the family to pieces. And I was so frightened. I just didn't want any of it. I made a silly mistake and, we believed, there was only one way out of it. My sister, and her husband, took you in.'

Elizabeth removed her hand. Her face was solemn. I could hear what was coming before she spoke the words, and it was paralysing.

'Payton, I am your mother.'

Time stopped.

She swallowed.

'Your... real mother.'

I sat, frozen.

My mouth went dry.

I felt sick.

'You... are my son.'

All of a sudden the ceiling shot up, and the walls exploded outwards. The space all around us expanded a thousand miles. I was pulled backwards, farther and farther until I was a tiny speck of nothingness. I couldn't speak - I couldn't breathe.

I couldn't do anything.

But I knew it was true.

Somewhere, far off, there were still words coming from Aunt Elizabeth's mouth, faint, hesitant words, impossible to make out. I tried to catch my breath, but there was no air.

I pulled my hands up to my chest, stood and turned my back on the woman in the bed. Somehow I found my way out of the room, all the way down the hall, out of the front door and into the street, where it was cold and spitting with rain. I embraced the cold and, coatless, ploughed down the pavement as quickly as I could, the freezing wind and rain soaking my face.

I walked and walked and walked - as far away as I could.

Interval

In which Payton Edgar holds the second round of disappointing interviews

The following morning I awoke feeling wretched.

I had returned home in the dead of night, crept into bed without washing, and barely slept. All I could think about was Aunt Elizabeth's terrible confession. I would've cried, were I not so lost.

Aunt Elizabeth.

A lie of a name.

And those four horrible words.

I am your mother.

I attended the bathroom, and spent some time washing my face - scrubbing all that turmoil down the sink. I dressed carefully and then, back in the bathroom, took in a deep breath and stood rigid. I lifted my chin and, to the man in the mirror, made a promise - a promise to push aside the horror of the previous evening, to rise above it - dry eyed - and to get on with it.

Ignorance was the only way forward.

Life must go on.

I had busy day ahead.

At nine o'clock, Irving and I sat down to hold our next - and hopefully last - round of interviews. My friend was being rather tiresome. He caught my sleeve.

'Are you alright this morning, Payton?'

'I am fine,' I replied quickly. 'One hundred percent. Absolutely super.'

Well, if you don't mind my saying, you don't look absolutely fine. You look tired. And you seem… distant.'

'I didn't sleep last night, that is all.'

'Didn't sleep? Well that's not at all like you-'

'Why should it matter whether I slept or not?' I snapped, despite myself. 'It's my business, not yours. I can be as tired and distant as I like, thank you! Now we are here to interview, so stop fussing and let's get on with it.'

On the way to the office I had occupied my mind by dreaming about the attributes of the perfect private secretary. How a typist looked and behaved was just as important as their clerical competence - probably even more so. The first impression a person has as they enter a reception area is crucial. If one is greeted by a giggly, distracted youth or a bull-faced witch then one is immediately put off the entire enterprise. And then there were the glasses - I had, fixed in mind, a mature, professional woman with glasses at the end of her nose.

That was what I needed to find.

We had two names on our list - Madison Perez of Chelsea, and Heather Blunt of Stepney. 'Madison Perez? What sort of a name is that?' I asked Irving doubtfully.

We soon found out.

Things started well. Miss Perez gave a polite nod and a smile as I greeted her at the door and, following her through to my office, I dared to think that she could be the one. I overlooked the garish orange coat which she unbelted and passed to Irving to hang on the hatstand, for underneath she wore a smart, well-pressed pin-striped trouser suit. Her hair was curled into a bob, with discreet, thin hooped earrings appearing at the sides. Most importantly, she wore glasses - not the fashionable horn-rimmed kind that I would have preferred, but a pair of small neat round red spectacles that were quite quirky.

I introduced myself and Irving, and then rattled off the first question. As I did so, I felt certain that it didn't matter too much about her replies, for she really did look the part. She was the one!

And then she spoke.

My heart sank.

She most certainly wasn't the one.

We got through to the end of the interview without too much bother. Her replies were sensible and considered, and after promising we would let her know a result by the end of the week, I allowed Irving to show her out. When he returned, he was smiling.

'Top hole, eh?'

'Absolutely not,' I replied. 'No, no, no!'

Irving grumbled.

'What? Her answers were pretty sound, and she looks the part. I liked her a lot.'

'No,' I said again, firmly. Irving was regarding me quizzically - as if he didn't know what I was about to say!

'Need I spell it out?' I asked. When my friend shrugged, it seemed that I needed to do exactly that.'

'Too American,' I said firmly. 'Far too American!'

Irving frowned.

'Too American?'

'I'm sorry, but I cannot and will not have an American as a private secretary. That drawl! And did you notice she said subway instead of underground?'

'So?'

'So? So she'll be typing eggplant in my reviews instead of aubergine - and greeting the mailman, in the morning, rather than the postman. Oh no! Not in my office, she won't!'

'I say mailman.'

'No you don't.'

'Potato and potahto!' Irving sang with an irritating lightness. I shot him a dark look.

'Nobody says potahto, Irving.'

'Well I liked her.'

'Like shouldn't come into it. No, my mind is made up. Let's hope Miss-' I checked my pad '-Miss Blunt is more eloquent.'

She certainly was.

Heather Blunt was another who looked the part. I caught Irving widening his eyes in approval as she settled herself. She was somewhere around the fifty mark, with a wide, friendly face and an appealing smile. She wore a pressed white blouse, a beige cashmere cardigan and an ankle-length grey skirt. Her shoes were clean and sensible. She spoke in an admirable clipped english tone, speaking clearly and precisely, and had the manner of the perfect secretary. She wore spectacles that were almost exactly in the style I had been looking for. She boasted many years of experience, and her answers to our questions were thoughtful and to-the-point, and, based on the interview itself , it was a text-book success.

But there was a problem.

It was only a small horror, but one that, once noticed, was impossible to overlook. She may have dressed smartly, but there was a yellow stain on her blouse, just above her left bust - approximately 3cm long and the shape of Italy. It looked like egg yolk, and, once I had spotted it, I couldn't take my eyes off of it.

I could never have a secretary who displayed her breakfast on her front for all and sundry to see, no matter how neatly presented and well-spoken she might be. Once Miss Blunt had gone, I was unsurprised to hear that Irving had failed to detect the imperfection.

'One must search for the detail, Irving! A tell-tale stain - and at a job interview, no less! Slapdash and prone to subtle disorder. An egg stain this morning, and then what's on her bosom at 1pm? The salad cream from her lunchtime bap, that's what! No, it won't do!'

He raised his hands in frustration.

'You will never - never - find the perfect secretary, Payton!'

'Oh, I will! Just give me time. I shall have to amend my advert once more in light of these developments. But mark my words , Irving - she is out there. And I will find her.'

I put pen to paper.

Wanted; efficient female secretary for city journalist. Must have typewriter skills and at least four years' experience in the field. Would suit quiet, mature and refined female with no current or planned family ties. Short nails preferred. Must speak Queens English, and have high standards of dress and hygiene. No tardiness tolerated. Punctuality essential. Non-smokers only. Must wear spectacles.

Contact P. Edgar, Pimlico

P.O. Box 2456

Act III

Part I

In which Payton Edgar's wicked plan goes somewhat awry

Dear Margaret,

My wife and I are writing to you with a query about dinner party etiquette. While we agree on many issues, such as the vulgarity of place names and the correct manner in which to slice celery, we come to blows when time comes for dessert. My wife insists on leaving the dinner table to announce the desserts herself, while I believe that this should be the housekeeper's responsibility. Much to my dismay, my wife even believes that she should portion and serve the sweet options herself! What is your opinion on this?

Mr and Mrs Bouffant, Purley

Margaret replies; How refreshing to receive a letter from a superior sort - a nice change from the usual monotonously trivial heartaches and pains. I was delighted by your stationary and lettering, Mr and Mrs Bouffant, and am only to happy to put you straight on this most pressing of topics. You may be unsurprised to learn that I share the opinion of the man of the house - the service and delivery of a meal should be down to the domestic staff, and not the host or hostess. Why else employ serving staff? Your wife should act as hostess only in terms of encouraging and maintaining entertaining repartee over the table. I hope that this clears up your query, and may I wish you many more delightful dinner parties together.

It was to be our final day at the Old Compton theatre.

None of us knew it as the day began, but this would be the last time the cast and crew of The Taming of the Shrew would assemble for rehearsal. It was a doomed production - doomed to end that day, and in the most violent of ways.

The horrific events of that dull, wet Friday morning changed everything.

It was a half past ten when I approached the theatre.

I was disgruntled to find Sir Maurice smoking at the stage door. He watched as I approached, his expression unwelcoming in the extreme. He then glanced at his watch pointedly, as if he were a prefect assigned to wheedle out latecomers at the school gates. He even spoke like one.

'What's this? You're late, squirt! Punctuality is the politeness of princes!'

'Excuse me! This from a man who rolls up late to every single rehearsal.'

'Oh, but I am a mere player, one of the many,' he replied in mock horror, with a hand to his breast. 'You are Artistic Director, are you not? Surely punctuality is part of the contract? You do have a contract, I'm sure.'

'Well, I have a very good reason for lateness today!' I replied as curtly as I could. 'I have been conducting interviews.'

'Interviews?'

'I am to recruit a private secretary.'

'Ah! Of course you are!' He puffed like a horse. 'Pity the poor wretch who takes on that position!' After a deep drag on his pipe he blew plumes through his cavernous nostrils, eyes wide, and I would have pressed on had he not blocked my path.

'Why are you still here, Edgar? Your presence is laughable!'

And then, as if to punctuate the point, he laughed, wildly. 'I should also say how much I adored your little piece in this morning's Clarion. Not your restaurant rubbish, but your darling page of advice.'

I bristled. That Sir Maurice knew the truth about the agony column was hard enough, without his mentioning it. There was a wicked glint in his eye, and he stepped closer.

'Your letter about dinner party etiquette was quite something! But I confess - I have been a little naughty. Oh, dear me! Perhaps I should introduce myself - for I am Mr and Mrs Bouffant! Yes, sweetheart! It was little me!'

I stood, speechless.

'I just couldn't resist the chance - the idea of penning some drivel to see if you'd bite. And you bit rather hungrily, didn't you? Fair snatched the bait - hook, line and sinker! Dear Margaret just adores her new well-to-do friends, doesn't she? I've purchased several copies of the rag- I shall enjoy sharing them with the company over afternoon tea. Perhaps you'd like to join me, to join in the chorus of roars, hoots and guffaws!'

A darkness descended.

Rage!

Fury!

Snitty!

How dare he! I balled my fists and watched as he crept away, that superior smirk fixed in my direction as he went.

Vile, rancid Sir Maurice! He had gone too far this time. Trying to steady my breathing, I vowed to have my revenge. After a minute, I gathered myself and moved slowly inside. As I walked through the building, I plotted a little. If only I could do something… anything to make him squirm and wipe that smirk off his face. There must be something that might embarrass the old fool in front of the company… something to make him forget the Dear Margret piece.

But what?

Then, as I passed across the stage I saw a small detail that ignited the first sparks of a marvellous idea. Suddenly the words Sir Maurice had said about his dressing room sprang to mind. 'I am hampered by my malady!' he had said. 'I suffer greatly with claustrophobia. It is a little known fact that many great artists have suffered in such a way.'

The man had a weakness - and suddenly I knew how to exploit it!

Emboldened by my secret, wicked plan, I joined Rosemary, to find her frowning over a copy of The Clarion. I said a cheery hello, only to receive a distracted grunt.

'Full of the joys today, I see.'

'What?' she said mindlessly and a little irritably. 'Oh, sorry. I'm just on the problem page.'

'And no smiles this time?'

'No smiles indeed. She's gone off the boil.'

'Off the boil?'

'I'm afraid so.'

'Who has?'

'Margaret Blythe.'

This was the last thing I wanted to hear, but Rosemary went on before I could steer the conversation away.

'Her responses have been less sharp and snappy of late. Far less interesting. Rolling out cliches - never happy with anything. There are letters I'm sure we've had before - and the way she sucks up to this well-to-do couple who write in about dinner parties, all rather unpalatable.' She closed the paper. 'I shan't bother with it again!'

Suddenly I felt the need to punish Rosemary, as well as Sir Maurice. I examined her discreetly. She wore a salmon-pink silk blouse with an unattractive rounded collar.

'Is that a new top?' I asked.

She fingered the collar. 'Why, yes, it is.'

I grunted.

'It looks like spam.'

I sat stiffly.

Gordon Farringdon started things up with yet another sparring session between his two principle characters. Sir Maurice bellowed through it all, full of self-righteousness as always, and, for once, Emma Drake seemed a little distracted and perhaps a little less comfortable with all the thunder her role required. Rosemary nudged me a little too sharply.

'She looks done in! Thought it was too good to be true. Got another of her colds coming on, I'll bet. She'll be wilting by lunchtime and gone for days, you mark my words.'

Soon Miss Pickford was up, playing her part with wide eyed innocence opposite Tony Trace. They were a compelling pair, and I almost got caught up in the drama.

Almost.

Playfair was absent, but by now the company was used to his tardiness. We all expected him to appear with tired excuses about bicycle clips at any moment. I remained alert, biding my time, and it was getting on for lunchtime when I seized an opportunity.

The piece had been halted for the umpteenth time for Sir Maurice and the director to exchange views on how the scene should play out. Miss Drake stood mute.

I cleared my throat noisily, and spoke up.

'Might I suggest an idea?'

Suddenly all eyes were set in my direction. Nobody invited me to continue, but I continued anyway.

'It seems to me that this scene is missing a little something – a little comedy, perhaps? Maurice is quite right about one thing; the scene is flat and uninteresting. We all know that his character wants to make an impression on our Shrew, am I right? He's trying to surprise her, isn't he? To catch her out? Well, in watching all this, I can't help but feel you have a bit of a problem with all those doors at the sides. There's so much coming and going, to-ing and fro-ing, in and out of all the doors, endlessly. In, out, in, out...'

Sir Maurice pushed his way in to the conversation.

'What you describe, Edgar, are classic features of the play we play. Bombastic entrances and dramatic exits are what it's all about - you might not know it, but it is the very linchpin of Shakespearian drama! You must understand that how one comes and goes adds the beat to the thing - the rhythm, the pace...'

'Quite so! But to an audience, all the coming and going can all get a little... stale.' I let this word hang in the air for a moment. 'Now, what about a different, unexpected entrance? A bombastic entrance, as you might put it, Maurice. Rather than simply bursting in through that door or prancing on from the other, wouldn't it be much better if, in this piece, he took the shrew completely unawares? That is his aim, is it not - to take her unawares?'

'What's your point, Edgar?' said Farringdon with ill-suppressed impatience. I continued confidently.

'Well, what about appearing in another way. He could... spring up from the floor!'

I let them take this in.

'The... floor?' Gordon groaned.

'There is a trap door in the stage, is there not? Why not use it?'

Sir Maurice took a step forward.

'Trap door?'

'It would be unexpected,' I continued, 'and, with the right actor, very, very humorous. It would improve the rhythm and pace, and I'm sure that Sir Maurice would make his entrance as bombastic and amusing as only he can.'

'Ridiculous!'

'Well I'm sorry, Maurice, but you said that actors thrive on bold direction - isn't that so?'

'Rubbish!' the actor spat, unsurprisingly. He went to speak but was drowned out by a swell of approval and understanding. My heart leapt. Rosemary and Gordon were mewing their thoughts, and Sir Maurice stood motionless, overpowered. Alex Drake was at the curtain as usual, chewing on gum like a cow on cud.

'See any problems with that, Alex?' Farringdon asked.

The stage-hand shrugged. 'One or two spiders down there, I'm sure. But no trouble wi' safety, like.'

'Let's try it, then!' said Gordon with renewed vigour. 'Take it from the top – Sir Maurice, into the floor with you!'

Sir Maurice hesitated.

'But, I can't …'

'Let's just try it!' Gordon pressed. 'Experiment, toss it around. Give it an airing.'

'B-but… I get… I can't- '

'Oh, come on! For your art, Sir Maurice, I'm sure you can do it,' I said, hugging myself a little. It was all very satisfying.

There was a rumble of agreement. I watched in glee as Sir Maurice pulled up the trap door by its ring, sat and lowered his legs down within. He paused, eyes lifted to the sky and cheeks flushing red. He wasn't so smug now.

'I… I really can't…' His words were lost, for everyone around him was chatting and gathering themselves. I watched on in silent glee. He was so full of nonsense. Claustrophobia - a most unlikely malady indeed. It was time to put this alleged affliction to the test.

'Into the hole, Maurice!' I shouted, unable to stop myself.

Once Sir Maurice's pale face had vanished under the floorboards and the door was flipped over by Trace, the players shuffled back into starting positions and Farringdon bellowed a few more orders. I suppressed a giggle. As the scene began all was calm, but only for a short while. It was some minutes until the leading man would be due to make his unconventional appearance.

And then, as Miss Pickford was twittering on, there came a dull thud.

I was listening out for something and so caught the noise with ease, but up on the stage the players continued.

Another thud - this time a little louder and with some urgency.

On the boards, the actors carried on regardless, it was not yet Sir Maurice's cue.

Suddenly the wild banging from below could not be ignored. It was as if a wild bull was caged beneath the stage and was kicking for release. I lifted my hand to my lips, allowing myself a private little titter. In the second row, Gordon Farringdon obviously didn't know what to make of it all, and was ordering the actors to continue, but the violence of the crashing from under the boards was too much for Miss Pickford, who issued a screech and jumped as if she were stood on hot coals. Sir Maurice was thrashing riotously below.

I smirked in the darkness. It couldn't have gone better! I might have felt a little sorry for the man, had he not been so horribly rude and bullying all the time.

Snitty indeed!

Within a flash, Trace was pulling open the trap door.

Sir Maurice sprang up out of the hole like a particularly devilish jack-in-the-box, eyes wide and screaming. The girls on stage followed his cue, and hysteria reigned. To my horror, bright red blood streamed down from the actor's crown, spots dripping from his beard. His hands and arms were bloodied, and we all stared in alarm as he tried to claw his way out of the hole.

He grappled desperately, but his wet hands slid across the boards of the stage. Alex Drake appeared, held out a hand and pulled Sir Maurice up onto the floorboards.

Rosemary let forth a shrill cry, and we both jumped up.

Once out of the hole, Sir Maurice pulled himself as far away as he could, staring at it as if it held the devil himself. As he moved he left a crimson trail on the boards in his wake. Even his trousers were bloodied. What on earth was down there? Razor blades?

Quick as a flash, Rosemary was up at the stage. I followed behind her a little hesitantly. Tony Trace was clasping Sir Maurice by the shoulders and ordering him to calm himself, but still the man screeched and squealed like a stuck pig.

'What happened down there, Mo?' Farringdon asked from his place in the second row. He was the only one of us who had not hurried up onto the stage.

'It's not mine… not mine!' wailed Sir Maurice. 'It's not my blood!'

Farringdon clutched the arms of his chair and hollered up at the screaming rabble before him.

'Calm down everybody! Calm-'

His words were cut short by the loudest scream, this time from Sylvia Pickford, who was standing closest to the trap door and peering down. We joined her. The hole was dark and foreboding, but there was one beam of light which sliced through the gloom, in which I could just make out a leg… and a face.

Down under the boards, crumpled in a bloody puddle, lay what was left of Christophe Playfair. His dead eyes stared up from the darkness in horror.

Part II

In which Payton Edgar ruminates upon the nature of scandal

Dear Margaret,

I have a terrible problem with mice and cannot seem to get on top of it. They have nibbled a hole in my favourite sweet-pea linen curtain panel and leave droppings behind my love seat. I have tried poison and even a cat, but they ignore the poison and the cat is so lazy it just sits there and watches them. Do you have any suggestions?

Yvonne, Hampstead Heath

Margaret replies; What on earth do you think I am, a rat catcher? I don't think for a minute that your biggest problem is mice - I think it is your lack of taste in home furnishings. Your vile sweet-pea panel sounds like it is better off devoured, and anyone who refers to their two-seater as a "love seat" deserves an infestation.

Following the grim discovery under the boards, there followed a half hour of absolute chaos before Rosemary and I sought solace in the comfort of the theatre bar.

Tony Trace had dragged a hysterical Sir Maurice to his dressing room, and Emma Drake had done the same for Miss Pickford, her wails and sobs echoing though the building as she went. Alex Drake, as stage manager, had taken some sort of control when Farringdon failed to act, closing up the trap door as respectfully as possible and suggesting that Chandler call the police.

It quickly became clear that this was no accident, for a bloodstained poker was discovered aside the corpse.

A poker!

Our body under the stage had been beaten and left for dead. Now, as his theatre swarmed with officers, Chandler was propping up the bar, his head in his shaking hands. Gordon Farringdon was at his side, searching fruitlessly for words of comfort. Rosemary and I had retreated to a corner of the room where we could chat without being heard.

'Poor, poor Dickie,' said Rosemary. 'First Toffee and now this. This might just kill him.'

'Well, it will certainly mean an end to the production,' I replied. Rosemary looked surprised.

'Do you really think so?'

'How could it not? That it survived the vanishing of the leading lady was nothing short of a miracle. Now one of the main players lies slain under the floorboards-'

'Payton, shhhh!'

'Er - hardly a secret, Rosemary!' I took a sip of my tomato juice. There was a nip of vodka in it. 'I only hope I might get a refund, after having given so generously-'

'How can you think of your wallet at a time like this?'

I flicked a wrist. 'A spade's a spade. All I'm saying is that where there is no more expenditure, any costs not incurred as yet, then well, I might see a few pounds back.'

'You amaze me, Payton. Poor Mr Playfair lies dead and you fret over a few pennies.'

'Hardly a few pennies now, is it?'

This bickering was getting us nowhere and so, in an attempt to get my confidante back on side, I leaned towards her ear.

'You do realise that this macabre development might answer our burning question from yesterday.'

'Which burning question?'

'Why nobody turned out to collect Chandler's ransom. I suggested that something happened to put a stop to the pickup, and perhaps I was right. Something… not to plan.'

'What do you mean?'

Rosemary was too unimaginative to catch my obvious insinuation. She really could be a bird-brain at times.

'If our felon found themselves tied up with matters of murder… well! That would explain the no-show. Which can only mean one of two things. One, that our kidnapper was Playfair himself, and somebody put a stop to things before he could make the collection…'

'And the second thing?' Rosemary asked when I left too long a pause.

'That Playfair got in the way, and our kidnapper to deal with him, thus missing the collection.'

Rosemary chewed this over. 'I can't see Mr Playfair being behind Toffee's disappearance. Such a nice, fine gentleman-'

I almost spat out my drink.

'I beg your pardon?'

'What?'

'What was it you called him only the other day? Ah - yes! A slithering creep!'

'Payton!'

'A slithering creep who makes your flesh crawl. That was the way you put it, as I recall.'

'Payton!'

'I think you also passed comment about his horrible turtle-necked jerseys, and-'

'Payton, the man is dead!'

'Death doesn't change who he was, does it? However, I do agree that Playfair wasn't behind Toffee's vanishing. It is all too easy to imagine, however, how a person like him might slither his way into people's private affairs and put himself in the firing line for want of some quick cash.'

'How so?'

'That curious declaration he made - that he had witnessed something… some gossip.'

'Gossip? About who?'

'He didn't say. You were there, Rosemary - you must remember! They know who they are, he said.'

'I do remember, and I think you have it a little wrong. He said scandal, not gossip. He made a point of it.'

'That's right - he did indeed. Is there a difference between the two?' I stopped to think. Beryl had said something about gossip and scandal - what was it now?

Across the room, Dickie Chandler raised his voice.

'Well, I'm sorry Gordon, but that's it - it's over. It's all over!'

Farringdon reached out. 'If we just try, wait until the dust settles…'

'Dust? Dust? That's all I'll have left, at this rate. No, it's all over… I'm done with it. And I'm not just talking about this production - I mean the whole enterprise! It's time now. I'm selling up!'

Rosemary had left my side and was approaching the two men.

'Dickie! You can't mean it…'

'I do mean it, and I should have done it a long time ago. I'm selling the Old Comp, and moving on. Might just chase the sun…'

'What about the show?' Farringdon whined.

'The show's dead, Gordon! Bows taken! Curtain's come down! No encores.'

'Oh, Dickie,' Rosemary whined beseechingly, 'don't make any rash decisions… with all you've put into the place!'

'Have to finish it sooner or later. And now, after all this, I'd rather it was sooner.'

'Then what about poor Miss Fudge!' said Rosemary. 'She's been with you since the start!'

'I will speak to Miss Fudge, when I can summon up the will. She will just have to understand. My mind is made up. I'm selling up, and that's that!'

It was then that a trench-coated inspector appeared at the door and asked gruffly if he might take our names and reasons for being there.

I made sure that I was the first in line - I had somewhere else to be.

Thistle house, Fleet Street.

Beryl Baxter's office was one of the largest in the building, and yet she made up for this by cramming it with wall-to-wall clutter. Why anyone needs two drinks trolleys in a place of work I'll never know. There were also three hatstands creaking under the weight of many coats, hats and scarves, and then, at the far wall, a counter boasted five dummy heads, each displaying an eye-catching wig of varying ridiculousness. In comparison, Toffee Morrell's hairpiece was altogether rather ordinary.

The typewriter on Beryl's desk was losing a battle amongst many towering pillars of correspondences and snapshots, and stretched across the far wall was a sea of black and white photographs of the great and the fashionable. I perused the many faces on the wall while I waited for her to return.

I didn't have to wait long.

'Payton, dear-heart!'

Beryl stood tall in the doorway laden with shopping bags, which she swung with an almighty heave into a pile on a chair. She was clearly returning from one of her epic lunches, and was as tiddly as a spun cat.

'Lucky me - a royal visit! You should've said you were dropping by!'

'I didn't know myself until this afternoon.' I gesticulated towards the hairpieces. 'Tell me… why do women wear wigs, Beryl?'

'Ha! You tell me, dearie.'

'To hide themselves?' I ventured. Beryl huffed.

'Or to reveal themselves,' she replied, eyes glistening as she slipped her fur from her shoulders. She was wearing a remarkable outfit - a pink, purple and brown striped skirt with matching jacket, topped off with a purple pill-box hat set at a jaunty angle upon a bobbed wig.

She studied my face.

'Something untoward at the Old Comp?'

'You could say that.'

As Beryl reached for her pad, I lifted a finger. 'I came for your advice, but strictly off the record.'

'Darling, I don't do off the record-'

'This time you will. I don't have tittle-tattle for the column, Beryl. What I came to discuss is highly sensitive.'

She dropped the pad. 'Well, alright then. But if I sniff one or two less sensitive details, I can't promise they won't make the next edition. What's the beef?'

I turned back to the wall of photographs. 'Something you said at lunch the other day has been swimming around in my mind… about gossip verses scandal. I need to understand the difference, and to consider the cast of The Shrew.'

Beryl issued a little cackle. 'The difference between gossip and scandal? Picture a pea and then a watermelon beside it - there's the difference.'

'A pea and a watermelon?'

'Not working for you? Alright then…' She reached for a copy of the clarion and set it down on the desk. She then pulled it open, and jammed a finger onto the page.

'Page eight - gossip. Page nine - gossip.'

She slapped the paper closed and placed the finger on the headline.

'Page one - scandal. Simple as that, dear-heart.'

I took a deep breath, and then told her that Christophe Playfair had been murdered. It was an unsavoury, sensational story, and yet she took it all in her stride. She even seemed a little disappointed.

'Well, Payton, a death in those circumstances is neither gossip nor scandal. It is merely news.' She approached the drinks cabinet. I was surprised that it had taken her this long. 'You do know that I shall have to tell Bilborough pretty sharpish? This is hot stuff.'

'Yes, I understand that. But it's not what I came to talk about.'

'Little drinkie?'

'No, thank you.' I cleared a chair of clutter and sat. 'Before he died, Playfair made a curious declaration - that he had witnessed something scandalous. He even made a point of saying it was not mere gossip, but scandal. I think he was on to something - that perhaps he witnessed something, and was killed for it. But what that something might be remains a mystery.' I took a moment to gather my thoughts, for there was much more to be said. 'It may relate to the disappearance of Toffee Morrell.'

'How so?'

As succinctly as I could, I told Beryl about the ransom demands and the failed drop off. She grimaced. 'So she didn't just do a bunk! Mmm, I thought it odd. Any girl like that was on to a good thing with Dickie Chandelier. Fancy - you holding out on me until now! Oh, I am itching for my pad and pen!' Instead she took up a glass of gin with lemon. 'That's the end of the whole production, then,' she added, not without relish.

'It's the end of the Old Compton! Chandler's selling up.'

'He never is!'

'And that's why I need you now. Playfair's scandal - what could it be?' I paused, daring myself to go on. 'It might involve Sir Maurice. There is something… something about him. How he likes … the company of … young men.'

'The boys he entertains, you mean?'

'You know about it?'

'A half of London knows about it, dear-heart - so it couldn't be your Mr Playfair's scandal. We wouldn't touch a story like that with a barge pole. We could never put anything so unappealing into print - Bilborough would have my head. Besides, I'm told they're of an age…'

'Mmm. If not him, then who? You'd already written about Sylvia Pickford and her torch for Tony Trace…'

'Ah - now there is a fine example of gossip,' said Beryl. 'A little nugget, a crush, a flirtation, nothing more. Far more commonplace than delicious scandal.'

When I failed to reply, her eyes twinkled. 'I can illustrate further.'

She stepped over to the wall of photographs, pointed a pencil at each photograph in turn, and spoke.

'Here - gossip. Gossip, gossip, gossip, gossip, gossip - and here - scandal. That one made a headline, caused a lovely kerfuffle! The row below - gossip, gossip, gossip, gossip, gossip, gossip, gossip - you're getting the picture? Gossip, gossip, gossip, scandal there - a real nine-days wonder, that one - and then more gossip. So you see how rare a good scandal really is.'

'But gossip is commonplace.'

'Indeed. It's usually easy to find when you know how, and everyone enjoys a gossip.'

'Not everyone, Beryl.'

'Codswallop!'

'I most certainly do not! I don't have time for tittle-tattle.'

Beryl moved in a little closer, tapping the pencil to her lip. 'May I share something with you, Payton? Did you know that the Home Secretary, St John Townsend, wears a lace bodice and suspenders under his suit at Westminster?'

I moved to the edge of my seat. 'What… really?'

'No, not really. But you can lift your jaw from the floor, dear-heart - I have made my point. Everyone enjoys a gossip, from a church mouse to Her Majesty on the throne. Not that we could put in print anything quite that lewd, more's the pity.'

I huffed a little.

'So what constitutes a scandal? That's what I need to know.'

Beryl went behind her desk and rummaged a little.

'Now what's that quote? I had a quote-a-day diary last year and kept one or two that made me smile.' Eventually she found what she was looking for - a torn page. 'Here it is! Scandal is gossip made tedious by morality. Oscar Wilde.'

'Meaning?'

'Morality is the key, dear-heart. Something that breaks laws or bends morals can be seen as a scandal. Sex usually. But not casual schoolgirl crushes like your little Miss Pickford. Scandal would be sex with a twist - age differences, infidelity, fetishism, incest.'

'Gosh!'

'Orgies…'

'Oh dear, oh dear!'

'You asked the question, Payton, you should be ready for the salaciousness of the answer. Unwind yourself! Don't be so uptight!'

I thought about the cast of the Old Compton. It was hard to imagine a sex scandal big enough to turn to murder to cover up. I said as much, and then something else suggested itself.

'Orgies, you say?'

Gordon Farringdon came to mind and I fell silent, deep in thought. After a while Beryl pounced.

'Well? What is it? Your face! What do you know? Tell Auntie Beryl!'

I went on to explain the display of depravation I had witnessed at the so-called Gentleman's Club in Whitehall. London's supposed finest figures groping and fumbling! The city's luminaries and so called "gentlemen" cavorting with bare breasted ladies! Abominable! Much to my surprise, Beryl remained unmoved.

'You don't have to explain any more, Payton. I know the W.G.C fairly well.'

'The W.G.C?'

'Whitehall Gentleman's Club. Referred to by some as the Writhing Girls Club. Quite frankly, I'm surprised that you're surprised. What else do you think goes on inside these places? Polite conversation, a cup of tea and a game of Bridge? I don't think so! The old chaps just like to unwind and have a bit of fun at the end of the working day, away from their despotic wives - that's all it is. They think they deserve it, what with all the terrible pressure of all their ministerial endeavours. It's certainly not the only establishment with such a program of entertainments, Payton, but it's rumoured to be one of the best. I've been there myself, actually.'

'I beg your pardon?'

'Not as a member - or a whore, I should add. I was a guest one evening, went with a contact of mine from the Ministry, curious to see what went on. I was relegated to the front rooms only, more's the pity. These things do go on, Payton - that's life in the city. Sex and money are the industrial cranks that keep London rolling on, and they go together like… like sausages and mash.'

'Sausages and mash?' I found myself parroting. What was the world coming to?

'I very much doubt Mr Farringdon being a club member would be the scandal your man Playfair referred to.'

'Then what?'

'Well, it might have nothing to do with sex whatsoever - it could be money. A good old financial scandal. Greed, embezzlement, bribery, bad debts, fraud, corruption, underhand jobbery… there are many kinds of financial impropriety.'

'I see.' I took a moment to mull this over. Money had certainly been an issue, often discussed. Especially between Farringdon and Chandler.

Beryl drained her glass.

'So that's what it comes down to, my friend - morality.'

'Mmm,' I hummed. 'And what about scandal striking twice?'

'Say what?'

'Something Playfair said about lightening… he implied that this scandalous event was not the first for this person. Do you know of any scandalous events in the past for any of the Old Compton lot?'

'Can't say that I do. But it's a poor soul who falls into scandal twice. Very rare.'

'Is it?'

'Scandal breaks backs, dear-heart! It ruins things, leaving carnage in its wake - marriages, families, reputations, careers, all ruined. A hearty, beefy scandal is a monster that chews a person up and spits out a broken soul.'

'Aunt Elizabeth said a similar thing…' The words were out of my mouth before I could stop them. Beryl arched an eyebrow.

'She was touched by scandal?'

I huffed. 'She ran from scandal.'

'Very wise!' Beryl replied proudly. 'Very wise indeed.'

I shook myself.

'Well what about the theatre and scandal? Are there any instances where the two have met?'

'Oh, yes indeed, but actually few and far between in comparison to other avenues of entertainment. The ravenous masses just aren't as interested in theatre. If it's film and Hollywood, turn over any stone and you'll find a hundred-thousand sizzlers… but theatre? Not so hot.'

'But there must have been some?'

Beryl winced, as if thinking hurt.

'There have been a few in the past who-knows-how-many years. There was that pretty young thing that took her life in her dressing room on opening night… I forget her name. More sad than scandalous, that one. Oh, and there was a girl, slight little thing, actress daughter of a back-bencher.... unmarried and ended up in the family way. Can't recall her name either, but I do recall that she had one or two indiscreet things to say about what goes on in Chambers. All very telling, and most definitely scandalous. And then there were the Swains, Yardley and Bessie...'

'Yardley Swain?'

'Husband and wife actors, trod the boards together. His was the bigger name, but both were very well respected, moved in all the right circles and all that. That's the thing about scandal - the higher you are, the further you fall. An affair with a pretty young thing was revealed and the brouhaha and subsequent divorce pretty much buried their careers.'

'Yardley Swain. I have heard that name before...'

'I think it was the wardrobe mistress he was caught out with. It was quite a while ago - I may be wrong. All I remember is that the girl was very young...'

I heard Playfair's lisping whisper. Mentored by the one and only Yardley Swain, an actor of much repute back in the day - before what happened to him happened, and things turned sour.

'That Swain tale sounds promising, and it has links to our murder victim. Do you think you could search the story out for me?'

'Search out?'

'There must be bountiful archives here, surely?'

'Oh! As if I have the time, dear-heart!'

'Well, what about a secretary or someone? Don't you have a person?'

'I do indeed have a person!' Beryl beamed. 'I have an office boy, a boy-what-does. Young Godfrey.' Her eyes sparkled. 'Dear Godfrey! But he's not in this afternoon.'

'Do you think you might ask him to look out the piece when he is back?'

Beryl sighed.

'For you, anything. I'll set him onto it first thing tomorrow.'

I said my thanks and watched as she massaged her temple.

'I feel a nap coming on.'

'Then I shall make a move.' I gathered myself to leave and, as I approached the door, Beryl spoke up.

'Remember, Payton, it all comes down to what's morally right or wrong, that's the thing. You want to find out what Mr Playfair's scandal was?'

'I do, desperately.'

'Well, if your intuition is correct, you find an amoral act, then you'll find your murderer.'

Part III

In which Payton Edgar deals with three-too-many phone calls

Dear Margaret,

My best friend is a habitual gossip, We belong to our local Women's Institute, and while I enjoy the baking, needlework and crafts, all my friend enjoys is gathering dirt on each of our club members and whispering about it in my ear. I hear about everyone's skeletons in their closets - the secret assignations, marital difficulties and personal strifes of each of the ladies. Some of it is quite shocking! How can I - politely - ask her to stop?

Kitty, Finchley

Margaret replies; It has recently been demonstrated to me that everybody enjoys a gossip, from a church mouse to Her Majesty on the throne, so why on earth would you want it to stop? In fact, I suspect that you enjoy having all the hot news whispered in your ear. I suggest that you be thankful that you even have a friend. In your overlong letter and rambling letter you sound unattractively prudish and - if you don't mind a slice of brutal honesty - a rather grim person to befriend.

After a day of high drama I was hoping for a little peace and quiet, only to find my evening ruined by a nagging nursemaid and three - three! - telephone calls.

I couldn't get the image of Sir Maurice drenched in Playfair's blood out of my mind. Sinking deep into my lounge chair, I closed my eyes and did all I could to dispel the thought. I tried to think of nice things, such as my lovely new cushion covers, or the birds in the park, but all the blood and chaos at the Old Compton kept creeping back in. I felt a pang of guilt for my part in the trap-door farrago, and decided that I should sincerely apologise to Sir Maurice when next we met. I would have to force the words from my lips, but it would be the right thing to do.

After a while Grace appeared, and it was immediately apparent that she was in one of her more pugnacious moods. She entirely failed to notice that I was emotionally exhausted and in little mood to spar.

'Your aunt needs to see you,' she said, a sentence which was quickly becoming her mantra. 'I don't know what you said to her, but she's been off again, not quite herself - unhappy, sulky, irritable…'

I shrugged, the very picture of nonchalance.

'Sounds very like herself to me.'

'It's like living under a cloud…' She hesitated, and then continued quietly. 'Payton, is there something I should know?'

The question was asked with some concern, and I wasn't sure how to answer. Thankfully, the telephone began to ring. Grace didn't move an inch. Granted, the phone was aside my chair and just within reach, but it was more proper for a member of household staff to answer calls, and she knew this. I waited, eyebrows raised until she did. After a mumble down the receiver, she thrust it under my nose.

'It's for you.'

'Who is it?'

'I neither know, nor care!'

I took the receiver. She shot me a look, and went away.

'Mr Edgar?'

'Speaking.'

'Mr... Peter Edgar?'

I am used to this most irritating of mistakes.

'Payton. May I help you?'

'This is Sergeant Niblet from Scotland Yard. Regarding the incident at The Old Comp Theatre. We missed you for questioning this afternoon.'

'Yes,' I replied vaguely. 'I had urgent chores to attend.'

Lucille jumped onto my lap.

'I see. Well, the Inspector should like to meet with you regarding the incident. Routine questions n'all. Wondered if you'd mind popping along to Scotland Yard tomorrow.'

'Is that a casual request, or a demand?' I asked. I disliked this particular officer's cheery tone.

'A casual request, Sir. So, we shall see you at eleven, or thereabouts? Good day.'

He was gone with a click. While some ordinary citizens might find it something of a thrill to be called to an interrogation, for me it was merely inconvenient and unnecessary. I nested in my chair and nudged my knuckles into Lucille's fur. Exactly what information might I have to tell about Playfair and what had happened? There was very little, for I was indirectly involved, a mere observer.

What details would they want to know? How did I know the man? He was hardly a friend nor confidante - quite the opposite. And as for reasons for clubbing the him to death with a poker, I remained in the dark. Yes, I might be able to spin out a few theories, but that was all they would be - vague theories.

No, I decided, I would not bother the police with unsubstantiated fancies. I would be of no use whatsoever.

The telephone rang again ten minutes later. I was still in the chair, enjoying Lucille. It was the police... again.

'Mr Edgar?'

'Speaking.'

'Mr Peter Edgar?'

'Payton. Who is this?'

'This is Constable North of Scotland Yard, I am-'

'Have I to be hounded by you and your colleagues at all hours of the day?' I roared. 'I have already received a call from another officer not ten minutes ago. I do wish you would speak to each other. You've already hounded me for my two-penneth worth, though what I have to tell you I couldn't say, and so I shan't attend tomorrow. You'd be better off probing into the dead man's personal life than wasting time with me. Yes, I may have disliked him and, yes, I may have inadvertently been involved in getting Sir Maurice in that bloody mess with his corpse, but there is nothing else to be said. I am no murderer, and have no information to give.'

There was a pause.

'That's all well and good, Sir, but I'm not sure what you're talking about. I was calling about your bowl.'

'My... bowl?' I asked, stupefied.

'That's right. Your retrieved goods will be ready for collection at Stepney Green Station, Monday morning. Please bring proof of identification.'

'My antique singing bowl?' I stammered, relief washing over me like a cleansing shower. There was a rustling of papers.

'Says "old red bowl" on m'docket. That's how it was signed in.'

'Yes, of course.' What would the constabulary know about ancient Tibetan artefacts? 'Is my briefcase also there? High quality blue leather - delightful cream stitching?'

At this Constable North hesitated and there was more flapping of papers.

'Ah, unfortunately not, Sir. Most of the goods reported were sold on by the perp, looks like. Seems your man took a shine to the bowl, though, kept a hold of it.'

I nodded.

'Yes. He wanted to see it sing.'

'Beg pardon, sir?'

'Nothing, Constable. I shall be there mid-to-late afternoon. Many thanks.'

'Good day, sir.'

An hour later, it was Rosemary's turn to call, and she launched into one of her unending monologues before I could draw breath.

'I can't stop thinking about it all! What on earth is going on? Dreadful, dreadful business. Gordon's in denial, of course, and driving me potty. He thinks Dickie will come around, and has convinced himself that we can weather this storm and get back to rehearsals by next week. He's like a dog with a bone. He's asked Mrs Damp to carry on with the costumes and Alex Drake the scenery and props, and has set his sights on bringing Nash in to the Baptista post and getting a new Hortensio. Naturally, he won't listen to a word I say! I am only his wife! Well, anyhow, he spent a long afternoon at Scotland Yard. Have you been called in?'

I went to speak, but wasn't about to get the chance.

'No, I didn't think so. I suppose they want to interview the important people first, but I dare say we'll be asked for our observations at some point. I don't know how I'll stop from telling them all about Toffee, do you, Payton? I've been thinking about it all - I can't see any evidence of a connection between our kidnappers and what happened to Mr Playfair, can you? And poor Sir Maurice! Had something of a breakdown by all accounts, after what happened to him.'

'Mmm. He won't be short of attention over all of this, will he?'

'That's a little uncharitable.'

'Is there a reason for your call, Rosemary?'

She chose to ignore my tone and gasped excitedly.

'We have been summoned, Payton! Dickie just rang - something has happened, and he has summoned the both of us to his flat tomorrow morning.'

'Why?'

'He wouldn't say - too upset. He could barely get his words out. Said it was about Toffee, asked me to call you, but that's all. A development, Payton!'

'I see.'

'Poor Dickie. We'll never see that girl again, I don't think. Not alive, anyway. But I could hardly say that to him, could I? I begged him again to tell the police, but he won't do anything that could complicate things. He still believes that she will simply re-appear at any moment. I think he's lost the plot, if I'm honest, Payton. He used to take such pride in his appearance, but he's been wearing that queer maroon velour for days now, and he doesn't bother with his hair like he used to. He just sits there, brooding. The poor man is completely off his onion!'

'Ah, well,' I said, smoothing down Lucille's thick coat.

'Is that all you can say? Ah, well? Have you no heart, Payton Edgar?'

'I'm terribly sorry, Rosemary, I must go. I think I hear my aunt calling for help.'

I could hear no such thing.

'Yes, I'm sure. I'll let you go, but I tell you what - one thing's for certain…'

'And that is?'

'Come tomorrow, we'll know more about Toffee - dead or alive.'

'Quite.'

I hung up sharply, rested the earpiece off of the hook and nestled into the chair. Lucille purred softly, and I allowed myself to drift away, with three words hovering in mind.

Dead or alive…

Part IV

In which Payton Edgar tolerates a dying duck

WE DEMAND PAYMENT, OR MORRELL WILL GO THE WAY OF PLAYFAIR. SAME PLAN, £5000 CASH. BROWN PAPER PARCEL. DROP BESIDE WASTE BIN, NORTH END OF BLUE BRIDGE. MONDAY, 6PM. COME ALONE, DROP AND LEAVE. MORRELL WILL BE RELEASED ON THESE TERMS ONLY.

I was rapping on the door to Dickie Chandler's flat when, rather dramatically, Rosemary threw it open. She had the kind of wild look on her face that dogs have when sparring, the whites of her eyes and all teeth showing. She almost growled.

I quickly realised that she was in a state of hysteria that required firm handling.

'Good morning, Rosemary,' I said, as calmly and firmly as I could. I was momentarily distracted by her choice of clothes - a blue and white striped trouser suit that put one in mind of Andy Pandy. 'Well? Are you going to let me in?'

'You're not going to believe what's happened!'

I pushed past her.

'I'll be the judge of that!'

I found Chandler in his lounge, plonked on the edge of his unusual, poppy-patterned eyesore, staring at nothing in particular. On the table was a letter, beside which sat Toffee Morrell's glasses.

'Dickie's received a demand!' Rosemary panted over my shoulder. 'A demand from a murderer!'

I greeted Chandler, who barely twitched an eyebrow. When nobody moved, I took up the note. I read the thing quickly - but it was the first sentence that said it all. We demand payment, or Morrell will go the way of Playfair.

Rosemary obviously felt it was her duty to fill the silence, and continued to twitter and coo.

'So, Payton, it's there in black and white! Whoever took Toffee killed Playfair! It's inexplicable! I've been telling Dickie, the police must be told about it now, mustn't they? They've killed once, they'll kill again, don't you think?'

I tried to block out her noise as I perused the note thoughtfully.

'Do you think they killed Playfair to prove something?' asked Rosemary.

This was a question worth considering.

'To prove what?'

'As a warning - to prove that they mean business!'

I weighed this up. 'I really don't think so. To go to the trouble of killing someone just as a message for Dickie? And, if you just stop to think about it, surely the very last thing they want would be to invite police to sniff around the theatre.'

Rosemary hummed. 'I suppose so. Nevertheless, we must take this to the police.'

At this, Chandler woke up.

'We will not go to the police,' he said simply. 'You are right, Rosie, these people are more dangerous than we thought. They will kill Toffee, if it comes to it. Silence and payment is the only way to get her back.'

Rosemary and I exchanged despondent glances. Chandler sank back in to his reverie.

'Cup of tea?' Rosemary asked, to fill the silence.

I was soon in the kitchen, pretending to help Rosemary make tea.

'Well, I can't get my head around it,' she said, setting down the kettle. 'It's all so… sordid. Death and drama… blood and murder. Nothing like this really happens. Not in real life.'

I huffed.

'Happens to me all the time.'

Teacups clattered onto saucers.

'Of course, the kidnapping could still have nothing whatsoever to do with what happened to Playfair.'

'Come on, Payton! It says in pen and ink that it does!' protested Rosemary.

'Yes, but we should entertain the notion that whoever took Toffee could be merely taking opportunity from the event. We have to at least consider that.'

Suddenly, a roar exploded from the darkness of the hallway. It was a deep, rumbling roar - the sound of a beast in torment.

'Oh, he's awake!'

Rosemary caught my startled expression. 'That'll be Sir Maurice,' she said. 'He's in the back bedroom in a dreadful state. He's gone bonkers!'

'Is that a medical diagnosis?'

'I should go and check on him,' Rosemary continued. 'He's awfully cut up over the whole affair. I'm not sure he'll ever be the same again…'

'I'll go,' I heard myself say. I couldn't fight that feeling of guilt - guilt for sending him into a pit of death.

I was already heading in the direction of the noise.

'You make the tea. I will see to Sir Maurice.'

In the spare bedroom, Sir Maurice Williams lay propped against a thousand pillows like a dying duck.

The door was ajar, and I entered gingerly. The air inside reeked of unwashed skin and stagnant pipe smoke. The curtains were drawn and a tiny bedside lamp was the only light. On the sizeable bed, Sir Maurice had the sheets up to his chin and a moist folded flannel balanced on his forehead.

'Sir Maurice?'

His right eye opened wide and blinked in my direction, and I did my best to summon up an apology.

'Oh, bloomin' piddle-pots, it's you!' he grumbled with undisguised disappointment. Despite his apparent woe the man still had the strength of Hercules in his thunderous tone. 'Make use of yourself - fetch me a beverage! I should like a gin and tonic, to ease my addled brain. And generous, mind - triple shots, one third tonic, easy on the ice.'

'Of course. And how are you?'

'How do you think I am? You really are a cretin, Edgar!'

My apology flew out of the window and over the hills.

'Traumatised - that's how I am! I have been in the depths of hell, quite literally. Those clamorous harbingers of blood and death!. I suffer flashes and… visions… of blood and torn flesh… the stench of decay ever lingering… '

'Oh, dear.'

He had more.

'Beware the swinging noose! Wraiths and demons hammer, hammer, hammer at the gates of hell! I lie, prostrate, in the clutches of terror. To dance so very close to death itself… so, so close. Oh, mercy me! The evil that men do!'

He punctuated this nonsense with long throaty groans.

'The visions will never banish. I lie paralysed by fear…'

'Well,' I said with cheer, 'perhaps the gin and tonic will loosen you up a bit.' I moved to the window. 'And let's open the curtains, let a little sunshine in-'

'Don't touch those bloody curtains! Nothing can anaesthetise my pain. Nothing!'

'Well, how about a nice milky Ovaltine, instead? Help you to settle…'

'Ovaltine? Can't stand the stuff! Gin, man!' Sir Maurice snapped his fingers. 'And tell that woman of yours that I need sustenance! A half-dozen sandwiches should do it. I have a wild hankering for fish paste!'

I balled my fists at my side.

'Any idea who did it?' I asked, brightly. 'Who would want to kill Playfair?'

'The devil himself!' came the reply.

'I see.'

It was clear that I was to get nothing sensible from the actor in the bed, and I made to leave. As I did, he lowered his tone and grumbled a grumble so low I barely caught it.

'Playfair saw the devil, and it came for him.'

At this, I stopped in the doorway.

'How so?'

'He said it himself. Said that he had seen evil at play. The devil incarnate in the theatre itself!'

'What had he seen?'

Sir Maurice closed his eyes. 'He didn't tell - he couldn't tell. Something… deeply unpalatable, that much is evident. Devoid of all morality…'

There was that word again - morality.

'Said he would make a deal…'

'A deal?'

'A deal with the devil.'

'Ha! The ravings of a particularly overt thespian…'

A grunt.

'The devil came for him!'

'The devil, Maurice, does not exist. Rather like the word "snitty", in actual fact.'

'What?'

'You heard me. Goodbye.'

I left Sir Maurice to his torment.

'How is he?' asked Rosemary, her eyes sparkling as I returned to the living room.

'Not too bad at all,' I smiled. 'I think he's cheering up.'

'Did he ask for anything? He must be hungry by now…'

'Nothing at all. Well, perhaps a nice warm mug of milky Ovaltine.'

'Right-o.'

There was a short sharp buzz, and Chandler jumped.

'Miss Fudge!'

Rosemary moved. 'I'll let her in.'

It seemed that I was finally to meet Chandler's elusive right-hand woman.

Dickie Chandler perched on the edge of his seat, suddenly furtive. 'Poor, devoted Miss Fudge - my front of house for so, so many years. If you'll leave us please, Mr Edgar? I invited her here because I have to break the news to her - gently - that I am selling the theatre. The poor woman will be devastated.'

I would have slipped discreetly away, had there not been something of a commotion on the stairs. 'Miss Fudge! Wait!' Rosemary was calling.

A tall, large-boned lady stormed into the lounge. She had shockingly wide features, high cheekbones and a firm jaw. Her hair was white and straight, pulled back by a thick band. She wore a sensible navy dress and grey cardigan, and had tears in her eyes and a Clarion in her hand. She failed to register my presence, and instead descended on Chandler.

'How could you, Dickie?' she bellowed. Her voice was delightfully baritone. 'How could you? When were you going to tell me?'

Chandler blinked, confused, and found the newspaper thrust in his direction.

'Society page! Beryl Baxter says you're selling up!'

His jaw dropped, speechless. I would have taken this opportunity to sneak away, but there was something about Miss Fudge that made me linger. The way she dressed and carried herself, and that delightfully deep, resonating voice. I barely noticed Rosemary glaring in my direction.

'Payton! On the hotline to Baxter again?'

Chandler was reaching out to Miss Fudge and making calming noises. As he explained his reasons I watched the woman thoughtfully. There was something arresting in her manner - despite her evident irritation, her poise garnered admiration. Her clothes were immaculate.

'You could at least have told me yourself!' she boomed. 'After years of dedicated service, and I read about it in the newspaper! What about me? What am I going to do now?'

I took this as my cue.

'Excuse me,' I said, stepping forward. 'We haven't been introduced. I am Payton Edgar, of the London Clarion. You may have heard my name - restaurant critic, wordsmith… journalist? Oh, and Artistic Director. So pleased to meet you.'

Disarmed somewhat, she shook my hand. I turned to Chandler.

'Mr Chandler, may I just take these?'

I took up Toffee Morrell's horn-rimmed glasses, and held them out for Miss Fudge.

'Would you mind putting these on, please?' She went to raise a question, and I lifted a finger. 'Humour me, if you would.'

After the briefest pause, she slipped the horn rimmed glasses onto the bridge of her nose and looked down at me a little sharply. She was a truly formidable figure - efficient and uncompromising. Her nails were short, her clothes clean, and the glasses finished the job. My heart danced.

My secretary! My perfect secretary!

'No need to worry about your future, Miss Fudge,' I declared with pleasure. 'I have just the job for you!'

Part V

In which Payton Edgar moulds his perfect secretary

Dear Margaret,

My fiancée is as blind as a bat - but refuses to wear glasses. She is very pretty, and rather vain with it, and feels that glasses spoil her look. I am forever guiding her away from lamp posts and trees and making excuses for her behaviour when in company. I love her no matter what she looks like, and I am worried that without me around she will come to trouble. How can I convince her to wear specs?

Mr P, Tulse Hill

Margaret replies; I wonder if you have ever heard of Darwin's theory of natural selection? Put simply, evolution separates the wheat from the chaff. I think the vain stupidity of your fiancée puts her firmly in the category of "chaff". I would let her run blind and free, if it is what she choses. Allow her to dance blissfully unaware into oncoming traffic, if she wishes to remain pretty but blind. The evolution of mankind may be all the stronger for it.

I couldn't wait to set my new secretary in her place at my office. I was quite literally shaking with glee. I even splashed out on a taxi to get us there.

I showed her around with pride - I would never tire of showing people around my office - and we ended up back at the front desk. Miss Fudge seemed to enjoy my pleasure and enthusiasm, and allowed me to fuss around her a bit. When I politely asked her to put on the glasses once again, she took them just a little hesitantly and slid them up onto her nose.

'Oh, my dear Miss Fudge, you really do look the part. I have been looking for you for so long! Now let's give it a try - a dry run, so to speak. Off you go!'

'Off I - what?'

I gesticulated towards the desk. 'If you could take a seat, in position, please.'

She did as instructed, smiling weakly. I moved one step back and took a moment to study the image. It was almost perfect.

Almost.

'You really don't have to smile like that, Miss Fudge, it pulls on your face. I suspect that you are not one of life's smilers, eh? Well then, be yourself - just a raised jaw with enquiring eyes is enough of a welcome. Now, let's give the welcome a go.' I took myself outside, closed the door, drew in a deep breath and knocked lightly before entering again.

'Good morning!' I said cheerily.

To my dismay, Miss Fudge froze, and then shrugged. 'What am I supposed to do?'

'Hardly the greeting one wants to hear, Miss Fudge. I am testing the welcome that persons of importance who come to keep an appointment might find. I expect a raised jaw, wise enquiring eyes and a polite offer of assistance. Warmish, perhaps, but there should also be just a slither of ice in that steely gaze. Do you think you might try that?'

She pursed her lips momentarily. There was certainly a slither of ice detectable.

'I'll try.'

I went back outside, knocked and entered.

'Good morning!'

'Good morning, Sir. How may I be of assistance?'

'Perfect!' I sang, for it was indeed perfect. The woman was drab and entirely without sparkle, and yet she had a natural air of professionalism, competence and efficiency. The glasses worked a treat. She went to speak.

'Regarding pay, Mr Edgar…'

'I shall happily double whatever old Chandler was paying you. You will be worth it.'

'And what exactly are my duties?'

I waved a dismissive hand in the air. I would, in good time, tell her all about the Dear Margaret column, alongside my restaurant reviews and personal correspondences, but for now, it was all about her look.

'In good time,' I replied kindly.

'Well, I do have one or two questions about the job, Mr Edgar, I just-' she stopped mid-sentence. 'What am I to call you? What is your name?'

'My Christian name is Payton, but I shall expect to be referred to as Mr Edgar.'

'Of course, Mr Edgar. My name is-'

'-hardly something I need to know! You are Miss Fudge, my private secretary, and you shall remain Miss Fudge, private secretary.' As she turned her attention to the floor, I wondered if I had appeared just a little bit finicky.

I softened.

'Tell me a little about yourself.'

She relaxed. 'Well, there's not much to say. I keep myself very much to myself.'

'An admirable quality. Any… family ties?'

'Not locally. I have a twin sister who lives in Clacton-on-Sea. I see her every other Christmas.'

How fitting.

'I have never married, nor have I wanted to.'

Perfect!

'And you are used to reception work?'

'I have been front of house for Mr Chandler for decades.'

'Well, you are my front of house now,' I declared happily. Suddenly, a detail came to mind. 'Can you type?'

It was perhaps a little late to be asking the question, and I was relieved when she nodded. 'I'm not a forty-per-minute whizz, but I can get by.'

I granted her one of my most brilliant smiles. 'I think we'll get along famously, Miss Fudge. Now… cup of tea?'

'Oh yes, that sounds like a very good idea.'

I headed towards my office.

'I quite agree. Two sugars, please.'

That evening found me in my slippers by a wonderful smouldering fire. I was dozing a little when Grace appeared and decided to harrang me all too rudely. This time, she had a letter.

'Your aunt has asked to see you,' she declared, for what was surely the umpteenth time.

'Ah, Grace - you will be pleased to hear that I have found my secretary!' I said breezily, steering things away as best I could. 'My perfect secretary!'

'Congratulations. Now, go and see Elizabeth.'

When I said nothing, an envelope was thrust under my nose.

'She said you wouldn't go, and so I was to give you this.'

I didn't take it - in fact, I couldn't even bring myself to look at it, never mind touch it. I imagined the words inside, and then stopped myself - I simply didn't want to know. But I knew Grace well enough to know that she would never give in, and so when she failed to move, I took the letter in pinched fingers. When she didn't shift, I raised an eyebrow.

'What are you doing?'

'Waiting,' she said in that efficient way of hers.

'Waiting?'

'I want to know what's in the letter.'

The cheek of it! I coughed and stammered a little.

'Payton, I am here day and night, and nothing gets past me. Yes, the incident with the revolver was terrible, but it made victims out of both of you. Your aunt is frightened, you are angry - it's not a happy combination. I just want to see that you are talking sensibly, and that you can iron this out so that we can all put all this behind us.'

'Putting all this behind us is exactly what I want,' I replied.

'Then go and talk to her!'

I searched for words.

'Least said, soonest mended!'

This was something my mother used to say - and I heard her brisk tone as the words left my mouth. My mother…

'That's absurd, and you know it!' said Grace.

I lost any patience I had left.

'Just go, Grace! I don't want you crowding me, and I certainly don't want you reading my private correspondences.'

She was itching to talk back and yet, to her credit, only nodded sharply and left the room. I sat motionless for some time, the letter rested on my knee. I may have hesitated, but I knew what I would do - there was no question.

I stood, tore the letter to pieces, and fed them to the flames.

Part VI

In which Payton Edgar experiences an epiphany

Dear Margaret,

My next door neighbours have despicable children - two rowdy girls who play at all hours of the day. They scream and giggle and whoop and I often develop a headache because of the din. I have complained to my neighbour, who insists that "children must play" and that they should be allowed to make as much noise as they wish. I adore where I live and wouldn't want this to drive me from my home, but I simply can't wait for years until they are older and quieter, so I can see no other solution.

Can you?

Juliet, St Albans

Margaret replies; Do you own a gramophone or a drum kit? There is only one surefire way to drown out unwanted noise - make some of your own. You must fight fire with fire. Whatever your din, make it loud and at the most inconvenient of times, especially late when the little dears are trying to get some sleep. It won't be long before your neighbour comes running to you begging for a compromise. Queen Victoria may have been a miserable old goat, but she was quite right - children can be seen and not heard.

On Monday morning, I collected my dear singing bowl from the police station.

I took it in my hands, enjoying the smooth curves and the fine craftsmanship, and almost kissed it. The mallet was still there and both were unharmed - and yet, as expected, the police had treated it like they might any old cereal bowl. I came prepared, and folded my third favourite tea-towel (birds of prey) around the thing and rested it in a lidless tin once used to house buttons. Nestling the tin carefully in my most sturdy of satchels, I took myself for a nice stroll in Green Park. It was an agreeable, almost spring-like day. The swans looked elegant and clean, and the trees rustled quietly in a gentle breeze. I sat for a while in my favourite spot - a clean new bench set back from the water - and daydreamed.

Usually, idle thoughts and random wonderings are all I have on such visits - a sort of harmonious mediation upon my surroundings and any concerns of the day. There have been one or two occasions when, in such a peaceful reverie, I happen upon something more urgent, a realisation or an idea - an itch to be scratched.

That afternoon, however, I experienced an epiphany. There is no other word for it.

From my bench I could see the Blue Bridge where whoever had taken Toffee Morrell would be collecting their cash later that day. It was irksome to realise that I was no nearer to the truth about what had happened.

I switched to more comforting thoughts, pondering vaguely about Miss Fudge, picturing her at the front desk of my office and contemplating the importance of image and first impressions. It was surprising the difference a pair of spectacles could make. I saw Miss Fudge and then Toffee Morrell, giggling and joking over lunch, her eyes sparking behind those specs.

A little way off, a world-weary woman collapsed onto the next bench, with children dancing at her feet. To my horror, the children moved in my direction, a boy and a girl of about six or seven. He wore a cap above round, rosy cheeks. She had tight yellow curls and thick round spectacles. They were both giggling furiously, and I might have shooed them away, had their actions not caught my attention. She pulled off his cap and fixed it on her head, playfully. He, in turn, removed her glasses and slid them onto his nose, and they both giggled as he staggered about, arms outstretched, as if blinded.

And then it hit me!

I almost jumped as the thought dawned, and I perched on the edge of the bench. Of course! The glasses! Why hadn't I questioned it at the time? Was I stupid? Had we all been stupid?

The birth of my revelation raised more questions than answers, but I was on my feet with my satchel over my shoulder, trotting - almost running!

I had to get to the office - and quickly.

Miss Fudge was somewhat befuddled as I arrived. She was sitting behind the desk, looking a little bored and flicking through a magazine. As I entered she slapped the pages shut and quickly apologised. The pitch of her voice was delightfully low.

'So sorry, Mr Edgar - good morning. I was just, erm… reading about home-baked crumpets-'

'No matter, Miss Fudge, you may browse a periodical during the quieter moments. All I expect is an affable yet economical greeting. You are wearing the spectacles, I see.'

She flushed. 'As instructed.'

'And you can read with them?'

'Yes. I quite like wearing them, actually. They feel like a part of my new uniform.'

'And you have never worn glasses before?'

'I've never needed to.'

'Well, I shall need them for the time being,' I said, holding out a hand. 'If I may?'

She passed over the horn-rimmed specs and then jumped again as the telephone on her desk rang out. 'Oh!' she gasped. 'My first phone call!'

I watched as she lifted the receiver.

'Good morning. The office of Payton Edgar, how may I help you?'

Perfect!

'Ah, hello, Mrs Farringdon. Yes, yes he's just arrived. If I may ask you to hold for a moment?' She covered the speaker. 'It's Rosemary Farringdon-'

'Wonderful! Tell her to get over here immediately, I have something urgent to discuss!'

'Of course.'

'And if she quibbles, tell her that I shall foot the cab. And pop the kettle on - we must have tea!'

In the end, we barely touched our tea, there was so much to discuss.

While waiting for Rosemary to arrive, I fiddled with the spectacles and mulled things over - but the more I thought about it all, the less I understood. I was hoping that Rosemary would prove to be a good sounding board, and that together we could make some sense of my news. When she arrived, she too was bristling with a nervous kind of energy, and I couldn't resist grandstanding for a while, so rapt was her attention. She sat, wide-eyed and spellbound, as I paced around the room excitedly.

'The revelation came upon me in Green Park - I have been so stupid! We have been duped, Rosemary - duped!'

'How so?'

'It's all about the spectacles - such a giveaway, right from the start!'

'I don't follow. Do you know where Toffee is?'

'Ha! I know where she isn't!'

'I beg your pardon?'

I held out the spectacles, and when I didn't speak, Rosemary sighed.

'Toffee's specs. I'm sick of the sight of them!'

'These, Rosemary, hold the key to all we need to know. Poor Toffee needed them - I am right about that? There was much discussion about how she could play the shrew with such an ailment?'

Rosemary nodded.

'Put them on!'

She hesitated, and I inched them closer. 'Put them on, now!'

She put on the glasses.

'What do you see?' I asked. Rather irritatingly, Rosemary shrugged.

'Just you. And the room.'

'Precisely! Blind without them, was she? I think not! These are costume glasses, Rosemary! Thick glass, but plain glass!'

Rosemary looked up, bewildered. With the glasses on her nose, her eyes amplified, she looked even more prudish than ever. 'What does it mean?'

'We've had them since the start, but we didn't look. We all passed them around, but didn't try them on… until now. I should have asked straight away why Miss Fudge, with perfect eyesight, could wear the specs so easily.'

'But what does it mean?' asked Rosemary again. 'That these aren't Toffee's glasses? That they were swapped somehow?'

'In what world would that make sense, Rosemary? No, you are making things far too complicated. The most simple explanation is the correct one. These are Toffee's glasses and she was not blind. They are a part of a costume. All the components of a costume were there - fake spectacles, heavy make-up, flashy clothes, that wig… all a costume. So we can draw the only natural conclusion - that Toffee Morrell was entirely fake. Nothing but a fake!'

Rosemary went to speak, but stopped and frowned.

'How well did you know Miss Morrell, Rosemary? How well did anyone know Miss Morrell? Hmmm? She came and went in a blink of an eye, didn't she?'

'Yes, but... it just seems nonsensical - the glasses, I mean. She would have been better suited to the role of Kate without specs, wouldn't she? Why lie? It makes no sense.'

'You are heading towards the crucial question, Rosemary. Come on, keep talking...'

'What?'

'I have arrived at a crucial question, and you will too.'

Rosemary bit her lip. 'I don't know...'

'Guess. Have a think...'

'Well, I guess that the plan was to create a character - Toffee Morrell - and then disappear herself, send a ransom and get the cash.'

'That is indeed my theory. But you haven't got to the question yet.'

'Well, just tell me the question!'

'It is the most obvious one, but with a significant answer!'

Rosemary flushed with irritation. 'Payton, your tone is patronising and I won't allow it! Just say what you need to say!'

'The question is - why the disguise?'

Rosemary blinked. 'Well, of course - and as I have just said, it was the creation of a character.'

'That can be done without going to the effort of fake specs and a wig. If I walked into a room full of strangers and wanted to pretend to be someone, I could do so without the need for an elaborate disguise, couldn't I?'

I savoured the moment.

'So... why would anyone wear such a disguise, Rosemary?'

'Well, to hide who they are?'

I slapped my hands together and she jumped in her seat.

'Precisely!'

I leaned in, my excitement barely concealed.

'Why the disguise? Because without it, she is someone we would recognise. She is someone we know.'

Barely a second passed before Rosemary let out a little shriek.

'Payton! Someone we know!'

'Undoubtedly.'

'Oh, dear! I feel quite giddy!' Rosemary cried as she fanned herself ineffectually with a limp wrist. They she stopped, sat bolt upright and shrieked unexpectedly.

'And I know who it is! I know who's behind the make up and the wig! Oh - it all makes sense! I know who Toffee Morrell really is!'

Part VII

In which Payton Edgar bears witness to a scandal

'Now I come to think about it, I thought it odd...'

Rosemary was up and out of her seat, pacing up and down, excited.

'Odd?'

'Well, Ethel just appearing like that.'

'Ethel?'

'Ethel Damp on costumes, Payton! Do keep up! When you said just then - costume glasses - well, costumes made me think of Ethel. She's new to the Old Comp, just popped up for this production. I think I told you that Dickie's previous wardrobe mistress left suddenly last year - some health problems or other. So up steps Ethel Damp! And then suddenly, after Toffee was gone, she was always around, costumes in arms and pins in her mouth - did you notice? What if, while we all thought she'd been back in the wardrobes beavering away on bodices and codpieces, she was out front playing Toffee Morrell?'

I thought this over. The tale of Yardley Swain came to mind. Beryl had said the wardrobe mistress was involved - could that be the past scandal Playfair had mentioned? It fitted, somehow.

'She puts me in mind of Mrs Punch,' I said, a comment which was not exactly helpful - but Rosemary saw something in it.

'Precisely! Picture pretty young Toffee in your mind - take away those glasses and wig, and wipe away the make up - and what do you have? A blank canvas. Add a false nose from a Macbeth witch, a stoop and heavy rouge and there she is! Ethel Damp!'

'Really?'

'And - oh, Payton! The shoebox from the kidnappers was from Horton and wotsit, those theatrical costumiers, wasn't it! It's Ethel - Ethel Damp!'

'Perhaps...'

'Oh, Payton!' Rosemary said again with relish, 'I really do think so! We must get to Dickie, tell him all about it - stop him from dropping off any cash. Then we must find Mrs Damp and challenge her!'

A sharp rap at the door pulled us from the moment. Miss Fudge entered with a small bundle.

'Second post's arrived, Mr Edgar. And something interesting from Fleet Street on top, hand delivered.'

I allowed her to leave before snatching up the top envelope and my smooth brass eagle-head letter opener. I loved my letter opener, a rare find that made the opening of even the most stubborn of envelopes a pleasure. Inside the envelope, I found two newspaper cuttings - Beryl's office boy had done as I had asked. Rosemary was moving closer with curiosity.

'Something interesting, Payton?'

'Interesting... and private,' I replied, shielding the cuttings from her view. I examined each one with interest. The first concerned veteran actor Yardley Swain and the announcement of a divorce from his actress wife. There was a photograph of a bow-tied and well-fed gent with a bulbous nose and dark, piggy eyes. The second cutting was dated a few days earlier and was sprinkled with a little more detail. But Beryl had been wrong - the young thing that broke the Swain's marriage was not the wardrobe mistress, but the understudy. The understudy - Emma.

But this couldn't be our understudy, our Emma Drake - this was one Emma Price. Miss Drake was unmarried and shared her brother's name. I set the cuttings down thoughtfully.

Rosemary made for the door.

'I shall have Miss Fudge call a cab right away. We must get to Dickie as soon as possible.'

Things were suddenly happening very quickly, and once we were settled in the taxi I began to plot a little. Rosemary's latest theory about Ethel Damp was not without merit, but something didn't quite fit. If the wardrobe mistress had indeed pulled off a kidnapping scam, where did the death of Playfair fit in to the equation? Bird-like Ethel Damp would have struggled to overpower the man. Either there was someone else involved, or else the wardrobe mistress was in the clear.

I didn't much fancy seeing either Dickie Chandler or dying-duck Sir Maurice again so soon, and was almost pleased when, as we passed the Old Compton, I caught sight of a red bicycle chained to the railings. The understudy was in. This in itself was odd, with the production frozen - why would she hang around?

Suddenly, I realised that, alongside Ethel Damp, there was another member of the crew who had come and gone at odd times… the sickly understudy.

Emma… Price?

After paying the driver, I suggested that Rosemary take herself to Dickie chandler's flat alone, and was unsurprised when she disagreed.

'Oh, no! You must come with me. You can help me to convince Dickie!'

'I'm quite sure you can do that alone, Rosemary. I have… something to pick up from the theatre. I'll come around to Dickie's shortly.'

And so, alone, I approached the theatre and slipped inside the stage door.

It felt right to do what I was doing - as if returning to the epicentre of recent events could, in some way, clear my muddied thoughts. Searching for the understudy, I noticed a dim light coming from a narrow corridor to the left, and followed after it. It shone from a small window at ankle height. It was a spot I hadn't visited before, and turned out to lead along to the wardrobes. I knew this because I could just see Ethel Damp sitting aside a sewing machine, head down over some darning, surrounded by hanging articles. The cloth on her lap didn't look like a costume, more like one of her husband's socks.

I left her undisturbed, and made my way deeper into the theatre. The place was ridden with shadows, and felt cool and empty. There was something unnerving, even spooky, about an empty theatre. As I stepped gingerly onto the stage the open space and the darkness closed in around me. There might have been people in the audience for all I knew, the auditorium was so dark.

I stood for a moment aside the trap door. The blood had been mopped up, but there remained some dark residue within the cracks on the boards. It seemed probable that Toffee Morrell had indeed been a fake - but where did the death of Playfair fit in? And what of the scandal he had brayed about?

A small triangle of light far away in the wings caught my eye and I moved towards it. A lamp shone at the far end of hallway that led, I think, to a fire exit.

Beneath the lamp were two figures, standing close together, shrouded in silence. Startled by the presence of other beings, I quickly shrunk into the darkness. I hadn't heard them because they weren't talking - they were entwined in a passionate embrace. Convinced that I was well hidden, I craned my neck.

Emma Drake pulled back and looked up at her lover. It was only as she shifted slightly that I saw who he was with.

Whatever I might have expected, it was not this.

Alex Drake loomed over his sister, pushing her back against the cold brick wall. He was unsmiling and somewhat predatory in his manner. He had one hand on her wrist, which he pinned against the brickwork. His other hand was clutching her shoulder, and he leaned in for another kiss.

Beryl's wise words drifted into mind - notes on a scandal. Look for an immoral act, she had said. Find your immoral act, you find your murderer.

Scandal would be sex with a twist, she had told me. Age differences, infidelity, fetishism, incest…

I had prepared myself for something more than tittle-tattle - but this! Most definitely scandalous, and in the most unexpected and unpalatable way. This can only have been what Playfair had witnessed. I scuttled back a few steps. It was all very uncomfortable.

What happened next only added to my befuddlement. They exchanged a few unclear words, hers high pitched and beseeching, his a warning growl. The stagehand moved to a door, pulled it open, and then took his sister by the wrist sharply and pushed her inside. I heard her squeal as the door was closed. He then turned the key in the lock and headed in my direction.

Thankfully, there were a number of tall panels set against the wall, depicting a dense forest glade. I hid behind the trunk of the largest tree and watched as Alex Drake passed by. He was a burly young man with a lumbering, powerful gait. Menacing would be the most appropriate word. For a wild moment I thought that I might pursue him - but to what end? I wasn't about to throw myself into any perilous position. Instead, I padded cautiously over the the closed door and rested my hand on the key in the lock.

After a moment of consideration I turned the key and opened the door.

The room was a storage room of sorts, with countless props and sets from old productions cluttering the place. A bright and rather jaunty giant toadstool sat in one corner, a suit of armour in the other. The woman inside must have been expecting her brother's return, for she cowered at the far wall, tears in her eyes. When she saw that it was me, however, the fearful expression melted.

'Mr Edgar? What are you doing here? You must get out now!'

'Who are you?' I asked, brazenly.

'What?'

'Emma Price, is it?'

For a split second the girl looked panicked, and then she relaxed.

'You must leave, Mr Edgar, quickly. For your own sake-'

'Is that a threat?'

'Believe me, you are in danger.'

'Believe you? I am more than a little inclined to distrust you, Miss Price, and with good reason. I won't go anywhere before you tell me about your brother... and about Yardley Swain.'

To my surprise, she laughed a little - but it was a tight, nervous titter.

'We really haven't time for that.'

I stood, arms folded, resolute. When she saw that I wasn't about to move, her shoulders fell and she gave a gesture of impatience with a flick of the wrist.

'Alright then. First thing - Alex is my husband, not my brother.'

'Ah.'

'I was Emma Price, now married, I am Emma Drake.'

'Then why lie? And what does Toffee Morrell and Yardley Swain have to do with all this?'

She shot out a hand.

'Can you please not mention that man again. I can't-'

'What? Yardley Swain?'

'Stop! Just... stop it! He doesn't deserve the breath it takes to say the name!' Her voice was shrill, almost a shout. Gone was the frightened lamb, her timidity replaced by a bubbling fury that was quite something to behold.

'Tell me what happened. I won't move until you do!'

She grizzled a little and tried to reign in her anger, with little success. She took a step past me, looked out along the corridor and, once she was satisfied we were alone, pulled the door shut behind us.

'Have you ever met the man?'

'Swain? No, but he sounds like a ghastly sort.'

'Ghastly? And then some. It was my first professional acting job. A glittering future, ruined by a passing flirtation with the leading man. The Swains were a horrid, vicious pair, forever sniping and trying to outdo each other, and then when it came out about Yardley and I - it was never more than a bit of an uncomfortable fumble in his dressing room - his wife swore I'd never work again. I am an actress, Mr Edgar, through and through. I have a rare talent, and I've always known it. An actress was all I ever wanted to be - and the scandal and those horrid people killed my dream! My name was dirt. I was tarred as a troublemaker, condemned forever to be behind, not on, the stage. Time passes, but theatre folk remember. Then I met Alex, and we began to share ideas. Mine were dreams... hopes.. aspirations. His were plots... moneymaking schemes and swindles. We ended up combining the two.'

I went to speak and then stopped myself. This was all coming out easily, and it seemed that she wanted to talk about it without prompt or query.

'We'd both love to get away from London - to escape to the sun - and our work doesn't pay much, and so Alex hatched a plan. When I joined the company, I was to woo Mr Chandler as myself, as Emma Drake. Of course, I had to be Alex's sister, not his wife, for it to work. Once I had won Chandler's heart we would make a play for his wallet. I would be taken, a ransom would be paid and we'd be off into the sunset. I flatter myself that I am not unsightly, and we were sure it would work. But there was a flaw in the plan - we got Chandler all wrong. I simply wasn't his type, try as I might. Chandler prefers loud, sexy, brash types. So… we created a loud, sexy, brash type. With raised heels, a wig, some specs and a ton of make up, Toffee Morrell was born.'

'You almost sound proud. It was a part you played admirably.'

'Well, of course. I was born to act, Mr Edgar. It wasn't hard - in fact, it was a fun performance. I liked Toffee, and was sad that she had to go in the end.'

'And so you stage a fight, a disappearance, and send for a ransom.'

'Exactly. It was a simple plan. The only problem being… well, with Toffee missing, as understudy I landed the lead role - wonderful, wonderful Katherine - and adored it. Strangely, I am a better actress that Toffee could ever have been. Finally, I had something to get my teeth into - and recognition too!'

'And your brother - sorry - your husband, didn't like it.'

'Not a bit. I tried to put a stop to everything, I begged Alex to drop it and let me carry on in the lead role. Toffee would have just simply done a runner, gone forever - and that would be that. But he wouldn't have it. He carried on the plan, and the ransom. Alex always takes things too far, and he did again - sending the specs made a silly kind of sense, but the wig covered in pigs blood? A step too far. And then…'

She stopped, and shuddered.

'Playfair recognised you, of course, having known Yardley Swain.'

'Oh, yes he did, right at the start of it all, when he joined the company. I begged him to keep quiet about it, which he said he would, but only in return for… a little flirtation. Alex was livid, of course, but couldn't do anything about it - in everyone else's eyes we were siblings, not spouses.'

'But then Playfair saw the two of you, together.'

'He turned nasty… said he would tell everybody about a sibling love affair unless we paid him well. Well, we daren't tell him the truth. If you lie about being siblings, what else might you be lying about? The whole story would unravel. I just wanted it to end there and then - we should have upped sticks and gone, leave it all behind as a plan turned sour. But Alex… Alex thinks with his fists. In the heat of the moment he… he…'

'You can say it!' I exclaimed. 'He murdered the man!'

'It all happened so quickly.' Emma lowered her tone, and continued beseechingly. 'From that moment on, Mr Edgar, I truly feared my husband.'

I scoffed. 'Not too much to tell the truth, though? To come clean…'

'You speak as if it is my fault! Can't you see how upset I am?'

'You said yourself - you are a fine actress. I think you are just as much to blame, Mrs Drake.'

'After all I have said?'

'After all you have said. You stayed aside your husband, didn't you? You kept quiet, and let it happen. You could, at any point, have gone to the police, or confessed to one of us…'

'I couldn't I really couldn't. I was frightened - petrified!'

She lifted her hand to her mouth to stifle a shriek. At first I thought it was a part of the act, the mewing of a frightened victim. I failed to notice that she was peering over my shoulder.

'Fear is not an excuse. We shall take this to the police and end it now. I-'

Sensing a presence, I turned my head.

Alex Drake stood tall in the doorway, frowning. I swallowed my words. His intent was clear.

'No, Alex - not again!' Emma Drake sobbed. His expression darkening, Alex Drake took a step in my direction, raising his ham-like fists.

Part VIII

In which Payton Edgar prevails

There is something to be said about the power of fear.

As Alex Drake loomed near, it was fear that galvanised my energies. I knew that I had to run, but the man stood in my way, and so, after a breath, I simply turned a shoulder and rammed forwards. I slammed into the mountain in the doorway with satisfying force. My swift action surprised the both of us, and he stumbled back into the corridor, tripping as he went. Miraculously, his head met a metal pipe that ran across the wall with a pleasing thud, and he sunk to the floor. My intention was not to stay and fight, but to flee to safety, and I inched alongside of him and made my way towards the stage. It was little Emma Drake that stopped me in my tracks. For all her involvement in the thing, I couldn't leave her in peril.

I returned to the doorway and held out a hand.

'Come with me!'

She shook her head, petrified. She couldn't take her eyes of off her groaning husband.

'Come with me!'

'I can't… I won't.'

I wasn't about to spend precious time talking it over, and so took to my feet again. To my horror, Alex was pushing himself up as I sped by.

I should have shot straight through the building and out on to the street. I should have run out into the bosom of Soho, screaming. Instead, rather foolishly, I dithered a bit. I could hear Drake grunting and staggering in the darkness, and it seemed like a long run through the building to the street. He was far fitter than I, and would run me down pretty quickly. The urge to hide in safety took hold. If I could find a spot, somewhere safe, give the man time to leave and then raise the alarm, everything would be alright. At first I hurried behind the panels depicting the doorways of Paduan houses, but couldn't quite set them in place to avoid a gap in between. I huffed and puffed a bit, and then gave up.

At the stage, the trap door sat tempting me inside. It could have been a perfect hiding spot, but knowing Playfair's fate and with the blood hardly dry, I would never go there. Thankfully, I immediately saw a more sensible hiding place - the flowing red velvet curtain which swept majestically from floor to ceiling. I vanished within its heavy folds.

I could hear Alex Drake moving in my direction, panting and cursing. I clutched my satchel close and pulled my feet in tight - the last thing I wanted was for him to catch sight of the toe of my brogues. He came closer and closer, coming to a stop just inches from the curtain. I daren't even breathe. And then the steps receded.

I don't know how long I stood there engulfed by the musty curtain, breathlessly still, but if felt like an eternity. And then, Drake called out.

'Are you there, Edgar? Come, face me!'

I would do no such thing - I would be pulverised! I bit down on my bottom lip, my heart beating ten-to-the-dozen. I had to give the man enough time to see that I had indeed escaped, and to give up pursuit. I waited.

It felt like an age.

Eventually, gathering my wits, I allowed myself a little peer around the curtain. The corridor stood empty, no movement or noise within. Gingerly, I came out into the open, and made my way towards the stage door. A muffled squeal stopped me in my tracks. It was Emma Drake, her cries were chilling.

I can be chivalrous at times. While it would have been all too easy for me to flee to safety, one cannot ignore a damsel in distress. I am, in many ways, a hero at heart.

And I came packed with the best of all weapons.

Alex Drake had returned to his wife. He had gone to the store room and taken her by her elbow.

'That's it, Em!' he was growling. 'You've let me down again. We'll pick up the cash and get far away from this bloody place.'

Emma Drake struggled and squeaked, helpless in his grip.

Suddenly a great weight was brought down upon his skull. The crack was sickening, and he collapsed to the floor in a heap. Emma covered her mouth and watched him sink, then peered up in my direction. I stood tall, and just a little breathless, with my dear singing bowl in my hand.

With shaking hands, I examined it in dismay.

A fine crack ran from one edge to the other! With boundless chivalry, I dropped it to the the floor and held out a hand for the weeping woman. She took it, blinking in shock, and allowed me to help her out of the room.

I closed the door and turned the key - securing a murderer within.

I was surprised to find something of a skirmish happening just outside the stage door.

Rosemary had, apparently, pulled Ethel Damp out of her wardrobe and out into the street. The seamstress was clucking like a chicken. To one side, Dickie Chandler looked on helplessly.

'You can complain all you like, Ethel!' sang Rosemary. 'We're on to you!'

I did my best to intervene.

'Rosemary - please stop-'

'Payton!' My appearance only served to galvanise her determination. 'Thank God you're here - we have her! I'm making a citizens arrest!'

'You really don't have to!'

Ethel Damp was pink-cheeked and confused. 'Please, Mrs Farringdon - let go of my wrist! I don't know what you're talking about!'

'Oh, you know all right! With that false smokers growl and that ridiculous, awful wig! And the fault in your disguise? That revolting nose! Where did you get it - a joke shop?'

And then, to everyones horror, Rosemary reached over and pulled on the woman's nose, quite expecting it to come away in her hand. When it didn't, Mrs Damp screamed, and we all jumped.

'Rosemary,' I said tentatively, 'you might have it… just a little wrong!'

Part IX

In which Payton Edgar visits his Aunt Elizabeth

Dear Margaret,

I decided to have my family history traced, and discovered that the woman I thought to be my older sister is in fact my mother. I have been in shock ever since finding out, and feel so betrayed. I can't bring myself to discuss it with her. Having said that, I can't go on pretending she is just my sister. What should I do?

Annie, Bromley

Margaret replies; Once the cat is out of the bag, it will never be the same again. There is no other course of action but to discuss your discovery with your "sister". She was quite wrong to keep this truth from you all this time, but once it is out in the open she may be relieved that the truth is finally out - and you might possibly, if you work at it, have an even stronger relationship because of it.

It took moment after waking to recall the drama of the previous day, my act of heroism and the praise in which I bathed. I had unearthed a dastardly plot, and deftly entrapped a violent murderer. That said, one can never have too much praise, and I felt the need for more.

With a happy heart, I dressed hurriedly.

Grace was in the kitchen enjoying some tea and toast, and I took up her offer of breakfast with enthusiasm. She eyed me suspiciously, and moved over to the pot. I sat at the table. Once the kettle was on, she placed a clean plate and knife on the table. I was about to tell her the story of my heroism when I noticed the jam jar, and pulled it closer. The jar lid was naked - I had removed the gingham cover some time ago, with vague intent. I slipped my hand into my pocket and pulled out the covers I had collected, one purple, one red and one orange.

Perhaps now - in my current frame of mind - was the time to act upon it.

Before Grace could present me with my tea, I was up and on my feet, uttering excuses and heading towards Aunt Elizabeth's room.

I knocked lightly on the door. A grunt came from within, and I entered. The woman in the bed's gaze was stony.

'What do you want?' she asked quietly, with a wounded affliction. I stood over her, my hands on my hips.

'You can sit down.'

'I'll stay standing, thank you.'

'So... what do you want then?'

'To bring you something... and to tell you some news.'

'Oh, yes? What news?'

'A trifling affair,' I began modestly, yet pride took over, and I continued with barely suppressed glee. 'I caught a murderer yesterday. A violent murderer...'

'Mmm, I'll bet you did.'

'It's the truth.' I sat and told her in broad strokes the tale of Mr and Mrs Drake and the kidnapping plot. I may have sensationalised a few details - especially the violence and peril of the finale. When she failed to respond beyond a raised eyebrow, I continued carefully. 'I thought you might be… proud of me.'

She sniffed.

'Perhaps.'

'I also found our burglar a while ago, and reported him to the police. Had a string of crimes under his belt. We won't see the likes of him again. We are safe.'

'A while ago, you say?'

'Well, yes. I-'

'And you haven't said? Didn't you think to tell me straight away?'

'I didn't want to… couldn't bring myself….'

'-to see me? You'd prefer to leave me lying here in fear?'

I stared at the woman in the bed. Words fell from my lips.

'I don't know what to say. I don't know who you are.'

'Hah! Of course you do. I haven't changed a jot.'

Hadn't she? My heart sank. Only one thing came to my lips, and I allowed it to pass.

'You… abandoned me.'

'Eh? What? I have never abandoned you! You've said yourself, time and again, I was always there. Always.'

'Mmm. Perhaps, in a way, you were…'

'I wish I could make you understand, Payton, why we did what we did. I couldn't have kept a baby, unmarried and alone… the scandal would have ruined us.'

I straightened upon hearing the word - scandal. There it was again, but this time, I understood. Scandal breaks backs. Scandal ruins reputations. I knew this now. But I wasn't about to forgive her everything, even if what she had done made a horrible kind of sense.

To my surprise, I found that I had a question.

'My father. What of my father?'

Aunt Elizabeth cast her eyes downwards. 'Unknown, to my shame.' She lifted a hand to her mouth. 'I didn't even know his name. As I said before, I was… a bad girl.'

I watched her for a minute, her furtive discomfort, her shame.

'I still don't know who you are,' I said, defiantly.

'Really? I know you, Payton. Better then you know yourself.' She craned her neck, her eyes suddenly mischievous and sparkling. 'I watched closely, all those years. I know things about you that nobody else ever will. I know your middle name, that precious secret you'll always keep.'

'Anyone who could sneak a look at my passport would know that.'

'I know how, ever since you were a tot, you've always loved your food.'

'Anyone who reads the Clarion would surmise the same.'

She raised her voice. 'Oh, don't be such a stick in the mud!'

I shrugged with as much nonchalance as I could muster, but in truth my shoulders were tight and my stomach lurched. It was all too much. I stood slowly, turned to the door and rested my hand on the handle. Aunt Elizabeth cleared her throat.

'I know how you missed your very first day at school. You had the mumps. Oh, how you wailed.'

I froze.

'I know that you've never forgotten it, Payton. You hated the fact you missed that first day. Hated it. And you've never forgotten it.'

Forever catching up…

I found myself looking down at the woman in the bed. She was smiling. It was almost a sweet smile.

'I have always been there, you see. Watching.'

Suddenly - unexpectedly - a strange calmness flowed through me from head to toe, and I lowered my shoulders. I reached into my jacket pocket and pulled out three gingham cloth jam jar covers.

'I have been collecting these for you.' I set them down on the eiderdown. 'I thought that they might make nice bonnets for your teasel… creatures.'

She took up the purple one, pulled the elastic a little and nodded.

'Make them look like they've got jam jar covers on their heads, you mean.'

I felt a flutter of vexation. 'Right-o. I hadn't expected thanks.'

'Good, then you won't be disappointed.'

And then she surprised me again with a light, playful giggle.

'They'll make good bonnets.'

She paused and then, as if coming to a decision, leaned over to her bedside table and retrieved an object.

'And now, I have something for you.'

It was one of her teasel creations, and she set it down on the bedding. It was a peculiar creature, round at the waist and adorned in tweed-effect fabric, with a hat, a stick and a down-turned mouth.

'It is a teasel Payton!' Aunt Elizabeth declared.

'I can see that.'

'Ha! You hate it don't you?'

'With all my heart,' I replied honestly.

She laughed again.

'… and you knew I would.'

The woman in the bed was grinning, and I surprised myself by joining her. I couldn't stop myself, and then I laughed - and as I did, tears came to my eyes.

'It was worth the effort for that look on your face, Payton! Now get out of my room.'

I picked up the teasel Payton. 'I suppose I will keep this. It can sit atop my bookcase.'

I stopped at the door. I had one last thing to say, and said it, carefully.

'I can never talk about this… about you … your secret. You are my Aunt Elizabeth. Only ever Aunt Elizabeth. You always have been, and always will. I cannot look back. Only forward.'

Aunt Elizabeth took this in, and nodded.

'Only forward,' she replied.

And then she flicked a hand.
'Now get out my bloody room!'

Part X

In which Rosemary writes a letter

Hotel De L'Hermitage
Calle Specchieri S.
Monte-Carlo
August 12th 1964

Dear Payton,

Well! Where to start!

I suppose I should begin by saying that I hope that you're well and enjoying a typically miserable British Summer. While the sun might peep out from behind a cloud once a week where you are, it's shining brightly here. I am in Monaco, darling!

As I'm sure you've heard, Gordon joined the great majority, as they say. He was never the same after his dream popped at the Old Compton. He died in March, almost peacefully. I hope you don't begrudge my not sending an invite - the funeral was a very quiet affair as Gordon insisted on only inviting those he liked. He may be gone, but I keep him with me - I have had his glass eye mounted into a pendant that I wear around my neck at all times, in remembrance of my dear departed.

But guess what? It turns out Gordy had hidden stock and shares one could only dream about. His idiot accountant kept that mum for too long - but that was where the money for his health pilgrimage was going to come from. Thank goodness he was too ill to go in the end. So it turns out we needn't have come to you to fund the Old Compton debacle in the first place! Still, all good news for me. I upped sticks from Chelsea (I never really did like it there). I am on an extended holiday at Monte-Carlo with a dear friend, and have just purchased a darling apartment on the Ile St-Louis in Paris! I shall live out my Autumn years in la belle France. Oh la-la!

I have some more news. The friend I am travelling with? It's dear, dear Dickie! It made sense, with the both of us alone and in need of companionship. But something unexpected blossomed, and we are to be married in November. Yes! I will be Mrs Richard Chandler! Carpe Diem, as they say! Aren't I lucky? Dickie isn't keen on inviting you to the bash, but I will insist. I shall send details as they are made.

We will have a gift list at Fortnum and Mason. I remember that the set of tea plates you sent for my wedding to Gordon were rather gaudy and not to our tastes - so I shall expect a top-tier present from you this time!

I must go - we have champagne cocktails at the poolside at six.

Yours with affection,

Rosemary

Epilogue

After all the excitement at the Old Compton at the start of the year, the following months were rather drab and uneventful. The summer was mostly cloudy and dull - but still I had one or two things to be thankful for. Miss Fudge settled in to her role well. She adored the fact that I was the voice behind Margaret Blythe and and quickly became indispensable. She wore Toffee Morrell's glasses with pride. Irving and I enjoyed a number of sub-par meals, and Payton's Plate and Dear Margaret continued to shine as jewels in the Clarion's crown.

It turned out to be something of an Indian summer, with the heat rising as September came along, and it was on a sunny September morning that I came cross a long overdue headline in the Clarion.

It was a Friday and, as always on a Friday, I purchased a newspaper and a quart of lemon sherbets. Just as I was handing over my coins, a few words in the lower half of the front page caught my eye. It was the very headline I had only ever dreamed about.

It read; Clarion Restaurant Critic shakes things up - sparkling contemporary cuisine! Page 4.

I had, in recent weeks, featured in an article about the changing face of British cuisine in Dear Lady magazine, the Clarions sister rag, and was expecting some delicious praise - but a banner on the front page? And my piece on page four? This was something else altogether! My report had been a little cheeky in places, and so it made sense for the editorial to focus on my more contemporary edges. I snapped up the paper and practically danced down the street.

Naturally, I called in on Irving to share my delight.

I could barely sit still as he dried his hands on a paint-spattered cloth and took the paper with a bemused smile. As he perused the piece, I couldn't hold my tongue.

'Of course, a feature such as this is long overdue, but I do like the way the headline defines me as a contemporary writer. Between you and I, I wondered recently if the style of Payton's Plate was, well, perhaps just a little stale - but this - well! I will probably be guaranteed more column inches in the paper and the magazine now. I always have more to say.'

I inspected Irving's latest painting, a vibrant affair that wasn't of anything in particular, merely dancing shapes and splashes. It was distracting enough, and it took me a minute to detect the silence in the room. I returned my attention to my friend, who was peering at me with a strange look on his face.

'What's up?'

'You haven't read the article, have you?'

I laughed. 'Need I?'

He held out the paper.

'Yes - you need.'

I took the paper and scanned the piece. It began just as I had hoped. Restauranting was a pastime becoming more and more en vogue, and the restaurant business was thriving. There were fabulous new establishments, but also a number of poor quality places. A strong voice was needed to guide the city's diners, and a new talent was being celebrated. A new voice, to right the wrongs and root out the worms from the apples.

'A… new voice?' I said, falteringly.

Irving nodded.

'A new voice,' he said, carefully.

'A new talent?' I whimpered. I let the paper drop.

'This isn't about you, Payton,' said Irving. 'It appears that the Clarion has appointed a new restaurant critic…'

I gasped, searching for breath. Irving retrieved the newspaper.

'One Mr Fenton Prentice.'

I felt dizzy.

'And you didn't know?'

I struggled to reply. 'I didn't know.'

'A new critic in town,' Irving continued, rather obviously. 'Writing exclusively for the Clarion.'

'But I write exclusively for the Clarion! They wouldn't have two, would they?'

'No, they wouldn't.'

'Then I have been… ousted?'

'It would appear so.'

'But who the dickens is this Fenton Prentice, anyway?'

I sank into a chair, with only one question in mind - a weak, pleading question.

How could they?

And then, as anger and indignation welled up in my chest, I rephrased the question and said it out loud.

'How dare they!'

Payton Edgar will return in "Payton Edgar's Nemesis"

Printed by Amazon Italia Logistica S.r.l.
Torrazza Piemonte (TO), Italy

13395677R00100